"I'm off men, you know."

"Yeah. I know." Tanner pulled Callie in, hard against his body.

She took two handfuls of his shirt. For balance, she told herself. But the truth was, she *wanted* to put her hands on him. He looked down on her face for another second, his brown eyes soft but full of intent as he slowly lowered his head.

"W-wait!"

He paused, eyes on hers.

She had her hands over his heart and could feel the beating beneath her palms. Slow. Steady.

The opposite of hers, of course.

"I…can't remember what I was going to say."

His eyes were smiling into hers. "So I can continue?"

She cleared her throat and nodded. "Carry on," she whispered.

He started with a brush of his lips against one corner of her mouth, a butterfly touch. And then the other corner.

She heard a soft sound, an almost whimper, and realized it was her. He slowly sank his fingers into her hair, and she melted. No other word for it—her bones just melted clean away. And then he proceeded to kiss the living daylights out of her…

Praise for Jill Shalvis and Her Novels

Once in a Lifetime

"Top Pick! 4½ stars! Shalvis never disappoints with her witty, comical and überromantic reads...should be on every reader's TBR list. Fans of contemporary romance will fall in love with Aubrey and Ben and find their sexual tension electrifying...Sweet and spicy—what more could you ask for?"

—RT Book Reviews

"As Aubrey grows stronger and more certain, readers will cheer for her—and for the love she deserves."

—Washington Post

"Nine books into this series and I still look forward to each one...There is no stress or that guessing game of will I or won't I like it when I open these books...The first three Lucky Harbor books will always be my favorite but *Once in a Lifetime* gave those books a run for their money."

—FictionVixen.com

"*Once in a Lifetime* is aww-inducing, entertaining, and all-in-all quite the charming love story. I love the characters, from the lovebirds to the regulars. I love the setting and wish I lived in a place like Lucky Harbor."

—DreysLibrary.com

It Had to Be You

"Engaging writing, characters that walk straight into your heart, and a town you can't wait to revisit make this touching, hilarious tale another heart-warmer worthy of Shalvis's popular series."

—*Library Journal*

"Four stars! A winner...Readers will laugh out loud as they rush to turn the pages."

—*RT Book Reviews*

"Ms. Shalvis has a gift for writing down-to-earth yet quirky heroines and swoonworthy, honorable heroes."

—**HeroesandHeartbreakers.com**

"A sweet and sexy romance to warm the heart, all wrapped in warm fuzzies and humor. If you love contemporary romance, you'll have to read Jill Shalvis."

—**DreysLibrary.com**

Forever and a Day

"4½ stars! Top Pick! Shalvis once again racks up a hit... laughter is served in doses as generous as the chocolate the heroine relies on to get through the day. Readers will treasure each turn of the page and be sorry when this one is over."

—*RT Book Reviews*

"[Shalvis] has quickly become one of my go-to authors of contemporary romance. Her writing is smart, fun, and sexy, and her books never fail to leave a smile on my face long after I've closed the last page…Jill Shalvis is an author not to be missed!"

—**TheRomanceDish.com**

"Jill Shalvis is such a talented author that she brings to life characters who make you laugh, cry, and are a joy to read."

—**RomRevToday.com**

At Last

"Full of laughter, snark, and a super-hot attraction between the main characters. Shalvis has painted a wonderful world, full of entertaining supporting characters and beautiful scenery."

—*RT Book Reviews*

"A sexy, romantic read…What I love about Jill Shalvis's books is that she writes sexy, adorable heroes…the sexual tension is out of this world. And of course, in true Shalvis fashion, she expertly mixes in humor that has you laughing out loud."

—**HeroesandHeartbreakers.com**

"A sexy, fun tale from the creative mind of Jill Shalvis…*At Last* will have you laughing, smiling, and sniffling…Another stellar read I highly recommend."

—**RomRevToday.com**

Lucky in Love

"Shalvis pens a tale rife with the three H's of romance: heat, heart, and humor. *Lucky in Love* is a down-to-the-toes charmer...It doesn't matter if you're chuckling or reaching for an iced drink to cool down the heat her characters generate—Shalvis doesn't disappoint."

—*RT Book Reviews*

"I always enjoy reading a Jill Shalvis book. She's a consistently elegant, bold, clever writer...Very witty—I laughed out loud countless times reading *Lucky in Love*...[It] is also one of the hottest books I've read by Ms. Shalvis. Mallory and Ty burn up the sheets (and the pages) with regularity and these scenes are sizzling."

—All About Romance (LikesBooks.com)

"Whenever I'm looking for a romance to chase away the worries of life, all I have to do is pick up a Jill Shalvis book. Once again she has worked her magic with the totally entertaining *Lucky in Love*."

—RomRevToday.com

Head Over Heels

"[A] winning roller-coaster ride...[a] touching, character-rich, laughter-laced, knockout sizzler."

—*Library Journal* (starred review)

"Healthy doses of humor, lust, and love work their magic as Shalvis tells Chloe's story...Wit, smoking-hot passion, and endearing tenderness...a big winner."

—Publishers Weekly

"The Lucky Harbor series has become one of my favorite contemporary series, and *Head Over Heels* didn't disappoint...such a fun, sexy book...I think this one can be read as a stand-alone book, but I encourage you to try the first two in the series, where you meet all the characters of this really fun town."

—USAToday.com

The Sweetest Thing

"A Perfect 10! Once again Jill Shalvis provides readers with a sexy, funny, hot tale."

—RomRevToday.com

"Witty, fun, and the characters are fabulous."

—FreshFiction.com

"It is fabulous revisiting Lucky Harbor! I have been on tenterhooks waiting for Tara and Ford's story, and yet again, Jill Shalvis does not disappoint...A rollicking good time."

—RomanceJunkiesReviews.com

Simply Irresistible

"Hot, sweet, fun, and romantic! Pure pleasure!"
   —Robyn Carr, *New York Times* **bestselling author**

"This often hilarious novel has a few serious surprises, resulting in a delightfully satisfying story."
                                 —LibraryJournal.com

"Heartwarming and sexy…an abundance of chemistry, smoldering romance, and hilarious sisterly antics."
                                 —*Publishers Weekly*

Also by Jill Shalvis

The Lucky Harbor Series

Simply Irresistible
The Sweetest Thing
Heating Up the Kitchen (cookbook)
Christmas in Lucky Harbor (omnibus)
Small Town Christmas (anthology)
Head Over Heels
Lucky in Love
At Last
Forever and a Day
"Under the Mistletoe" (short story)
It Had to Be You
Always on My Mind
A Christmas to Remember (anthology)
Once in a Lifetime
Lucky Harbor (omnibus)
It's in His Kiss
He's So Fine

Other Novels

Blue Flame
White Heat
Seeing Red
Her Sexiest Mistake

One in a Million

Jill Shalvis

GRAND CENTRAL
PUBLISHING

NEW YORK   BOSTON

Grand Central Publishing
Hachette Book Group
237 Park Avenue
New York, NY 10017

www.HachetteBookGroup.com

Printed in the United States of America

OPM

First edition: October 2014
10 9 8 7 6 5 4 3 2 1

Grand Central Publishing is a division of Hachette Book Group, Inc.
The Grand Central Publishing name and logo is a trademark of Hachette Book Group, Inc.

The Hachette Speakers Bureau provides a wide range of authors for speaking events. To find out more, go to www.hachettespeakersbureau.com or call (866) 376-6591.

The publisher is not responsible for websites (or their content) that are not owned by the publisher.

ATTENTION CORPORATIONS AND ORGANIZATIONS:

Most Hachette Book Group books are available at quantity discounts with bulk purchase for educational, business, or sales promotional use. For information, please call or write:

Special Markets Department, Hachette Book Group
237 Park Avenue, New York, NY 10017
Telephone: 1-800-222-6747 Fax: 1-800-477-5925

One in a Million

Chapter 1

♥

I want a hoedown wedding."

Callie Sharpe, wedding site designer and planner, was professional enough to not blink at this news. "A hoedown wedding."

"Yes," her client said via Skype. "The bridesmaids want to wear cowboy boots and Jimmy wants to eat pigs in a blanket at the reception. You okay with that?"

"Sure," Callie said to her laptop. After all, she loved pigs in a blanket so who was she to judge? "It's your day, whatever you want."

Her bride-to-be smiled. "You really know your wedding stuff. And you always look so wonderful. I love your clothes. Can I see what shoes you're wearing? I bet they're fab too."

Callie didn't let her easy smile slip. "Oh, but this is about your wedding, not my shoes. Let's talk about your invitations—"

"Please?"

Callie sighed. For the camera, she wore a silky cami and blazer. Out of camera range, she wore capri yoga pants that doubled as PJs and…bunny slippers. "Whoops," she said. "I've got another call. I'll get back to you."

"But—"

She disconnected and grimaced. "Sorry," she said to the client who could no longer hear her. She went back to work, clicking through page after page of the season's new wedding dresses, uploading the ones she liked best. She switched to the latest invitation designs next. And then unique party favors and stylish accessories.

You really know your wedding stuff.

Unfortunately this was true. She'd been a bride once, the most silly, hopeful, eager bride ever. Well, an almost bride. She'd gotten all the way to the church before getting stood up, and since that memory still stung, she shoved it aside. She'd married something else instead— she'd united her strong IT skills with her secret, deeply buried love of all things romantic—and had created TyingTheKnot.com. On a daily basis, she dealt with demanding, temperamental, and in lots of cases, batshit-crazy brides, all looking for their happily-ever-after. She'd made it her job to give them the dream.

It was exhausting. Standing, Callie stretched and moved to the wall of windows. Her apartment was one of three in a battered old warehouse that had once been a cannery, then a salt water taffy manufacturer, and then, in the fifties, a carnival boardinghouse. The building wasn't much to write home about, but the view made the lack of insulation and insufficient heat worth it.

Mostly.

Today the waters of Lucky Harbor were a gorgeous azure blue, dotted with whitecaps thanks to a brutal mid-November wind that was whistling through the tangle of steel rafters, metal joists, and worthless heating ducts above her.

Callie had grown up in this small, quirky Washington coastal town sandwiched between the Pacific and the Olympic Mountains, and once upon a time, she hadn't been able to get out of here fast enough. There'd been more than one reason for that but she was back now, and not exactly because she wanted to be.

There was a man in the water swimming parallel to the shore. Passing the pier, he moved toward the north end and the row of warehouses, including the one she stood in.

Transfixed, she watched the steady strokes and marveled at his speed. He might as well have been a machine given how efficiently and effectively he cut through the water.

Callie had been in those waters, although only in the summertime. She couldn't even swim to the end of the pier and back without needing life support.

But the man kept going.

And going.

After a long time, he finally turned and headed in, standing up in the water when he got close enough. After the incredible strength he'd shown swimming in the choppy surf, she was surprised when he limped to the sand. Especially since she couldn't see anything wrong with him, at least from this distance.

He was in a full wetsuit, including something covering

his head and most of his face. He peeled this off as he dropped to his knees, and she gasped.

Military-short, dark hair and dark eyes. And a hardness to his jaw that said he'd had the dark life to go with.

He looked just like…oh God, it was.

Tanner Riggs.

While she was standing there staring, her cell phone started ringing with the *I Love Lucy* theme song, signaling her grandma was calling. Eyes still glued to the beach—and the very hot man now unzipping his wetsuit—she reached for her phone. "Did you know Tanner Riggs was home?" she asked in lieu of a greeting.

"Well, hello to you too, my favorite nerd-techie grand-daughter."

"I'm your only granddaughter," Callie said.

"Well, you're still my favorite," Lucille said. "And yes, of course I know Tanner's in town. He lives here now. Honey, you're not reading my Instagram or you'd already know this and much, much more."

She didn't touch that one. The sole reason she was back in Lucky Harbor and not in San Francisco was because of her grandma.

Callie's dad—Lucille's only son—had been an attorney. Actually both of her parents had been, and even retired, they still liked things neat and logical.

Grandma Lucille was neither, and Callie's parents were pretty sure her grandma was no longer playing with a full set of marbles. Callie had drawn the short stick to come back and find out what needed to be done. She'd been here two weeks, staying in the rental because she needed to be able to work in peace. Her grandma had loaned her the car since she'd been soundly rejected by the DMV for a license renewal. The two of them had daily meals—mostly lunches, as Lucille's social calendar made the queen of England look like a slacker. But there'd been no sign of crazy yet.

Not that Callie could give this any thought at the moment because Tanner shoved the wetsuit down to his hips.

Holy.

Sweet.

Baby.

Jesus.

Back in her high school days, a quiet brainiac like Callie had been invisible to him. Which had never gotten in the way of her fantasies, as the teenage Tanner Riggs had been rangy, tough, and as wild as they came.

He'd filled in and out, going from lanky teen to a man who looked like every inch of him was solid muscle, not a spare ounce of fat in sight.

Was he still tough and wild and a whole lot of trouble?

Oblivious to both her musings and the fact she was drooling over him, Tanner moved to the fifty-foot sport boat moored at the dock where he came face to face with a teenager who looked just like him down to his dark hair, dark eyes, and that air of wildness. Callie actually blinked in shock. Unless time travel was involved and Tanner had come back as his fifteen-year-old self, she was looking at his son.

The two males spoke for a moment, the teen's body language sullen and tense, Tanner's calm, stoic, and unreadable. Then still shirtless, his wetsuit low on his hips, Tanner hopped lithely onto the boat and shimmied his way up the mast, moving seemingly effortlessly on the strength of his arms and legs. He had something between his teeth, a rope, she saw, and damn if her heart didn't sigh just a little bit at watching him climb with heart-stopping, badass grace.

"He's certainly romance hero worthy," her grandma said in her ear, nearly making Callie jump. She'd forgotten she was on the phone.

"Tall, dark, and a bit attitude ridden on the outside," her grandma went on, "but on the inside, he's really just a big softie."

Callie couldn't help it, she laughed. From her view, there was nothing soft about Tanner Riggs.

Nothing.

Not his body, not his mind, and certainly not his heart. "I remember him," she said softly. And what she remembered was getting her teenage heart crushed. "I need to go, Grandma. But I'll come by for lunch."

"Good. I want to introduce you to the guy I think I'm going to take on as my new boyfriend."

Callie tore her gaze off Tanner and looked at her phone. "Wait—what? I've been here two weeks, and you haven't mentioned this."

"Yes, well, sometimes you can be a little prudish about these things."

"I'm not prudish."

"And you think I'm losing it," Lucille said. "That one might be true."

"Oh, Grandma."

"I mean, just the other night I lost my glasses. And they were right on my head. Someone told me I needed to eat more blueberries to boost my memory. Which reminds me to ask, why couldn't it be drink vodka, or something good, to regain some memory?"

Callie rubbed the headache brewing between her eyes. "Back to the taking on a boyfriend thing…"

"Well, I'll need your definition of boyfriend first," her grandma said.

Callie stared at the phone. "Maybe we should forget the blueberries and have your hormone levels checked."

Lucille laughed. "I didn't tell you about the boyfriend because my sweetie and I like to keep things on the down-low. And plus it was a test. A test to see if you've got skills to sniff out the dirt like I do. You failed, by the way."

"You mean because I'm not a snoop?" Callie asked, trying not to picture her eighty-plus grandma having a "sweetie." "And you do realize you have a reputation as the town's unofficial media relations director, right?"

"Yep. Although I'm lobbying to make it official—as in a paid position." She laughed when Callie snorted. "I swear, honey, it's like you're not even related to me. And anyway, how is it that you're the one who taught me how to work a computer and what social media was, and yet you don't utilize them to your favor?"

"You mean manipulate them?" Callie asked. "And I taught you all that because I thought you were getting elderly and bored and your mind would go to rot. I didn't know you were going to terrorize people with it!"

Lucille laughed. "I've got a bunch of good years left before I'll even consider getting elderly and bored. And no worries, my elevator still goes to the top floor. Come on over, honey. I've got to put the new registration sticker on the car; it just came in the mail. Nice that the state allows me to pay them for the car they won't license me to drive, huh? To sweeten the deal, I've got dessert from Leah at the bakery. She makes the best stuff on the planet."

Callie blew out a breath. "Okay, I'll bring the main course, something from the diner."

"I could make my famous fried chicken."

Last week, Lucille had set her fried chicken on fire and had nearly burned her house to the ground. Hence the "famous." Which was really more like infamous. "I'm on a diet," Callie fibbed.

"That's ridiculous," Lucille said, obviously outraged. "You don't need to go on a diet to catch a man. You look fantastic! I mean, you're a little short but your curves are all the rage right now. And sure, you can come off as a little standoffish, but I blame your parents and their inability to love anyone other than themselves for that, not you."

Callie choked back her laugh. It was true; she was the product of two college sweethearts who'd been so crazy in love with each other that nothing had ever really penetrated their inner circle—including their own child. They'd raised her kindly and warmly enough, but her quiet upbringing had left her introverted and preferring the company of a computer rather than people. "I'm not trying to catch a man," she said.

"Well, that's a shame. And not to add any pressure but you do know Eric's around too, right?"

Eric. Damn. Just the sound of her ex's name made her stomach cramp. "Eric who?" she asked casually.

Lucille cackled. "Atta girl. Perfectly normal tone. But next time, no hesitation. That was a dead giveaway. Just be forewarned that your ex-fiancé—may his soul turn black—has married and has a kid on the way."

Callie told herself she didn't care that the man who'd left her at the altar due to a sudden severe allergy to commitment had apparently managed to overcome said allergy.

"And I'm not sure how long you're planning on staying in Lucky Harbor," her grandma went on, "but I doubt you'll be fortunate enough to avoid him. He's the only dentist in town. So the question is, how are your teeth? In good condition? You flossing daily? You might want to make sure you are."

Callie thunked her head against the window, and when she looked up again, she was startled to realize that Tanner was back on the dock and looking right at her.

For a minute, her heart stopped. "I've got to go, Grandma." She needed to be alone to process things. Like the fact that Eric was in town. And also that her very first, very painful, very humiliating crush was as well, and he'd grown into the poster child for Hottest Guy Ever.

"Wait," Lucille said. "Bring salads because you might be right about a diet. The one of us who is going to get lucky needs to stay hot and all that."

Oh boy. "Salads it is." Still on the phone, Callie forced herself away from the window, heading directly to her refrigerator. More accurately, her freezer, where she had two choices. "Ice cream or vodka?"

"Tough decision," her grandma said. "But I'd go with vodka."

It *was* a tough decision, but as it was still early and she wasn't the one trying to look hot, she passed over the vodka and reached for the ice cream. Breakfast of champions, right? She had a wooden spoon out of the drawer and the lid off the ice cream when she remembered. Ice cream was sugar. Sugar was bad for her teeth. And bad teeth required a dentist. "Crap."

"What?" Lucille asked.

Screw it, she needed this ice cream. "Nothing."

"Did you hear what I said about Eric?"

"Yeah." Callie took her first bite. "I'll floss." She was older and wiser now. No big deal. And plus her hefty armor of indifference and cynicism toward romance and happily-ever-after would help. "I'll be fine."

"Do you want me to set you up with another hottie? 'Cause no offense, honey, but you could do a lot better than Eric anyway. Listen, I'll start a poll for you on my Tumblr asking who people want to see you with—"

"No!" Callie nearly went back to the freezer. "No," she said again, firmly. "No men."

"A woman then?" Lucille asked. "Being a bisexual is in style."

Forget the vodka. She needed a new life. Maybe on Mars. "Grandma, I love you," Callie said. "I love you madly, but I don't want to discuss my love life with you."

"You mean your lack of?"

She sighed. "Or that."

"Fair enough," Lucille said. "But for the record, we can discuss mine anytime you want."

"Noted."

"I mean, it's amazing what those little blue pills can do to a man, let me tell you. He can just keep going and going like the Energizer Bunny—"

"Really gotta go," Callie said quickly. "I'll see you later." She disconnected, and she and the ice cream made her way back to the window.

Tanner was gone.

Chapter 2

♥

The ice cream didn't cut it. Needing caffeine, Callie went back to her kitchen before remembering her coffee-maker had died and gone to heaven the day before.

Damn. This was going to require a trip into town. And possibly seeing people. Which in turn meant kicking off her slippers and shoving her feet into her fake Uggs. Quite the look, but she wasn't planning on socializing. This was purely a medicinal trip.

In light of that, she skipped the diner and hit the bak-ery, thinking she'd get in and out faster. What she hadn't planned on was the amazing, mouthwatering scent of the place and the way it drew her straight to the doughnut dis-play. A pretty brunette was serving behind the counter. "How can I help you?"

"You Leah?" Callie asked.

"Yep."

"Perfect. It's rumored you make the best desserts on the planet."

"True story," Leah said.

"I'll take a small coffee and two of those powdered sugar doughnuts then," Callie said, pointing to the display.

"Excellent choice. They solve all problems."

"Yeah?" Callie asked.

"Well, no. But they taste amazing."

"Good enough," Callie said.

Two minutes later, lost in a doughnut-lust haze, she'd forgotten her resolve to get in and get out. Instead, in a hurry to ingest the sugar, she looked for a seat in the crowded place. She finally snagged the last table and tried to look busy so that no one would ask to share it. But given the long line, the odds were against her. Which in turn meant she was going to have to be social.

Damn.

That should be in her game plan, she decided. Help out her grandma and also learn to be social with something other than her laptop and vibrator while she was at it. Shaking her head at herself, she dug in, taking a huge first bite and maybe, possibly moaning as the delicious goodness burst onto her tongue. Oh yeah. Definitely the best powdered sugar doughnuts on the planet.

She took another bite, eyeballed the place, and then nearly did a spit-take across the room when she caught sight of the man at the front of the line. His back was to her, but there was no mistaking those broad shoulders.

Tanner had changed from his wetsuit and now wore dark, sexy guy jeans and a light windbreaker that said LUCKY HARBOR CHARTERS across his back. He was talking to Leah but he was also scanning the place as if by old military habit.

Don't look at me, she thought. Don't look—

He looked. In fact, those dark eyes lasered in and locked unerringly right on hers.

Her first reaction was a rush of heat. Odd, as she hadn't had one of those in relation to a man in a while—but not completely surprising as Tanner was hotter than sin. An ice cube would've had a reaction to him.

Self-awareness hit her, and reality. She looked down at herself. Yep, still wearing capri yoga pants and fake Uggs. Perfect. She was dressed like she didn't own a mirror. Even worse, she wore no makeup and her hair...well, mostly the long, strawberry blond waves had a serious mind of their own. The best that could be said this morning was that she'd piled them up on top of her head and they'd stayed. Thank God the messy topknot was in this year.

Not that this knowledge helped, because when a woman faced her first crush, that woman wanted to look hot—not like a hot mess.

"Is this chair taken?" Tanner asked.

Callie promptly swallowed wrong. Sugar went down the wrong pipe and closed off her air passage. When had he left the line and moved to her side? And damn it, why couldn't she breathe? Hiding this fact, she desperately went for a cool, unaffected look—difficult to pull off while suffocating.

His dark eyes were warm and filled with amusement. "Yes?" he asked. "No chance in hell?"

That's when she realized there was something worse than asphyxiation in public—he didn't recognize her.

Damn. In a single heartbeat, she was reduced to that shy, quiet, socially inept girl she'd once been. Talk, she ordered herself. Say something. But when she opened her mouth, the only thing that came out was a squeak.

And a puff of powdered sugar.

"It's okay," he said, and started to turn away.

This surprised her. The cocky, wild-man teenager she'd once known would've sent her a lazy smile and talked her into whatever he needed.

But it'd been over ten years and she supposed people changed. She'd certainly changed. For one thing, she was no longer that quiet, studious dork with the foolishly romantic heart. Nope, now she was a suave, immaculately dressed professional...She kept her legs hidden and decided this could be a good thing. His not recognizing her meant that she could make a new first impression. She didn't have to be a nerd. She could be whatever she wanted. Or more correctly, whatever she could manage to pull off. "Wait!" she called out to him. Maybe a little too loudly.

Or a lot too loudly.

Half the bakery startled and stared at her. And then in the next beat, everyone seemed to find their manners and scurried to look busy. Lowering her voice, Callie gestured to the free chair. "Sit," she told Tanner. "It's all yours."

He kicked the chair out for himself and sprawled into it. Sipping his coffee, he eyed her over the steam rising out of his cup, all cool, easy, masculine grace.

She tried to look half as cool but she wasn't. Not even close. And she had a problem. A twofold problem.

One, the table was tiny. Or maybe it was just that Tanner's legs were long, but no matter how she shifted, she kept bumping into a warm, powerful thigh beneath the table.

And two, his eyes. They were the color of rich, dark, melted chocolate.

God, she loved dark, melted chocolate.

But he had no recollection of her. A definite blow to her already fragile, powder-sugar-coated self-esteem. She wished she didn't care.

But it was the damn high school crush.

How did one get over a crush anyway? Surely the statute of limitations was up by now. After all, he'd devastated her and hadn't even noticed.

To be fair, he'd had other things on his mind back then. She'd been a quiet, odd freshman, and he'd been a senior and the town's football star. She'd loved him from afar until he'd graduated and left town. She knew his story was far more complicated than that but her poor, romantic heart had remained devastated by his absence for nearly two years. Then in her last year of high school, Eric had moved in across the street. He and Callie had become a thing. They'd stuck, and by their last year of college, she'd had their wedding completely planned out—and she did mean completely, from the exact color of the bridesmaids' dresses, to the secluded beach where they'd say their vows, to the doves that would be released after they did…

Yeah, there was a reason she understood her client brides as well as she did. She'd once been a batshit-crazy bride too. But she'd honestly believed that Eric would be the perfect groom and the perfect husband. After all, he'd spent years making her happy.

Until the moment he'd stood her up at the altar.

"You okay?" Tanner asked.

"Sure." Just lost in the past. But she was done with the

past and took a bite to prove just how okay she really was. Bad move. Turns out it was hard to swallow correctly once you've already choked. She then promptly compounded her error by gulping down some hot coffee on top of the sore throat and lump of doughnut that wouldn't go down and commenced nearly coughing up a lung.

She felt the doughnut being removed from her hand and then the coffee. Tanner had stood up and was at her side, patting her back as she coughed.

And coughed.

Yep, she was going to die right here, in yoga capris and fake Uggs.

"Hang on," Tanner said, and strode to the front counter of the bakery.

From the dim recesses of her mind, she saw that he didn't bother with the line, just spoke directly to Leah behind the counter, who quickly handed him a cup of water.

Then he was back, pushing it into Callie's hands.

Nice and mortified, she took a sip of water, wiped her nose and streaming eyes with a napkin, and finally sat back. "I'm okay."

Tanner eyed her for a long moment, as if making sure she wasn't about to stroke out on him, before finally dropping back in his chair.

She opened her mouth but he shook his head. "Don't try to talk," he said. "Every time you do, you nearly die."

"But—"

He raised an eyebrow and pointed at her, and she obediently shut her mouth. And sighed. She wanted to ask him about his limp but he was right; she probably couldn't manage talking without choking again.

Way to wow him with a new first impression.

A woman came into the bakery, eyed Tanner with interest and intent, and unbelievably he leaned in closer to Callie, as if they were in the midst of the most fascinating of conversations.

"You settling into town okay at your new place?" he asked.

"My new place?"

"I see you watching me from your window."

Damn if she didn't choke again.

Seriously? She lifted a hand when he started to rise out of his chair, chased down the crumbs stuck in her throat with some more water, and signaled she was okay. "Sorry, rough morning."

"Let's go back to the not-talking thing," he said.

Yeah, she thought. Good idea.

A few minutes went by, during which Callie was incredibly aware of his leg still casually brushing hers. And also a new panic. Because now she realized she was trapped, forced to wait until he left first so that he wouldn't catch sight of her wardrobe.

But he looked pretty damn comfortable and didn't appear to be in a rush to go anywhere.

She drew out her coffee as long as she dared and eyed her second doughnut. She wanted it more than she wanted her next breath but she didn't trust herself. And what did he mean, he'd seen her watching him? She didn't watch him. At least not all the time. "I don't watch you," she said.

He slid her a look.

"I don't. I can't even see you from my window." She waited a beat to be struck by lightning for the lie. "I watch the water," she clarified. "It calms me."

"Whatever you say." He looked amused as he drank the last of his coffee. "So if I get up and go, are you going to choke again?"

Funny. "I think it's safe now," she said stiffly. "And anyway, I'm going to be good and give up doughnuts." Forever.

Or until he left.

"Good luck with that," he said, still amused, damn him. "But as you already know now, Leah's stuff is addictive." He cast his gaze around the room, watchful. He caught sight of the perky brunette hovering near the door. "Can I walk you out?" he asked.

Absolutely not. If he was afraid of the perky brunette, he was on his own. No way was Callie going to reveal her bottom half. With what she hoped was a polite, disinterested smile, she shook her head. She wasn't moving again until he was gone, baby, gone.

Just then, the little toddler at the table behind her dropped his pacifier. It rolled beneath her boots.

He began to wail.

Pushing her chair back, Callie picked it up and handed it to the mom with a smile before realizing she'd moved out enough for her body to be seen. With a mental grimace, she quickly scooted close to her table again and stole a glance at Tanner.

He was smiling. "Cute," he said.

She blew out a breath. "I was in a hurry."

"No, I mean it," he said. "Cute."

Cute? Puppies and rainbows were cute. Once upon a time she'd spent far too much time dreaming about him finding her so irresistibly sexy that he'd press her up against the wall and kiss her senseless.

And he found her cute.

"Maybe you should steer clear of the dangerous powdered sugar doughnuts next time," he said. "In case there's no one around to rescue you."

"I like to live dangerously," she said, and because this was such a ridiculous statement, not to mention wildly untrue—she lived the opposite of dangerous and always had—she laughed a little.

He smiled at her, and it was such a great smile it rendered her stupid and unable to control her mouth. "You don't remember me."

"Sure I do," he said, and pushed away from the table as he stood. His gaze met hers. "Seriously now. Be careful."

And then he headed to the door.

Nope. He really didn't remember her. Still, she watched him go.

Okay, so she watched his fantastic butt go. After all, she was mortified and maybe a little bit pissy to boot, but she wasn't dead.

Chapter 3

♥

Tanner Riggs had been born an adrenaline junkie. It'd seen him through playing balls-out football to being a Navy SEAL to being the guy in charge of planting explosives on an oil rig, and there was little that he hadn't seen or done.

So he should've seen the signs that the day was going to go to shit before his client freaked the hell out twenty feet below the choppy surface of the ocean.

Tanner ran Lucky Harbor Charters with his two closest friends, Sam and Cole. They gave coastal tours, took people deep-sea fishing, scuba diving, whale watching, you name it, they did it, and though the business had taken off, it was usually tame in comparison to their past jobs.

He'd descended with their latest client, one Michael Soder, a certified scuba diver on his honeymoon. They were both in dry suits in deference to the November chill and cold Pacific Northwest waters and had just gone through an arch section made up of sandstone and rocks.

Michael had moved in close to the seawalls to examine some sea life and had bumped his face mask on a rock.

Not the end of the world, as the mask itself had nothing to do with his ability to breathe. Except now his nose wasn't covered so if he tried to inhale that way, he was going to get an unpleasant lungful of seawater. But all the guy had to do was reset his mask. An easy, basic skill and Tanner remained at the ready, waiting for Michael to do it.

But he didn't. Bubbles began to escape in increasing agitation and Michael lost grip of his mask entirely. Freaked out, he knocked himself into the rock wall, eyes wide as his mask drifted away.

Tanner snatched it, caught Michael by the arm, and held out the mask to him.

But Michael was gone, flailing around like a fish on a hook, completely mindless with panic.

Shit. Tanner tightened his grip and pressed the mask to Michael's face himself.

The guy continued to thrash a bit until Tanner took him by both arms and put his face right up against his, his own expression calm and steady, the idea being that it would sink into his client to copy that calm.

It took a long moment but finally Michael relaxed slightly. At the first sign of sanity back in his client's gaze, Tanner guided him out of the arch area.

Once more in open water, he stopped and checked Michael's mask. It was on solidly now, but his eyes were still wild and panicky. Shit. Tanner checked the guy's SPG—submersible pressure gauge—and found it lower than it should be, probably because he'd sucked down half his air during his panic attack.

It was easy enough to set him up with Tanner's own alternative breathing source, but it was game over at that point. There was no way Michael was going to recover in time to enjoy this, and Tanner wasn't willing to take the chance anyway. His gut feeling was confirmed when he pointed to the surface and Michael readily nodded.

Sharing Tanner's regulator they swam closely together, with Tanner eagle-eyeing the air pressure as they made it to their designated safety stop, where—per protocol—they would stay for three minutes before hitting the surface.

Twice Michael tried to go early, which made it three extremely long minutes.

If it'd been a true emergency, Tanner would've let it happen, but Michael was no novice. He knew the ropes. Which is what made this such an anomaly. They'd done a review on the boat beforehand, and Michael—showing off for his bride, who wasn't certified and was therefore safe and warm on board above them—had acted all manly and cocky. Tanner should've canceled the dive right then and there. He was kicking himself in the ass now for not doing so.

And actually, he'd kicked himself in the ass a whole hell of a lot lately, such as yesterday morning at the bakery in the presence of one adorably sexy strawberry blonde choking on her doughnut.

Sitting with her had been the highlight of his week. Hell, his month. And he wished he'd stayed longer.

He was an idiot.

When they finally surfaced, Michael gasped and sputtered and inhaled a bunch of water. Done with it, Tanner got a firm grip on him, pulling out his own mouthpiece.

"Relax," he ordered as Michael instinctively began to fight. "I'm going to tow you to the swim platform at the back of the boat."

"I can do it," Michael said stubbornly.

Hell, no. He'd had his chance. "I've got this," Tanner said with a level stare that helped get the no-more-bullshit point across.

Tanner swam them to the boat and Cole, captain and head mechanic, was right there waiting to lift Michael out of the water.

That was the beauty of a partner whose instincts were honed sharp as razors. They never let you down.

"What the fuck?" Cole murmured to Tanner.

"No idea," he said. "But I'm going to find out." He looked over at Michael, now huddled in the blankets that Cole had wrapped him in.

Tanner crouched beside him, ignoring the sharp protest from his bad leg. "What happened back there?"

Behind them, Cole was on the radio to Sam, head of operations. Sam wanted to know if they needed an ambulance waiting on shore. Cole looked to Tanner.

But Michael shook his head vehemently. "I don't need medical attention. I need a lobotomy."

No argument from Tanner. "Talk to me."

"I had a bad dive in Mexico last year," Michael said. "Gave me claustrophobia. I wanted to get past it."

Over his head, Tanner met the cool gaze of Cole. If you didn't know the guy, you'd never guess he was pissed off. But he was, and Tanner was right with him. Every single client of theirs was required to fill out multiple forms. One of the many questions was: Are you claustrophobic?

Clearly Michael had lied. Nothing to be done about it

now. They were just lucky it'd turned out as well as it had.

Michael's bride was smiling and taking pics as they got out of the water. "You weren't down for long," she said, clueless to what had gone on below. "You have fun?"

Michael slid his sheepish, apologetic gaze to Tanner. "Yes," he said.

His bride beamed.

"How do you do it?" Michael asked Tanner quietly. "Always stay so calm?"

For one thing, scuba diving was as natural to him as breathing. So was swimming. For another, his life hadn't exactly been a walk in the park. That he was now a one-third owner of a charter company consisting of a warehouse, yard, waterfront, dock, hut, and fifty-foot Wright Sport boat, where he was the resident scuba diving instructor and communications expert, was a piece of cake compared to where he'd been. "It's my job," he said.

"Your job gave you nuts of steel?"

"Actually," Cole said helpfully, "his life's given him nuts of steel."

Michael looked like he thought this was really cool. And once upon a time, Tanner might've enjoyed being thought of that way. Back in high school, for instance, when he'd lived on adrenaline rushes.

He no longer thrived on being stupid. In fact, he'd made it a lifelong goal to never be stupid again.

An hour later he, Cole, and Sam were at the Love Shack, Lucky Harbor's local bar and grill. They had a stack of hot wings and a pitcher of beer. As always, they all raised their glasses and clinked them together. "To Gil," Sam said.

"To Gil," Cole said.

"To Gil," Tanner echoed, and felt the usual tug in his gut at the name.

Gil had been, and in many ways still was, the fourth musketeer of their tight-knit group. He'd been gone and buried for two years now, but that hadn't erased the hole he'd left in Tanner's heart. Losing Gil in the Gulf after a rig fire had changed Tanner's life. Or maybe that had been because he'd nearly lost his own at the same time. At the reminder, he rubbed his leg, which was aching like a sonofabitch today.

Sam's gaze slid to the movement.

"I'm fine," Tanner said.

Sam and Cole exchanged annoying "right" glances.

"I am," he said.

"Uh-huh." Cole dove into the wings. "Saw Josh last week. He said you were overdue for an appointment."

Probably true. But Dr. Josh Scott, an old friend and excellent physician, couldn't fix his leg. All that could be done had been done. "Subject change."

"Fine," Cole said. "How was dinner with Troy last night?"

Troy was Tanner's fifteen-year-old Mini-Me and until two weeks ago, he'd lived in Florida with Tanner's ex, Elisa. "Good," he said. "I think I actually got four whole sentences out of him this time."

"Progress," Cole said.

"He's a teen," Sam said. "Four sentences is a miracle."

Plus it was a hell of a lot better than Tanner and Troy had managed in the past. He might not be Father of the Year but, unlike his own dad, who'd taken off when Tanner was five, he was trying.

"And it's not like you were a joy at fifteen," Cole reminded him.

Tanner eyed him over his beer. "What was wrong with me at fifteen?"

Cole laughed but when Tanner just looked at him, he turned it into a cough instead. "You were a real punk ass. Wild. Uncontrollable. Always looking for trouble." He turned to Sam. "Right?"

Sam stuffed a fry into his mouth. Sam pleaded the fifth a lot.

"Whatever," Cole said in disgust, and pointed a finger at each of them in turn. "You were both shitheads."

"And yet you hung out with us," Tanner said.

"Well, someone had to keep you two assholes in line. And you know how teenagers are," he said to Tanner. "It's just going to take you time to connect with him. Time and effort."

Tanner was more than willing to put in the effort. In fact, he'd never tried harder at anything than he had at being a dad, but in truth there were times when it'd be easier to part the Red Sea. This parenting-a-teenager shit was not for the faint of heart.

"Heard he got fired from the pier," Sam said. "Something about having a bad attitude with his boss at the arcade."

"Yeah," Tanner said, and shook his head. When he'd been fifteen, he'd gone to school, then football practice, and then he'd bagged at the grocery store for gas and car insurance money before finally going home to handle the house for his single mom. In comparison, his son's life was a walk in the park. "That's not why I'm pissed."

"Is it because he was taken to the police station for

filling the principal's car full of packing peanuts?" Cole asked.

"I bet it was that he posted a pic of his handiwork on Facebook after," Sam said.

"He says he didn't do it, that someone hacked into his account and put up the pic to get him in trouble." Tanner scrubbed a hand down his face. "But even if he did, Jesus. At least I was always smart enough not to document my own crimes."

Sam shook his head. "Not always, you weren't. Seventh grade, when you had a thing for the mayor's daughter. You stole the town's Christmas tree lights and used them to decorate her front yard, and then when everyone freaked out about the theft, you got caught in the act of trying to return the lights."

Cole started laughing at the memory and spilled his own beer. Tanner supposed it was wrong of him to hope that he choked on it. "Okay, fine," he said. "So the apple doesn't fall far from the tree."

"Maybe it's karma," Sam said. "You were wild and stupid and now he's following in your footsteps."

Sam was only kidding but the way Tanner saw it, Troy's bad 'tude was all on him. He could remember all too well the inner fury of being a kid who'd been dumped by his dad. And no, Tanner hadn't dumped Troy, but the kid didn't see it that way.

Tanner had been a teenager himself when he'd found out he was going to be a father. As a seventeen-year-old with no means to support himself, much less the girl he'd slept with on the beach after a party one night, he'd done the best he could. This had involved marrying Elisa to give her and their baby his name, throwing away a lucrative football scholarship to ship off to the navy, and growing up pretty damn fast.

Elisa had dumped him shortly after Troy's birth and moved with the baby to Florida to live with her grand-parents, but Tanner had still done what he could, making sure that he'd provided for the both of them along with his mom.

When he and the guys had first come back to Lucky Harbor from the Gulf of Mexico, he'd asked Elisa for custody, or at least partial. She'd refused, and for the past two years Tanner had done the best he could from three thousand miles away, visiting Troy as often as possible, calling, emailing...

And then two weeks ago Elisa had changed her tune, showing up in town with Troy in tow, as well as Boy-friend Dan. Suddenly she'd been all about sharing custody of their son.

No idiot, Tanner had jumped right on that, but there'd been problems he hadn't foreseen. Such as Troy's bad attitude, resentment, and basic hatred of all authority figures—of whom Tanner was apparently the king.

"If the kid's anything like you," Cole said, "and we all know he's exactly like you, then keeping him busy is the key. He just lost a job. Why don't we give him one?"

"I like it," Sam said. "The boat needs a massive detail-ing, the dock needs a good bleaching, and the equipment needs its seasonal going-over—every single inch of every single piece of equipment with a fine-tooth comb."

"And you trust a pissed-off-at-the-world fifteen-year-old to do all that?" Tanner asked in disbelief.

"It's better than us doing it," Sam said pragmatically. "He's already grounded from anything except school, right? He probably thinks his life is over. You'd be doing him a favor, and you need that. You need him to owe you."

"It's a great idea," Cole said.

Actually, Tanner couldn't think of a worse idea. But his so-called friends just grinned at him. "Shit," he said, and they out and out laughed at him. He pointed at Sam. "You're next, you know. You're getting married in a month. This kid thing is coming for you, and I can't wait. I'm going to laugh my ass off."

"That's just mean, man," Sam said.

"You'll get the hang of daddy duty," Cole told Tanner, clapping a hand on his shoulder. "Sooner or later."

God, he hoped so, but sooner would be better than later. The problem was, Tanner had undeniable survival skills, an arguable amount of life skills, and absolutely no known dad skills.

Chapter 4

♥

Callie was woken before the crack of dawn by a call from a panicked bride who'd decided she wanted to elope instead of face her elaborate wedding in two days.

"I don't know what I was thinking," Lacey wailed. "All this crazy fuss. I just want to cancel."

Callie had a lot of experience with these sorts of calls. But up until yesterday Lacey had been over-the-moon ecstatic about everything, down to the color of the nail polish she planned on using on her Yorkshire terrier. "What happened?" Callie asked, stumbling to her kitchen for coffee before remembering she no longer had a coffeemaker.

"It started last night," Lacey said. "Joe said all I ever talk about is the wedding and he's sick of it. Can you believe it? All this work I've done and he's over it before it even happens!"

Callie opened her freezer and stared at the ice cream. No, she told herself firmly. You are not having ice cream for breakfast. "Sometimes grooms feel a little left out, that's all," she said. "You could involve him in some of the decisions that have to be made. Maybe he could help arrange the flowers at the reception site or—"

"He can't be trusted with the flowers!" Lacey cried. "He thought we could do without flowers, said he didn't see the big deal. And then he tried to tell me that the seating arrangements are all wrong, that his Uncle Bob can't sit next to his Aunt Judy because they'll kill each other. But now's a fine time to tell me that! Do you know how difficult it is to work with tables that only seat six?"

Yes, Callie knew exactly. With a sigh, she shut the freezer. "I'll rework the seating arrangement for you."

"Great. But can you give my fiancé a personality transplant?" Lacey asked. "No? Then I want to elope! You're my virtual wedding planner, can you help me elope or not?"

Callie drew a deep breath. "Yes. But I want you to do me one favor. Remember how Joe proposed? It was just as you'd asked him to do, in front of all your family and friends on the beach at sunset. He even got you the exact ring you wanted, the one with the bigger diamond that he couldn't really afford."

Lacey sighed dreamily. "Yes. He did do that for me."

"He'd do anything for you," Callie said. "And if he's voicing his thoughts to you, you're already ahead of the game in the marriage department. It means you're communicating. All you have to do now is listen and hear him. He's feeling left out, Lacey, that's all. Find a way to let him help you."

"You really think that'll solve the problem?"

"Absolutely," Callie said. "Talk to him. And if you still

want to elope afterward, we'll make that happen. Call me tonight."

"Okay. Thanks, Callie. You're like magic."

Yes. She was. She was magic at creating the illusion that romance lasted forever in spite of the fact that the statistics were stacked against Lacey and Joe making it to their second wedding anniversary.

God, she really needed a new job. And possibly a new life.

She showered and pulled on another "work" outfit—a pretty blouse and blazer and…comfy sweatpants for a few Skype calls. An hour later her stomach was grumbling loud enough for her clients to hear. Her famously bad instincts warred with her desire to go back to the bakery to feed her newfound doughnut addiction.

And maybe also to see if Tanner was there again. A mistake waiting to happen, of course.

She'd had lunch yesterday with her grandma. She'd met the boyfriend candidate, who'd turned out to be Mr. Wykowski, an eighty-plus retired rocket scientist who resembled a pipe cleaner with eyes. A stooped pipe cleaner. But he was warm and kind and very patient. He had to be, to be thinking of dating her grandma.

Lucille had filled Callie in on the latest gossip in town as well as what she knew about Tanner. Finding out that he'd been in an oil rig fire and had nearly lost his life had made it difficult for her to breathe, but he was okay now. She'd seen this for herself. Yeah, he still obviously had trouble with his leg, but from what she understood, he was lucky to have the leg at all.

She couldn't begin to imagine what he'd been through, but hearing about his bravery had only fueled her curiosity about him. Which meant that she couldn't trust herself not to act like that pathetic little bookworm she'd once been.

In any case, she couldn't go to the bakery. She had plans for breakfast with her two neighbors, Becca and Olivia. The three of them were becoming friends, and Callie was grateful to have them in this town that no longer felt like home.

When she'd grown up here, she hadn't had a lot of friends. Her best friend from school, Hannah, had died of cancer five years ago. Her loss had made it easier to stay away.

She left her apartment and knocked on Olivia's, right next door. Olivia stuck her head out wearing a man's white button-down and what looked like absolutely nothing else.

"A new look?" Callie asked.

Olivia laughed and stroked a hand down her definite bedhead hair. "Yeah. Um, was everything okay last night? You slept good?"

Callie leaned against the wall. "You mean did I hear anything coming from your love nest after you stuffed something in the pipes?"

Olivia grimaced. "Socks. I used socks this time. Better than the rolls of toilet paper."

"Worked like a charm," Callie said. "Even more efficient than the insulation we don't have."

"Good." Olivia gave a relieved smile. "Didn't want a repeat of the other night. I'm still sorry about that, by the way."

Unfortunately, the warehouse was so poorly constructed they could hear each other sneeze. And more.

And in Olivia's case there'd been a lot of that *more* lately, thanks to her new relationship with Cole, one of Tanner's business partners.

"No worries," Callie said. "I put on my headphones as a precautionary measure."

Olivia groaned. "We've really got to get the landlord to put in some insulation. Listen, about breakfast…I've got a…thing."

"Uh-huh," Callie said on a laugh. "Let me guess. A six-foot, gorgeous, green-eyed thing that goes by the name of Cole?"

Olivia bit her lower lip. "He didn't dock until three a.m. and we need a few more hours of shut-eye."

"Go for it," Callie said. "I'll just get Becca. We'll make it a wedding planning breakfast."

Becca was marrying Sam, Tanner's other business partner, and Callie had promised to step in for this last month before the wedding and help however she could.

"You didn't get her text?" Olivia asked.

"No, I—" Callie looked down at her phone. "Oh." Indeed she'd missed a text from Becca:

> The guys didn't get in until 3 a.m. Sorry to bail on you, but I'm toast. I owe ya breakfast and I have a feeling Olivia does too.

Callie laughed. "Got it," she told Olivia. "Go back to bed."

"Thanks. Have a doughnut for me, will ya?" Olivia asked. "Try one of Leah's old-fashioned chocolate glazes this time. You shouldn't choke on those."

Callie opened her mouth to ask how she knew, but

Olivia shook her head. "It's Lucky Harbor," she said. "You know how it works. You can leave your front door unlocked and no one would ever touch your stuff, but you can't keep a secret."

"There's no secret," Callie insisted. "I just had coffee."

"And doughnuts." Olivia paused. "With Tanner Riggs."

"The tables were full," Callie said. "He sat down because there was nowhere else to sit."

"That's not what I heard," Olivia said.

"What did you hear?"

"That he was smiling and laughing. Which is a big deal because he hasn't had much to smile or laugh about in a while."

"He was smiling and laughing because I made an ass out of myself," Callie told her. "And to prove it, ask your source what I was wearing. Yoga capris and Uggs. Fake Uggs. That's not a hot-mama look, in case you were wondering."

"Yeah, I heard that too." Olivia grinned. "And, um, not to be critical or anything, but today isn't all that different."

Callie looked down at herself—nice blouse, blazer, and sweatpants—and groaned.

Olivia laughed but then her smile faded. "Listen, Tanner's been through a rough time. You're going through a rough time." She paused and waited for Callie to say something. When she didn't, she said, "Do you really not see where I'm going with this?"

"It was coffee," Callie repeated. "And you should know, even given what I do for a living—or maybe especially because of what I do for a living—I'm not at all sold on the male race."

"I get that," Olivia said gently. "But just think about it." And then she blew Callie a kiss and shut the door.

Callie shook her head and started to head out of the building. She stopped short and once again looked down at her "work outfit." Since Sam and Cole hadn't gotten in until three in the morning and Tanner had probably been with them, she wasn't going to run into him this morning. Right? Right. So there wasn't a reason to change her clothes. She wasn't trying to impress anyone.

She went back to her apartment to stuff her backpack with her laptop and wallet and rode to the bakery on the bike she'd bought on a whim the weekend before at a garage sale. She was crap on a bike, but in the name of getting herself a life, she'd decided that more exercise was a definite place to show improvement.

Her mission was threefold. Objective A: not thinking about her two friends, the both of them in bed with their big, sexy, hot men keeping them warm in their icy apartments.

She wasn't jealous, exactly. She didn't want a big, sexy, hot man to call her own.

But she wouldn't mind one for a single night.

Or two...

Objective B: caffeine and a doughnut—chocolate glaze. Make that two doughnuts.

Objective C: not hiding out behind her computer in Lucky Harbor but getting out and living.

The morning was startlingly clear and bright and sunny. But true to November in Washington, her breath made little puffs of cloud in front of her face, and she couldn't feel her fingers and toes as she rode.

She came to the pier and stopped, gazing up at the Ferris wheel jutting into the sky. She'd gotten her first kiss there from Jonathon Walters in sixth grade, but only because it'd been dark, really dark, and he'd thought she'd been the very popular Jessica Bentley.

"Well, look who's back."

Callie eyed the guy painting the closed ice cream stand. "Lance," she said with a big smile. They'd gone to school together. "How's it going? Are you a painter?"

"Nah. I run this place in the good weather months with my brother."

Thanks to cystic fibrosis, his voice was thick and almost hollow sounding, and her smile faded. "You doing okay?"

He lifted a shoulder. "Hanging in," he said simply.

She felt her throat get a little tight and was figuring out how to ask if she could hug him when he spoke again.

"Your granny's been up to no good."

Uh-oh. "Such as?" she asked.

"Meddling." He grinned. "She's pretty good at it too, running a gossip circuit between Instagram, Twitter, and Tumblr. She was on Facebook for a while but got booted for inappropriate pics. That woman's on top of technology for being a couple hundred years old. How did she learn all that?"

Callie laughed a little but she was horrified as well. "I might have taught her."

"Yeah? Well, you created a monster, babe."

"Is it really that bad?"

He grinned. "She's got a geriatric gang behind her and has armed them all with tablets that she got donated to the senior center. Mostly because they couldn't navigate smartphones since they're all over seventy and blind as bats. Anyway, they pretty much run the town."

"This explains a lot," Callie said.

"There's even word that she plans to run for mayor."

"Oh my God."

Lance laughed, which sent him into a coughing fit. When he could talk again, he just smiled, though it was a weak one. "No worries, she can't win. Most people think she has enough power as it is."

This did not make Callie feel any better. She gave Lance a hug and a kiss on the cheek. "Take care of yourself," she said, and pushed off on her bike.

Five minutes later she was inside the bakery, which was once again crazy crowded. She ordered a coffee and stared at the doughnuts. Resist.

Leah smiled a greeting. "Hey. Heard you're Lucille's granddaughter."

"Yep," Callie said. "That's me."

"My grandma plays bingo with your grandma. Which is probably one of the more innocuous things they do. The seniors are all very excited you're in town. They're hoping you're going to teach Lucille some new tricks." She laughed at the look on Callie's face. "Yeah," she said. "And you probably don't know even the half of it."

"That's what I'm afraid of," Callie said. "I'm back in town to see how bad it's gotten and if she needs help."

"It's probably a matter of opinion," Leah said on a laugh. "But if you're asking if she's sane? Sane as Batman."

Not helping. Callie slid another look at the doughnut case. "So how are your old-fashioned chocolate glazes?"

"Out of this world."

Callie bit her lower lip. "I read that chocolate comes from a tree called cacao. Which makes it a plant. Which means it's practically a salad."

Leah grinned. "You want one or two?"

"I'll be good and have just one."

A minute later Callie took the only table available—by coincidence the same one as the other day. She pulled her laptop from her backpack and opened it, and kept her head down as she stuffed her face and pretended to be engrossed so that no one would bother her. It was okay to need to work up to being social, she told herself.

Someone pulled out the chair across from her with their foot and sat.

Crap.

She inhaled a breath for patience and lifted her head. And then stilled.

Tanner raised a brow. "You're not going to choke again, are you?"

Chapter 5

♥

Don't you dare choke, Callie ordered herself. "No, I'm good," she said to Tanner with what she thought was remarkable calm. "I must've been catching a cold yesterday or something."

He flashed her a knowing grin.

Damn it. Deciding to look busy, she went back to her keyboard rather than let her eyes wander over him. Which wasn't necessary since she already had him memorized. Battered boots, faded and ripped jeans riding low on his narrow hips, and a navy blue thermal, the sleeves shoved up on his forearms and stretched taut over his broad chest and shoulders. A build like that came from years of physical labor, and it had done a body good. His dark hair was damp and he smelled faintly of some really great-smelling soap. She found herself inhaling deeply just to catch another whiff.

"Yeah, it smells great in here, doesn't it?" he asked.

She did her best not to give herself away with a blush.
"Really great."

"It's the vanilla," he said.

Actually it's you, she thought but didn't speak. Didn't
dare. She was already tongue-tied again. It was the way
he had of focusing in on the person he was talking to, she
decided. He gave his full attention, totally present. Rare
in today's electronic world. When Tanner Riggs looked at
you, you knew he wasn't stressing over his grandma driving everyone batty or whether his hair looked good today.
Which, for the record, it did. It looked dark and silky soft
to the touch— Her phone buzzed with an incoming text
from one of her brides and she nearly jumped out of her
skin.

Is it hard to get a plane flying over my wedding with
a banner that reads HE FINALLY PUT A RING ON IT
AND JUST IN TIME TOO as the minister says "I now
pronounce you husband and wife"?

Oh boy. Callie hit REPLY and typed out her response:

Do you really want your 350 guests to know you're
having a shotgun wedding?

While she was waiting on a response to this, already
mentally preparing to figure out how to do the banner as
tactfully as possible, a white bag appeared between her
eyes and her screen.

Tanner, offering a daring smile if she'd ever seen one.

"A Boston cream," he said.

"Are you trying to make me be bad?"

He smiled, slow and wicked, and Callie's face heated. "You know what I mean," she muttered, looking around to find no one paying them any attention at all. The fakers.

"Just eat," he said. "Enjoy."

"Why?"

"Suspicious thing, aren't you?" He stretched out his left leg with a long, slow exhale as if he were in pain. She thought of what her grandma had told her about the guys losing one friend and nearly Tanner as well, and her heart ached for him. She wanted to ask him if he needed anything, Advil, or…a massage. But just before she could make a total fool of herself, he shifted and his right thigh bumped hers.

He didn't pull back. She doubted if Tanner knew the definition of pulling back.

"Consider the doughnut a bribe to let me share your table," he said. "And a thank you for doing so."

"I didn't say yes."

"Take a bite and you won't say no."

She narrowed her eyes. "Everything you say sounds dirty."

His head went back and he laughed softly. The amusement transformed his features, and she found herself staring openly at him.

Still smiling, he leaned in. "You know what this means, right?"

She had no idea, and still staring at him, she shook her head.

"It means you're the one with the dirty mind."

She bit her lower lip and when he laughed again, she took a bite of the Boston cream—in spite of already eating the old-fashioned chocolate glazed—and moaned in pleasure.

Tanner stopped laughing. He looked at her mouth and his eyes went black, and right there in the middle of the crowded bakery Callie felt herself go damp. It was crazy. She sat staring at him, mentally tearing off his clothes, when her phone buzzed with another text from her bride.

You're right. Disregard banner.

Callie smiled. She'd long ago discovered that most of her brides needed the ideas to be their own. Thinking she was in the clear, she started to set her phone aside but it buzzed again.

I do want to be carried in, though, on a fancy litter. Can we do that? And I was thinking of 3-D invitations, delivered with 3-D glasses. What do you think?

"Good Lord," Callie muttered.

"What?"

"I'm dealing with a bride who wants me to design her three-D invitations to be delivered with three-D glasses, which I can totally do. But she also wants to be carried down the aisle. On a litter."

He smiled. "Interesting job you've got there."

"Yep. Always lots of fires to put out." She went still as it sank in what she'd just said and how that would sound to a man who'd actually been in a fire for his job. Literally. "God. I didn't mean…"

"I know."

She met his gaze. "I realize that next to the jobs you've

held, mine's a piece of cake. I don't even have to leave my house to do it."

"Or wear pants," he said.

Crap! She'd forgotten. She felt her face go hot. "Bad habit. I usually only dress from the waist up for Skyping clients," she admitted.

"I'm liking this story," he said. "Tell me more. Slowly. In great detail."

Her face got even hotter. "You're playing with me."

"Yes," he said, and flashed that killer smile.

Good Lord, he was potent. She had to shake it off. "Um, I should tell you I'm not interested in playing. My life's...full." God, she was so awkward. She'd like to think it was the clothes she was wearing but she knew better. It was her. "It's just that I'm not interested in love," she blurted out. "I don't believe in it."

He just sipped his coffee all calm and relaxed. "No?"

"No. Not at all. Not even a little, tiny bit." God, Callie. Just shut up. "It's not for me."

"Makes two of us," he said easily. "Eat your doughnut."

She stared into his unfathomable eyes and found herself unwilling to let this go. She knew why she wasn't interested in love. It was because love was a romantic fiction and, with the exception of her crazy parents, didn't last.

But why wasn't he interested in love? Was it his failed marriage? To keep herself from asking she shoved in another bite. Heaven. She licked the sugar off her lower lip and watched his eyes follow the movement of her tongue. She stilled, swallowed, and then was tempted to do it again if only to get another one of those delicious shivers his gaze had invoked. "If I gain a single ounce over this," she murmured, her voice a little husky, "I'm coming to find you."

His eyes gleamed, speaking as clearly as any words could have.

He'd be fine with that…

And she? Well, in spite of her ridiculous I'm-not-interested-in-love speech, she knew she was in trouble here. Big trouble. Because love she could resist. Lust, as it turned out, not so much. And she was sinking in lust fast, going down without a raft or life vest in sight. "We shouldn't make a habit of this," she said. "Sharing a table. I like to be alone with my coffee."

"And your doughnuts." He laughed again when she blushed. "And I disagree about making this a habit," he said. "We're providing each other a service by sharing a table."

"How so?"

"If we sit together, you don't have to pretend to be working to be left alone," he said, "and I don't have to answer the incessant questions."

"Questions?"

"If my leg hurts, how come Troy's bound and determined to be as wild and reckless as I was, why don't I remarry, blah blah."

She was afraid to admit she'd like to ask him all those same questions and more. "I wasn't pretending to work to be left alone," she said. "I really was working."

He grinned, his teeth white against his tanned skin and stubble. "Good. Go with that. It's almost believable."

Yeah. She had a problem. Because her high school crush? Fully reinstated.

Chapter 6

♥

That night Tanner got home after a long day on the water with clients to find his voicemail loaded.

"Call me," Sally Taylor, the high school principal, said, and brought back all sorts of memories from his own high school years, where his mom getting calls from the principal had been a weekly thing.

Tanner let out a long breath. This couldn't be good. It couldn't be anywhere close to good. His second message was from Elisa.

"Call me," she said.

Shit. Definitely not good.

The third and last call was from Troy himself. No message.

Yeah. So not good. Tanner called his son first. "What's up?"

There was a long, weighted pause. Then a tentative "What did you hear?" from Troy.

Tanner felt an eye twitch coming on. "Spill it," he said.

"It wasn't my fault."

Oh, Jesus. He'd heard this before. "What wasn't?"

"The almost fight," Troy said.

Tanner put a finger to his twitching eye. "Keep talking."

"It's cliquey here. You're either an athlete or a nobody."

Tanner got that compared to Miami, where Troy'd grown up until a few weeks ago, Lucky Harbor was probably the equivalent of moving to the moon. "I thought you wanted to play football," Tanner said. "I talked to the coach for you."

"Yeah," Troy said, "and he told his quarterback son, who isn't excited about me joining the team just in time for the playoffs and stepping all over his toes."

"Ignore him," Tanner said. "He's a punk ass. Don't get drawn in to the drama."

Silence.

"Troy? You hear me?"

"Yeah. I gotta go."

Disconnect.

Now both of Tanner's eyes were twitching. Either he was getting an embolism or he was irritated as shit. Maybe both. He called Elisa.

"He's out of control," she answered with. "His grades are slipping. He talks back. He won't do what I ask. And the principal called today."

"I know. What did she want?"

"I don't know. I missed her call too," she said. "I came back to Lucky Harbor for the sole purpose of getting you to help me, but honestly? I think you need to do more. You need to take custody."

"Done," Tanner said.

Elisa paused. "Well, that was easy."

"Why are you surprised? The day I left the Gulf I asked you for joint custody."

"You were in the hospital and recovering from a life-threatening accident, remember?"

He wasn't likely to forget as he'd also been mourning losing Gil. "You said there was no way in hell you'd give him up."

"That was before your son insinuated to my boyfriend that Dan wasn't old enough to shave."

Tanner didn't say what was on his mind at that—which was that it seemed like a fair question to him as Dan was a decade her junior.

"So you'll take custody?" Elisa asked.

Tanner frowned. "Why do you keep forgetting to say joint?"

"Right. Joint."

"Wow, that's convincing."

"Hey," she said, her voice angry. "The absentee dad doesn't get to judge. Now I'm in desperate need of a week off. Are you going to help me or what?"

"Yes," Tanner said immediately. Hell, yes. "I'll come get him right now. I can be there in ten minutes."

"No, he's grounded. He's already in his room for the night. I'll bring him to you tomorrow."

"Before school," Tanner said. "The docks. I've got a job for him."

"Ha. Good luck."

Tanner stared at his phone for a long time after she disconnected and then at his ceiling. He was trying not to take offense at the absentee dad comment, since basically it was true.

But shit, he'd had little choice. Their circumstances

had been dire. He'd been seventeen when he'd gotten her pregnant thanks to a bottle of "borrowed" hootch and a technical foul on condom use. He'd been eighteen when Troy had been born. Going into the navy had been the only way to make enough money to support them all.

Elisa had known it. She'd been all for it.

Until Tanner had actually gone, that is, and then suddenly the reality of being alone with a baby had set in. She'd moved to Florida without consulting Tanner, and he'd had little choice but to agree that being with her grandparents was good for both Elisa and Troy while he was away.

Unfortunately, absence hadn't made the heart grow fonder. That year he'd gotten divorce papers for his birthday delivered to his base.

But that was all in the past. Tanner was a here-and-now kind of guy, and he was going to take what he could get. In this case, it was a second chance with his son—teenage alien or not.

Tanner woke before dawn. Both the military and the rig job had required brutal hours, so it was second nature by now.

He showered and dressed and left his house in the pitch dark, heading to the harbor. Sam arrived at the same time, and so did Mark, Sam's dad, who worked for them on a part-time basis answering phones, dealing with clients, whatever was needed.

"Troy starts today," he warned them.

"Oh, boy," Mark said. "Batten down the hatches."

"Dad," Sam said.

"Maybe we should fingerprint him," Mark said, warming to the subject.

"Dad," Sam said again.

"Put up nanny cams," Mark said, grinning, getting into it. His grin faded when he realized neither Sam nor Tanner was smiling. "Too far?"

Sam gave Tanner a look that said *I'll trade you a teen for a dad.* "You've got this," he said.

Tanner exhaled. "You think so?"

"Just remember what you were like at fifteen."

He'd been an ass. "Not helping."

Sam clapped him on the shoulder. "We've got your back." Then he headed to the warehouse to work on the boat he was building.

"Hey," Tanner called after him. "How are you going to have my back holed up in the shop?"

"Call me if you need me."

"But you don't answer your phone," Tanner said.

Sam vanished. Tanner sighed and eyed Mark, who was still grinning.

"Now maybe you guys will see that this daddy shit ain't all it's cracked up to be," Mark said.

"This isn't funny," Tanner said.

"A little bit it is." Mark had recently come back into Sam's life. He was good at handling the office crap that none of them wanted to do, and even better at annoying Sam. But Tanner got that it was important for Mark and Sam to spend some time together—as long as it was supervised. No need to tempt fate and risk Sam going to jail for murder one.

Tanner drew a deep breath and headed to the dock. Thirty minutes later a car pulled into the lot and Tanner walked up to the warehouse to meet it.

Elisa didn't stay to chat when Troy got out of her car with two duffel bags.

The teen eyed Tanner, not looking super thrilled. Then he eyed the sign hanging off the warehouse door that said: NINJAS & PIRATES & LASERS & SHIT—STAY OUT.

He blinked. "You've got lasers?"

"Sam doesn't like company in there when he's building a boat," Tanner said. "The sign is supposed to scare people off. He changes it every week or so."

Troy looked disappointed. "Mom said I'm going to stay with you for the rest of the week and that I had to give you an hour of work every day before school." Eyes hooded, his 'tude dialed to Sullen Teen, his face was closed off.

Tanner knew it matched his own face, from the square jaw to the hard set of his mouth, to his dark hide-everything gaze. "Glad you showed," Tanner said.

Troy hunched into his jacket. "I don't think she wants me at the house right now."

"That's what happens when you're a shithead."

"Maybe it's because of her boyfriend, Dale."

It was Dan, and they both knew it. But if that was true, that they didn't want Troy around, Tanner was going to be seriously pissed off at Elisa. The problem was that he had no real faith in either Troy's or Elisa's version of the truth. They were both acting Troy's age.

"I want you here," Tanner said, and when Troy looked up, vulnerability and uncertainty flashing across his face, Tanner's heart squeezed as he nodded reaffirmation.

But the kid was good and he masked his emotions real fast—something else he'd gotten from dear old dad—giving a casual shrug like he didn't give a damn, staring down at his shoes as if they held the secrets to life. "You gotta say that."

"No, actually, I don't," Tanner told him. "I never say anything I don't want to. I've always wanted you with me."

Troy didn't respond to that other than to make a noise that suggested Tanner might be full of shit.

Yeah. He got that. Hell, he'd been there, right there in Troy's shoes, so he didn't bother to try to convince the kid. Words couldn't do that anyway, only actions could. "You lost your job at the arcade and you got in trouble at school again," Tanner said. "Yeah?"

Troy shrugged.

"If nothing else, a Riggs always owns up to their own shit. Got me?"

Troy hesitated. "I get you."

"And?"

Troy stared at him for a long beat and Tanner held his gaze, hoping Troy was going to step up.

Troy blew out a breath. "And I got fired," he admitted. "And in trouble at school."

Tanner nodded. "You've got a job here. You'll make more money than you did at the arcade, but your responsibilities will be more important. You on board with that?"

Troy was showing some interest now. "You're going to pay me?"

"Yeah, we're going to pay you, though you're going to work your ass off for it. Yes or no?"

Troy blinked. "I get a choice?"

"I'm not into slave labor, Troy."

"Do I have a choice since I have to live with you for a week?"

Tanner blew out a breath. There was no gain in telling him that Elisa had dictated that decree. All it would do was hurt him, something Tanner was going to make sure didn't happen on his watch. "I'm your dad," he said. "That means this is more of a dictatorship than a democracy. So yeah, you're with me this week. My rules include: respecting your mom, respecting your employer— whoever that may be—not getting in trouble at school, and in general being a decent human being. It does not include you being forced to work for me. That's your choice. Now I've got a lot of shit to get to so I'm going to ask you one more time. Yes or no?"

Troy shoved his hands in his pockets. "I get grounded for saying the word 'shit.' Or 'hell.' Or 'fuck.'" He said this last with great defiance, and Tanner decided to pick his battles.

Besides, he and Cole and Sam swore like it was their job, so he didn't have a soapbox to stand on with this one. "Yeah, well, when you're as old as I am no one'll ground you for swearing," he promised.

"That's not fair."

"Nope," Tanner agreed. "But life isn't fair. Yes or no, Troy."

Another shrug. "I guess."

Tanner studied him a moment. "I'll take that as a 'oh, thank you, Dad, yes,'" he finally said dryly. "You'll be scrubbing the deck today."

As if he'd just been asked to make molehills out of mountains, Troy blew out a breath and rolled his eyes. Which was just about the kid's favorite thing to do, and if he persisted at it, Tanner was going to put those eyes in a jar and roll them for him. "The equipment's in the hut."

The hut was what they used for the front office of Lucky Harbor Charters. "Mark's already in," Tanner said. "He'll get you what you need."

"The old guy?" Troy asked. "He tells stupid stories and never stops talking."

"Mark is Sam's father," Tanner said, "and you'll need to give him the same amount of respect that you'd give me, Sam, or Cole." Tanner held Troy's gaze for a long beat, but apparently Troy was smarter than he looked because he didn't quite dare roll his eyes again.

But neither did he look happy or thrilled, or any of the things Tanner had ideally hoped to see. Apparently, getting Troy's head out of his own ass was going to take some time. And just as apparently, the two of them working together was going to make them or break them, though Tanner would accept nothing less than success—God help them both. Because there was no going back. Like the explosives Tanner had worked with for so many years, he had one chance to get this right, to avoid blowing things sky high with his son.

He received an email and glanced at it. It was from his mom.

Honey, I stopped by the B&B spa and picked up a deep muscle tissue cream for your leg. You remember Chloe Traeger? Well, she's Chloe Thompson now, married to the sheriff, and she runs the spa. She says to come by so she can massage the knots out of your leg. She said you need to be doing this weekly. Also, she wants you to do yoga with her for PT.

Tanner did remember Chloe, vividly. She'd been as wild as he, and a lot of fun. But he would do yoga with her over his cold, dead body.

Troy read the email over his shoulder and snorted.

Tanner slid him a look. "What?"

"Grandma's pretty bossy for a nice old lady."

Tanner couldn't help it—he had to laugh. "Don't let her hear you call her old or you'll really see bossy."

"You going to do the yoga?"

Hell, no. But he didn't want to form the kid's negative opinions. "There's nothing wrong with yoga."

"Yeah, if you're a girl," Troy said.

Tanner deleted the email.

"You think she'll be baking brownies again anytime soon?" Troy asked, an unmistakable note of hope in his voice.

Tanner met Troy's gaze. "She told you she baked those brownies herself?"

"Yeah."

Tanner laughed. "She buys them at the bakery from Leah."

"Really? Why did she lie about it?"

"She didn't. I guarantee you she heated them up in her oven specifically so as to not be lying." He shrugged at Troy's confused expression. "Look, for most of your life, you've lived far away from her and she didn't get to spoil you. She wants to be the grandma who bakes. But she can't bake, she burns everything, so she buys the brownies and reheats them."

"For me," Troy said.

"For you."

Troy chewed on that for a minute. "Mom doesn't even try to cook," he finally said. "So I don't care that Grandma buys the brownies instead of baking them herself. I just love to eat them."

At this much of Tanner's amusement faded. He really

didn't have any business judging Elisa. He didn't care that she hadn't baked their kid brownies. But he cared that Troy had been robbed of his mom's nurturing company. "As much as you love to eat them," he said, "that's how much she loves to provide them for you. And she likes you thinking she made them, so pretend you don't know otherwise." He lifted a hand when Troy started to respond. "Look, I can't explain the female mind to you. There aren't enough hours in the day."

Troy's mouth quirked at the very corners in an almost smile and Tanner felt like he'd been given a winning lottery ticket.

An hour later, he dropped Troy off at school with a "Try to stay out of trouble."

The teen slid out of the truck and had to hike up his too-loose jeans or lose them.

Tanner shook his head. Been a damn long time since he couldn't walk for risk of mooning everyone around him.

Troy vanished inside the school, and Tanner sat there watching him go, feeling everything his own mom must have felt every single day—a terrorizing love and an equally terrorizing fear that he'd somehow screw up this parenting gig.

Finally he pulled out of the school and headed to the bakery. He needed his day's fix of coffee, and possibly a lobotomy for his inexplicable desire to see Callie again.

Up until a week ago he could've gotten coffee in the hut, but Cole and Sam had gotten into a paintball fight and the machine had been the only casualty. There were other, closer places than the bakery to get coffee.

Eat Me Diner, for one.

The town's bar and grill, the Love Shack, for another.

But Tanner took the extra block, parked, and strode into the bakery, unable to pretend he was doing anything other than hoping for another glimpse of the awkwardly sexy strawberry blonde who'd made him smile for two mornings running.

The tables were all filled, even the back corner one that he already thought of as "their" table. A woman was seated there, head down, eyes glued to her laptop.

Callie.

She was in real pants today, skinny jeans tucked into black leather boots that revved his engines, and a long, soft sweater the exact color of her jade-green eyes. She was chewing on her lower lip, staring at her screen, seemingly oblivious to the rest of the world.

But thanks to the military Tanner was a master of reading the tiniest minute details, and he caught on to the fact that she was watching him out of the corner of her eye. Not so oblivious to him at all, a fact that was somehow both cute and hot at the same time.

As he watched, a guy walked up to her, gesturing to the empty chair at her table, clearly asking if he could sit.

Callie blinked up at him and shook her head.

The guy moved off.

Someone else immediately moved in, and she waved them off as well, a frown on her face.

Most definitely a lobotomy, he thought, and drawn to her like a magnet, he bought two coffees, four doughnuts, and moved in close. "Morning."

She jumped and looked at him, her cheeks going pink. "Um. Hi."

"Hi."

She paused and, looking endearingly nervous, offered him a rather self-deprecatory smile.

And he realized...

She'd been saving the chair for him.

He liked that.

He liked that a whole hell of a lot.

And that's when he thought maybe his day was going to get better after all. "That guy you turned away wanted to buy you a coffee," he said.

"He would've had more luck if he'd been offering doughnuts."

Yep. Definitely getting better, he thought, and handed her his bag of doughnuts.

Chapter 7

♥

By the time Tanner grabbed the empty chair and pulled it out for himself, Callie's heart was knocking hard against her ribs in panic.

And okay, a little bit of lust as well. Or, you know, a lot.

In checking up on her grandma, she'd been through Lucille's social media pages. Instagram, Tumblr, Twitter… and she'd inadvertently learned a lot about Lucky Harbor's citizens.

One in particular.

Tanner Riggs was Lucky Harbor's current most popular bachelor. Actually, Lucille had called him the Last Hot Single Guy for Two Hundred Miles. Callie wondered if he knew. Not that she was going to be the one to tell him if he didn't.

"Real pants today," Tanner noted. "I like the boots."

She'd argued with herself earlier when she'd gotten out of the shower and stared into her closet. Yoga pants or jeans? Don't care or care?

Turned out she cared. Hence the jeans.

And the boots. "They're my kick-ass boots," she said.

He smiled and she forgot how to breathe. Just plain forgot.

"You plan on kicking any ass today?" he asked.

"Too early to tell," she responded. Look at her, all smooth and cool. "But I wanted the odds balanced in my favor if anything comes up."

"I like the way you think." He straightened out his leg, letting out a long, careful exhale as he did.

"You okay?" she asked quietly.

"Yes." He drank deeply of his coffee and her gaze was drawn to his throat as he swallowed.

And then his broad chest.

And flat abs.

And the way his jeans—faded and threadbare in some of the good spots—fit him. Which was perfectly. "I meant your leg," she said.

"It's fine."

"Huh," she said.

He slid her a look. "Huh what?"

"Well, it's just that 'it's fine' is a typical guy response. Men tend to use 'fine' as a catchall."

"A catchall."

"Yeah," she said. "You know, a noun, adjective, adverb, whatever. Tell me the truth—your leg could be literally falling off and you'd still say it was fine, right?"

"Nah," he said. "When it was actually threatening to fall off, I was most definitely not fine."

Her smile faded and she regretted her flippancy. "I'm sorry."

He shrugged. "Shit happens. You were saving me a seat," he said, back to teasing.

"No," she said in automatic denial. "I—"

He flashed her a knowing grin that was so innately Tanner-Riggs-of-the-Past—all cocky, popular football star, aka the guy she'd never been able to say two words to without tripping over her own tongue—that she once again found herself momentarily tongue-tied.

"What are you working on?" he asked, gesturing to her laptop. "Ordering a litter? Designing three-D wedding invitations?"

"Both," she managed to say in what she hoped was a perfectly normal voice.

Because you are perfectly normal, she reminded herself. You are not just a computer geek. You are so much more. You…ah, hell. She couldn't think of a single thing when he was looking at her like that, like maybe she was amusing him again.

"Your job suits you," he said.

"What does that mean?"

"You have this sort of…" He waved his cup at her. "Dreamy, romantic air about you."

She let out a low laugh and he set his cup down, sitting forward, at attention. "You going to start choking again?" he asked.

"No," she assured him. Or she hoped not anyway. "And it's not a romantic job. It's a technical job."

"How are hearts and flowers and chariots technical?" he asked.

"Okay," she conceded. "Maybe it's romantic for a minute or two, if you believe in that sort of thing."

"And you don't?" he asked.

"My job is to create the right setting to culminate their romance," she said, trying to explain her job. "That's all I can do. I can't guarantee a happy ending."

He grinned.

"Not that kind of a happy ending!" she said, and laughed in spite of herself. "The stats are completely against a real happily-ever-after, not that anyone wants to think about it while planning their wedding. Which means that TyingTheKnot.com should really be called AnotherOneBitesTheDust.com. But I doubt I'd be able to make a living with that."

"Huh," Tanner said, cocking his head as he studied her. "Didn't see that coming."

"What?"

"You're a cynic." He gestured at her with his cup. "All wrapped up in a sweet, warm package."

He thought she was sweet and warm.

Don't get excited, a little voice inside her warned. He also thought you were cute. Like a puppy. And he doesn't remember who you are. "I earned the cynicism," she said.

"Someone break your heart?"

He didn't say this with a mocking inflection. Nor did he sound like he was pitying her. She looked into his eyes—those hot-as-hell eyes—and saw that he was just genuinely curious. Which was the only reason she answered him. "Yes, actually," she said. "But it was my own fault."

"How's that?"

His voice was low and a bit morning gruff, and she found herself staring at his mouth. "That's a little bit personal, don't you think?" she asked, her own voice low, too, but not because it was morning.

It was more because he was turning her on with little to no effort.

He leaned in and smiled. "You don't want to get personal with me?"

Her breath caught. Her pulse skipped another beat. Or a hundred. And there were other reactions, too, things that really shouldn't be happening in public. But once upon a time she'd dreamed about him wanting her. She'd even gone as far as to send him a secret Valentine, one of those anonymous lollypops with a heart that you paid a dollar to the student body fund for and then it was delivered to the recipient's homeroom class in front of everyone.

Except Callie hadn't sent hers anonymously. She'd signed her name.

And he'd never said a word about it.

And suddenly that bugged the crap out of her. Love sucked. Romance sucked. And even if that hadn't been true, there was no way she was going to admit her failures out loud to a guy she didn't really know. She shook her head. No, she didn't want to get personal.

"You really don't believe in love?" he asked.

Did he think she was just being coy? "Let's just say that I know that love isn't enough," she said. "And I'm not interested in it. Not for myself." She knew this without a shadow of a doubt. After all, she'd had the perfect guy and the perfect life, and had planned the huge wedding to celebrate it—and it'd ended with her heart crushed.

Nope. Love was not enough. Not by a long shot.

Tanner startled her by running a finger along her temple, tucking a wayward strand of hair behind her ear. "A definite cynic," he said softly, meeting her gaze. "I like it."

"You do?"

"Not exactly a romantic myself," he said, and leaned back. "And no disrespect to your work, but I think love was something made up by Hallmark for Valentine's Day and…well, wedding websites."

She laughed. Touché. "So I guess you think Valentine's Day cards are pretty dumb, too. Even if, say, you got one from a girl who had a crush on you." She held her breath for a beat, and then someone bumped into him from behind and the moment was broken.

The cute brunette who'd done the bumping sent a big smile Tanner's way. "Sorry," she said breathlessly. "My fault. Let me buy you a coffee to make up for it."

Tanner lifted his coffee. "Already taken care of."

The woman looked disappointed but moved on and Tanner turned back to Callie. "Sorry, what were we talking about?"

Well, she'd been about to admit that she'd once sent him a Valentine's Day card, which meant she'd also be admitting to her painful crush.

And that would lead to him saying out loud that he didn't remember her. So she was eternally grateful they'd been interrupted. "We were discussing you being a cynic too," she said. "You're not…involved."

"No," he said. "I was married once, for about ten minutes."

She knew all about him and Elisa. It'd been the talk of the town back then. "It didn't work out?"

His laugh was mirthless. "No. I got beat all to shit."

So she did have something in common with this big, built, tough, gorgeous man. "I'm sorry."

"It was a long time ago," he said. "And I did get something really great out of it. My son, Troy. But it's not anything I'd repeat."

She understood that. She lifted her coffee and touched it to his in a toast, acknowledging that they were in perfect sync on this sentiment.

"If it makes you feel better," she said, "I got all the way to the altar before I got beat to shit. Didn't actually say the I dos but it was close enough to teach me that happily-ever-afters are for fiction." She smiled. "Don't tell anyone, though. It's not exactly good for business."

He didn't smile back. In fact, his gaze was dark and unreadable but also somehow…warm. Commiserating without pity. "Your secret's safe with me," he finally said softly, and they finished their coffee in comfortable silence.

Well, Tanner was comfortable anyway, at least going by his kick-back, sprawled posture in the chair.

Callie, not so much. She was wishing that she believed what she'd said about not wanting romance for herself because as she watched him, while pretending not to, she found herself aching just a little bit.

Damn, she really wished he remembered her.

"Gotta get back to work," he said and rose.

"Right," she said. "Me too." She slipped her laptop back into her bag. Then she stood up and…knocked over her coffee.

Tanner grabbed a stack of napkins and efficiently cleaned up the mess in about three seconds, during which time Callie ordered herself to get a grip. "Sorry," she said.

He shook his head. "No need."

Good. Great. No need for her to be sorry that she was an idiot. A clumsy idiot. She gathered the rest of her things, trying to keep her hands busy.

And her brain.

Just get out the door without further incident, she told herself. But Tanner was standing close, looking down at her, his dark, dark eyes holding hers prisoner.

"What?" she whispered.

Again he ran a finger along her temple, letting the touch linger. "I'm sorry I never thanked you for that Valentine," he said quietly. "I should have."

And then he was gone.

Chapter 8

♥

Callie was still shocked that Tanner had known who she was all along. It was the end of the workday, and she'd just met with Becca and gone over more of her wedding plans. Everything was nearly handled. She and Sam were going to get married at the B&B and then jet off to Greece where they'd rent a boat and island-hop for their three-week honeymoon. But first up was the bachelor/bachelorette party. This would take place at Lucky Harbor Charters on the boat and dock.

With all that planning dancing in her head, Callie helped Becca with some of the details and then picked up dinner from Eat Me and brought it to her grandma's house.

Halfway up the walk, she stopped short at the sight of Lucille standing in her garden smooching Mr. Wykowski like they meant business. "My eyes," Callie said, and covered them.

The lovebirds laughed. "Gotta get it when you can," her grandma said.

Callie clapped her hands to her ears next. "Grandma!"

"Do you think they let you have sex in the old people's home?" Lucille asked Callie. "Because I'd really miss it."

Callie blinked at her. "What?"

"Well, you're here to make sure I'm not crazy, and I'm pretty sure I totally am crazy. I just want to make sure, if I end up in a home, I can bring my cutie pie here and get it when I want."

Callie gaped.

Lucille just smiled sweetly.

"That's probably not funny to your granddaughter," Mr. Wykowski said in a gently chiding voice, and her grandma laughed.

While Callie tried to recover, Mr. Wykowski greeted her warmly, murmured "Be good" to Lucille, and left them alone.

"I didn't mean to interrupt anything," Callie said. "But you're so busy I practically need to make an appointment to see you."

"No worries," her grandma said. "We save the good stuff for after *Jeopardy* anyway. When you get to be our age, the dark is your friend."

Callie was doing her best trying not to let the image of that form in her head as her grandma peered into the bag of food.

"Should've gone to the Love Shack," she complained. "Jax—you remember Jax, right? The hottie master carpenter? He's co-owner of the place, and he just announced his adorable wife Maddie is having their third baby. I bet they don't wait for *Jeopardy* to be over, know what I'm saying?"

"Yes," Callie said. "But I really wish I didn't."

Her grandma grinned as they dug into the food. "Anyway, everything's half off at the Love Shack to celebrate. Although really, I should get to eat there free all the time since I had a hand in them getting together."

"You did?"

Lucille smiled smugly. "You don't know this about your dear old grandma, but I'm known as being quite the matchmaker. In the past five years alone, I've been responsible for…Let's see…" She counted on her fingers. "Jax, Ford, Sawyer, Ty, Matt, Josh, Luke, Jack, Ben, Sam, and Cole." She beamed with pride. "All found their happily-ever-afters with a little help from *moi*—even if most of them have no idea I helped them. Really, I should go into the business with you."

Callie blinked. "You mean…"

"Yep," she said proudly. "Matchmaking. It'd make a great addition to TyingTheKnot.com, don't you think?"

She stared at her grandma until her phone buzzed with an incoming text from one of her brides.

I know you said animals at the wedding wasn't really a great idea but my bridesmaids all want to walk down the aisle with their pets. Okay with you?

Callie blew out a breath.

Her grandma leaned in to read and then grinned. "You going to let her do it?"

Callie pointed at her. "You don't get to change the subject. Hold on a sec, one emergency at a time." She typed in a response to her bride.

It's your day. You get to decide. But isn't your maid of honor's pet a cow?

The response was immediate.

Yes but Sweet Pea is potty-trained.

Lucille chortled in delight, and Callie again pointed at her. "No comments from the peanut gallery." She gave her thumbs a workout dealing with the bride, and five minutes later they'd settled on animals at the reception but not the actual wedding.

"You should let her have the cow down the aisle," her grandma said. "You could give out little air fresheners as party favors."

Callie blew out a sigh. "That's not a bad idea."

Lucille hooted with laughter. "Gotta love your job, honey. It's a beaut."

"It's something anyway. Now about you."

"What about me?" her grandma asked innocently.

Uh-huh. "You can't interfere with people's lives like you've been doing," Callie said.

"Why not? It works. And aren't you essentially doing the same thing?"

"Yes, okay, fine. But at least I get paid for it," she said.

Lucille beamed. "That's because you're smarter than I am. Have I told you lately how very proud I am of you?"

Callie's frustration drained away. Her parents had always been so wrapped up in each other. She'd long ago gotten used to being a third wheel at her own family dinner table, but she'd always had Lucille who, quirks and all, had never let her down. "I love you, Grandma," she whispered, and came around the table to squeeze her tight.

"Aw. Aren't you the sweetest," her grandma said, hugging her back. She barely came up to Callie's chin and smelled like roses and baby powder and felt a little bit like a bag of bones, but Callie held on for a long moment.

"I suppose it might be time for me to face facts."

Callie's heart stopped. "What facts?"

"I'm losing it."

Oh God. "Grandma—"

"The desire is just…gone," Lucille said sadly.

Callie reached for her grandma's hands. "The important thing is to realize that you're not alone."

"Oh, honey, you're such a joy to me. But I can't help how I feel. I'm going to—"

"—I'm here for you, to the end."

"—Retire," Lucille said, and frowned. "What?"

"Retire?" Callie asked.

Lucille stared at her. "What did you think I was going to say?"

"Nothing," Callie said.

Lucille smiled. "You thought I was telling you I was going nuts, right? That's a conversation for another day."

"So you are going nuts?"

"Another day," Lucille repeated.

"Okay," Callie said. "But we're going to definitely discuss, sooner rather than later."

"So you can go back to San Francisco?"

"Yes," Callie said. "And my life."

"Your life." Lucille rolled her eyes. "Your life is here, with your family—me, in case you were wondering. But I'm talking about retiring from the matchmaking game, not from my sanity." She pointed at Callie. "Right after I match you."

"Oh, no," Callie said. "No. No, no, no."

"Well, why ever not?"

"I don't want to be matched," Callie said. "I'm good as I am. I don't need a man."

"Honey, we all need a man. Whether we keep him or not, that's personal preference."

"Grandma, seriously," Callie said. "No matchmaking me, I don't need or want it. You hear me?"

Lucille was suddenly very busy cleaning up.

"Grandma."

"Hmm?"

"You heard me, right?"

"Of course, dear. I'm old, not deaf. I can hear you just fine."

Which wasn't the same thing as listening, Callie knew.

"You get onto my social media accounts and do your research?" Lucille asked.

Callie went still. "What research?"

"You wanted to know more about Tanner. I left you a bunch of stuff to find. You learn everything you needed?"

Yes. And more. "I'm not interested in him that way," she said.

Lucille grinned.

"What?" Callie asked.

"You're pretty good at fibbing. But don't forget who taught you how. Word is that you're sitting with him in the mornings at the bakery pretending to drink coffee."

Oh, for God's sake. "We sit together so that we'll be left alone," Callie said. "Big difference."

"Honey." Lucille *tsk*ed, all disappointed. "The last thing Tanner needs is to be left alone."

"What does that mean?" she asked.

Lucille sighed. "Tanner's daddy left him when he turned five."

Yeah. This wasn't news to Callie. She'd known that back in school.

"And that boy has been wild ever since," her grandma said. "He's got his hands full now with the people in his life, but he's not doing a damn thing for himself. So let me repeat—being alone is not what Tanner needs. What he needs is you."

Callie stared at her grandma. "Even if that was true, which it's not, what about what I need?"

"Oh, you need him too, honey."

"I don't," she said, shaking her head. "I'm doing just fine."

"See now, that's the beauty of it," Lucille said. "Of course you don't *need him* need him. You support yourself, blah blah. But you've been hurt by life too, and let down. Your parents did the best they could, but they could've done better by you. You deserved more."

"I had you," Callie said, and had the pleasure of seeing her grandma soften and put a hand to her heart.

"Aw, honey," she said. "I love you so. But truth now. You've felt alone and vulnerable. With Tanner, you'd have something you've always been sorely missing."

"What's that?" Callie asked.

"An 'us.'"

For a single heartbeat, Callie's chest tightened in

yearning, but the feeling faded quickly. If she was being honest, she was a little afraid of the us. She busied herself with cleaning up for a long moment. "I do love you, Grandma," she finally said. "So much. But you're wrong. I'm good as I am. I don't need the complication in my life right now." Maybe ever. Bending, she kissed Lucille's cheek. "I gotta get home. Please stop meddling in people's lives, okay? For me? Promise?"

"Hmm?"

"Grandma."

"Oh, all right, sure. I'll try."

The next day Callie had meetings straight through breakfast and she skipped the bakery. She told herself it was for the best but she had to admit she really missed the doughnuts.

And maybe also Tanner.

That afternoon she walked down to Lucky Harbor Charters to take measurements for decorations for Becca and Sam's bachelor/bachelorette party.

The docks were a perfect spot for a party. As she got there, the late-afternoon November sun was just touching down on the water, casting a halo glow on everything.

Gorgeous.

She stood there taking in the view thinking that, with outdoor space heaters, this could really work. The lighting was perfect for pictures, the kind of lighting that would make anyone and everyone look good. It'd be a wonderful spot for their wedding photos too, which made her laugh a little. Here she was thinking to eventually move on from this job when she had decent savings and yet her eye for all things romantic and wedding-perfect never seemed to stop.

She was so messed up.

She heard a boat and shaded her eyes to see that it was the Lucky Harbor Charters' boat.

Cole was behind the controls. When he navigated close to the dock, Tanner leapt off the boat, limped to the stern, and caught something tossed to him by his Mini-Me still on board.

A rope.

Tanner crouched low and tied the boat to the dock, then straightened and caught a second rope.

Callie found herself frozen in place, watching him move with confident ease in spite of the clear fact that his leg was bothering him. She watched as he efficiently and effortlessly tied that rope off as well and then looked up and said something to his son.

The body language of the two males told her that all was not well on the home front. Troy said something to Tanner.

Tanner spoke back calmly.

Troy said something else, not calmly.

Tanner didn't speak again, just held his ground with steady, firm eye contact.

Troy broke it, spun on his heel, and stormed off.

And only when he was gone did Tanner's expression change. From that easy calm to…deeply troubled.

Hollow.

It was a deeply personal moment, one Callie knew there was no way he wanted to be caught in. So she started to back up and go home, but then he turned his head and met her gaze.

Sorry, she mouthed. He gave the slightest head shake, nothing more. He didn't approach her and she didn't make a move toward him. And though she had the oddest urge to hug him, she left him alone.

That night, with Becca and Olivia sitting on her kitchen counter keeping her company, Callie made them all grilled chocolate sandwiches. It made her think of Tanner.

Okay, that was a lie. She'd been thinking of him since she'd left the docks earlier.

"I didn't know you could cook," Olivia said, chowing down on her second sandwich.

"I do okay," Callie said. "If the recipe has chocolate in it."

"Yeah, I'm going to need you to make a lot more of these," Becca said.

"Is that why you're stuffing them into your mouth like you haven't eaten in days?" Olivia asked.

Becca grinned. "Been burning lots of calories lately."

Olivia laughed softly and Callie sighed deeply. Then she realized they were both staring at her. "Sorry," she said. "Sex envy."

"Listen," Becca said earnestly. "I know that being around the two of us when we're stupid in love has got to be superbly annoying, but I promise you, you'll find the right guy too."

"I've already got one for her," Olivia said.

Becca stared at Olivia and then laughed as a light bulb apparently went off. "Yes! I don't know why I didn't think of him sooner."

"Because you're having too much sex," Olivia said, tapping a finger to her temple. "Sex brain."

Callie sighed. "I really wish you'd both stop talking about sex. And I don't want to find a—"

"Tanner's perfect," Becca said.

"—guy," Callie finished.

"Yep, perfect," Olivia said to Becca as if Callie hadn't spoken. "They're meant for each other."

"Yeah, they are," Becca said.

"No," Callie said.

"Please tell me you think he's hot," Becca said. "Those eyes…Gah."

Callie sighed. He did have some damn amazing eyes.

"I don't know why we didn't think of this sooner," Becca said.

"We?" Olivia asked. "I already thought of it." She pointed at Callie. "And your grandma thought of it too. She's out there lobbying for the two of you."

"Lobbying?"

"Trying to get everyone involved in matchmaking the two of you. It's on her Tumblr."

Well, crap. Callie hadn't had time to check her grandma's social media yet today. "I told her to stay out of it."

Both Olivia and Becca burst out laughing.

"I don't see what's so funny," Callie said.

Becca got herself together but was still grinning when she spoke. "Honey, your grandma…she doesn't know how to stay out of it. Have you ever met her?"

Callie gritted her teeth. "I'm going to have to hire a babysitter."

"You're not mad, are you?" Becca asked.

"Yes," Callie said. "But only a little bit at you."

"Okay, good. So you'll still make us more grilled chocolate sandwiches, right?"

Chapter 9

♥

The next morning Callie told herself she had absolutely no reason to go into town. She could stay in bed and work from there. She certainly had plenty of it to keep her busy. Hell, she could bury herself in work if she wanted.

But she'd been doing that for years now, and that hadn't gotten her anywhere.

Besides, she was hungry. And she hadn't told Becca and Olivia, but grilled chocolate sandwiches were pretty much the only thing in her wheelhouse.

She could go to her grandma's house and get breakfast and while she was there she could demand to know why she was doing exactly what Callie had asked her not to do.

But that was an argument she couldn't have without doughnuts.

Which meant she needed doughnuts.

So go to the grocery store. She repeated this to herself as she dressed—in real clothes—and then again as she put on mascara and lip gloss. She had a hard time justify-

ing that part but, hey, one never knew when she'd have to
take a Skype call today, right? Might as well be prepared.
She drove toward town. When she passed the grocery
store, she said, "Whoops."

And then kept going until she hit the bakery.

Just for the coffee and doughnuts, she told herself. And
absolutely nothing else, like, say, sitting there waiting on
a certain gorgeous, funny, ex-super-crush named Tanner
Riggs.

She got out of the car and checked her hair in the mirror.
And maybe applied more lip gloss. When she opened the
door to the bakery, the delicious scent of coffee and baked
goods immediately assaulted her. She paused to inhale
deeply and then froze when she heard a blast from her past.

And not a good blast.

It was a male laugh that once upon a time had been the
laugh of her fiancé. It was now the laugh of the guy who'd
left her at the altar.

Whipping around, she eyeballed the street and found
Eric about fifteen yards away, holding hands with a cute
blonde as he walked up the sidewalk toward her.

An unreasonable panic gripped her. Or maybe it was
dread. Without thinking, she ducked the rest of the way
into the bakery, pressed herself behind the door, and
peeked out the window.

It was early, she told herself. Maybe they were just on
a stroll. And Eric was a dentist. No way would he come
into the bakery. Surely he was bound by some dental decree to not step into sugar-infested bakeries. Besides, her
luck couldn't be that bad.

He headed for the bakery.

Damn it. She hated that after all this time she could

still feel the humiliation of what he'd done to her, but there it was. And damn, that pissed her off. He'd literally left her at the altar, for God's sake. And the only thing worse than that was everyone in town knowing it.

She'd assumed it no longer mattered, that she would be ready to face him if that happened, but apparently not.

She was not ready.

But she couldn't deny that there was also a little part of her that hoped he'd seen her and he'd felt…what? Did she want him to feel guilt? Regret?

Yeah. She kind of did.

She also wanted him to feel…yearning. And a desperation that he'd let her go. Yeah, desperation would work just fine.

Eric and Blondie stopped a few feet from the bakery door. They were laughing, having a great time, and Callie held her breath, hoping they'd go away. Far, far away.

Instead, Eric pulled the woman in close and kissed her. Gently. Sweetly. He held her face while he did it and when he pulled back, he smiled into the woman's eyes like she was his entire universe.

He'd never once kissed Callie like that.

Fine. Whatever. The good news was that now they were walking again, and with relief, she turned away from the window.

The bakery line was long as usual and she got into it, reminding herself to breathe as she casually eyeballed the room.

Tanner was at "their" table. He was watching her, head cocked, like maybe she was a fascinating and ridiculous reality show.

Terrific.

She tried to look normal. Like nothing to see here…

"Callie. It *is* you."

This came from right behind her, and she nearly jumped out of her skin. Whipping around, she came face to face with—oh, perfect—Eric and Blondie. How had that happened?

"Hey there," Eric said with an easy smile. And not a single flicker of guilt or regret or yearning or desperation.

Damn him.

"It's great to see you," he said, standing very close to the woman next to him. "Tina, this is Callie. I've told you about her."

"Lovely to meet you," Tina said, smiling with freakishly straight, white teeth.

But her smile was genuine and Callie tried to act normal. "Nice to meet you too."

"I didn't know you were back in town," Eric said.

"Just for a bit," she heard herself say. "Checking in on my grandma."

He gave a fond smile. "Lucille. As insane as usual, I'm guessing?"

"She has reasons for her ways," she said in quick defense. Apparently Callie could be irritated by her grandmother, but no one else—especially an ex—was allowed.

And speaking of her ex, he had the nerve to look pretty damn fantastic.

He also had a hand on the small of Tina's back. A casual, affectionate gesture that insinuated intimacy and ease. Except he'd never been into PDA before, and certainly not with Callie.

And suddenly she didn't want a doughnut.

No. She wanted an entire baker's dozen.

*   *   *

Tanner had watched with some amusement as Callie had
bolted into the bakery, plastered herself to the wall, and
stared out the window as if the hounds of hell had been
on her heels.

When she'd relaxed and gotten in line, he'd still been
watching. So he'd had eyes on her when the couple had
gotten in line behind her.

Ah, he thought, watching as he drank his coffee. Stiff
posture. Fake smile. Quick hand over the hair.

Either an archenemy or an ex, he guessed. And since
this was real life and not a comic book, he crossed archenemy off the list. An ex then. The guy had his arm
around the blond woman next to him and Tanner winced
in sympathy for a pale-faced Callie. Her lips were curved
but she wasn't showing any teeth, and she also looked like
she'd just swallowed something really sour.

That, or the ex was stinky.

Then the woman said something and the ex leaned in
close to catch every word before tossing his head back
and laughing.

Callie looked like she wished she had powers and
could vanish.

Or maybe she was plotting the man's murder.

She said something and started to leave the line without coffee or a doughnut, which told Tanner more than
anything else how off axis she was, but it was her turn at
the front of the line and Leah called out to her.

Callie stared blankly at Leah as if she couldn't remember why she was there.

Leah's smile faded a little bit and she reached over

the counter to squeeze Callie's hand. Then she quickly brought her a coffee and a box of doughnuts.

A box.

Tanner had to smile. Leah was good people. Really good.

Arms loaded, Callie turned to go but the guy reached out and stopped her with a hand on her arm.

Why didn't the asshole back off? It was pretty obvious to Tanner that's what Callie wanted, so why wasn't he getting out of her face?

Instead, the guy said something to her, smiled, and then leaned in even closer, looking like he planned on kissing her cheek.

Callie instantly recoiled, her body language screaming "go away." Jesus. How was the asshole missing the fact that she didn't want him to touch her, much less kiss her?

Then it went fubar.

As Callie pulled back, she tripped over the blonde's foot and stumbled. Her coffee went flying one way, her box of doughnuts the other way. Luckily neither hit anyone, just the floor, but the mess was pretty spectacular.

People scattered, including the ex and the blonde. They walked out together arm in arm, holding their coffees, not paying much attention to the carnage they'd left behind.

Shit. Tanner rose and moved toward Callie, who was now attempting to clean up.

"Don't," she said when he crouched at her side to help.

He took the box from her and scooped up the last of the mess.

"Tanner—"

"Shh," he said. He took the entire mess to the trash.

When he got back to Callie, she was standing right where he'd left her. She had crumbs down her front along with a few splatters of coffee.

"Did you burn yourself?" he asked.

She shook her head.

"Sure?"

She stopped shaking her head to nod it.

"Come on," he said. "I'll get you another breakfast."

This seemed to snap her out of it. "No," she said. "Thanks, though. I think I'm just going to go back to bed and start the day over another time. Like maybe next year."

He smiled and ducked down a little to look into her pretty green eyes. "You're not that person," he said softly, taking her hand. "You don't bury your head in the sand."

"Oh, you'd be surprised," she said with a humorless laugh. "I can bury my head with the best of them." She pulled free, but she did it slowly, almost reluctantly, not jerking away as she had with that other guy. "And you *do* remember me from high school." She said this in an accusatory voice that told him she'd been steaming about that since he'd last seen her.

"Of course," he said.

"Of course." She snorted.

"That's funny?" he asked

"No one remembers me from high school. I was the nerd, the bookworm."

"*I* remember you," he said firmly.

"Yeah, probably because some of your fellow football players paid me to do their homework."

"Yeah, they did," he said. "Because you were cute."

She blinked as if he'd stunned her speechless and he smiled. "But you were off limits to me."

"Why?"

"For one thing, you were *way* too good for the likes of me," he said, and had the pleasure of seeing her quick smile.

She had a really great smile when it included her eyes. "So who was he?" he heard himself ask.

"Who?"

He gave her a get-real look.

"Oh, you mean that guy who was just here?" she asked.

"No, I mean the Easter Bunny."

She sighed. "My ex-almost-husband."

He remembered what she'd said during their love-wasn't-for-her talk. *I got all the way to the altar before I got beat to shit.* Hell. "That was the guy you were engaged to?" he asked.

"Right up until the day he got cold feet," she said way too casually.

He craned his neck and eyed the door. He couldn't have gotten far. "Want me to go beat the shit out of him?"

She laughed. "Yes, please." Then she stared at him. "Wait. You're kidding, right?"

Not in the slightest.

She took in his expression and laughed again, this one low and a little bit ragged. "That's the nicest thing anyone's asked me in a while," she said, but she shook her head. "And thanks but no. I'm good. I'm actually going to get going. See you." Then she turned and ran right into two people coming in the door.

Tanner grimaced for her as she backed up, apologized profusely, and tried again.

To be safe, Tanner stepped forward with her, setting a

hand on her back, guiding her out after opening the door for her.

"Sometimes," she muttered, "I'm pretty sure my guardian angel drinks."

Tanner spent the rest of the day on the boat with Cole, working on the boat's mechanics. They were head deep in the engine compartment, grimy from head to toe, when Cole suddenly piped up with "So you're going for Callie?"

Tanner lifted his head so fast that he cracked it on the boat frame. "Shit. Damn. Fuck."

Cole grinned. "Yeah. It's true."

"What's true, that you're an asshole?" Tanner asked, holding his head. "*Sonofabitch*, that hurt."

"Did it knock any sense into you?" Cole asked.

"I've got more sense in my pinkie finger than you have in your whole body," Tanner said.

"You know, she'd be good for you."

Tanner stared at him. "How the hell do you figure that?"

"I hear from Olivia that she's funny, smart, and won't put up with any of your shit."

"We're so not having this conversation," Tanner said, lowering his fingers from his noggin to check if he was bleeding. "Shit."

"Come here, you big baby." Cole cupped Tanner's face and tilted it down to look at the top of his head. "Okay, so there's good news and bad news."

"Just tell me," Tanner grated out.

"The good news is your head's still attached to your shoulders," Cole said.

"And the bad news?" Tanner asked.

"The hit doesn't appear to have knocked any sense into you."

Tanner gave Cole a shove that didn't budge him. Cole often came off all casual and easy, but in reality he wasn't either. He was just as tough as Sam or Tanner himself, and he was also the glue that held them all together. And sometimes, like now, he acted like a chick. Tanner shoved him again and Cole shoved back, and then the men had each other in a headlock.

"Hug me like you mean it," Cole said. "And I'll let go."

"I'm going to kick your ass."

"Hug me like you love me, bitch."

"Uh…I can come back." This was from Troy, who'd apparently shown up from school as he'd been instructed to do since he was still grounded from everything else. He was standing on the dock, backpack hanging off one shoulder, staring at them. "If you wanna be alone."

Cole laughed a little and from his hunched-over position craned his neck to look up at Tanner. "He thinks we're—"

"Hey," Troy said, backing away, lifting up his hands. "There's nothing wrong with that."

"Of course there isn't," Tanner said. "But we're not."

"There's a kid in my class that has two moms," Troy said.

"That's great," Tanner said, shoving free of Cole. "But it's not…Cole and I aren't like that. Not that it wouldn't be fine if we were."

"Speak for yourself," Cole said, straightening his sweatshirt. "You're not even close to my type."

Tanner gave him another shove and Cole blew him a kiss.

"Knock it off, you idiot," Tanner said. He looked at Troy. "He's kidding."

"Oh." Troy nodded. "That's good because Tumblr says you're having a thing with some chick named Callie."

"I am not having a thing with Callie," Tanner said, though he had to admit he wouldn't mind having a thing with her. Maybe a couple of things. He turned to Cole. "And what the hell do you mean, I'm not your type?"

Tanner took Troy fishing. He took the boat out to his secret sweet spot and showed the kid how to get one on the line without fail.

The entire time Troy looked like he was getting a root canal.

So much for bonding.

After nearly three hours of silence, Tanner gave up. "Is there a problem?"

No answer.

"Hello," he said.

Troy pulled out an earbud. Tinny music blared out. Tanner stared at him and then shook his head. Jesus. "Not your thing, fishing?"

Troy looked relieved. "Fish suck."

Okay, so maybe they weren't two peas in a pod after all.

That evening they sat at Tanner's kitchen table and worked on Troy's chemistry homework due to the D he'd come home with.

"Chemistry sucks," Troy said an hour later when he still hadn't gotten halfway through. "Sucks hard."

"Working sucks," Tanner said. "Fishing sucks. School sucks. Let's try this—what *doesn't* suck?"

"Here? Nothing," Troy said sullenly.

Tanner pushed the books aside. "Come on. I've got something we need to do."

"What now?"

Tanner pushed open the door to his spare bedroom, the one he'd given over to the kid. It'd been pretty sparse when Troy had first arrived, just a futon. But Tanner had picked up a bed, a dresser, and a desk.

"Great," Troy said, looking at the desk. "A place to do more work. In a white room. It's like my own private padded cell."

Tanner ignored the sarcasm. "You don't like white? Then pick a color. We'll paint this weekend."

"Dark purple," Troy said without hesitation.

Tanner swiveled his head and stared at him. "Dark purple?"

"Dark purple."

Tanner rubbed a hand over the top of his head and winced at the bump there from hitting it earlier. "Look, I get that you're pissed off at having to be here, that it feels unfair and you want to strike out and all that, but you're the one who has to live with the color. So I'm going to ask you again. Dark purple? You sure?"

Troy just stared at him sullenly.

"Okay," Tanner muttered, and shook his head. "You're sure." He started to leave and then stopped. He remembered after his dad had left, how his mom had picked up two jobs to make ends meet, and he'd felt so helpless and furious all the time. "Listen," he said. "It will get better here."

More nothing and Tanner shook his head. "Fine. Life sucks. Go with that, it's a great attitude."

Troy moved past Tanner and stretched out on the bed. He closed his eyes and for a moment looked so painfully young and so painfully vulnerable.

"'Night," Tanner said quietly and turned to go.

"Um," Troy said.

Tanner turned back. "Yeah?"

Troy hesitated. "Thanks."

It was possibly the first time Troy had ever said that word to him, and Tanner felt an ache from deep in his chest. The kind of ache that was either a heart attack in the making or he was having a bona fide, real dad moment. He wanted to press Troy for more but knew that wasn't the right thing to do.

As for what was the right thing, he didn't have a clue. So he nodded and left the kid there on his bed and hit his own, where he dreamed of a green-eyed, strawberry blonde who lit up at the sight of a doughnut and hadn't a single clue that she was the hottest woman in the room.

The next morning he sat at the bakery for an hour but she never showed.

The pretty brunette from the other day was there, though. She came up to his table with a try-me smile. "Is this seat taken?" she asked.

"No," he said, and rose. "And this one isn't either."

"But…" She stared at him as he started to walk away. "Don't you want to finish your breakfast? We could make it a date."

"Sorry," he said genuinely. "But I already have one."

Chapter 10

♥

Callie figured out the way to battle her doughnut demons. She stayed in bed. It wasn't bad as far as offices went, and the dress code—PJs—really worked for her. She'd gotten up long enough for a teeth-brushing mission and to grab her laptop, and then she'd crawled back into bed and gone straight to work, telling herself that she didn't need caffeine and sugar to get going.

Her humiliation did that just fine.

She worked like a fiend. No one could deny that she knew how to throw a hell of a good party. She just hoped her brides enjoyed it because odds were that the reception would be the highlight of their marriage.

An hour or two later she decided that this working from home thing was a decent gig. In fact, maybe she wouldn't ever go into town again.

That's when someone knocked on her door.

She went still, frozen like a deer in the headlights.

Then she glanced at the clock. It was ten in the morning. Both Becca and Olivia were at work by now. She hadn't ordered a pizza for breakfast—though she absolutely would have if anyplace in Lucky Harbor delivered pizzas for breakfast. Hey, maybe she could quit her job and do that.

In any case, she wasn't expecting company.

The knock came again and she looked down at herself. A double-extra-large men's sweatshirt that kept falling off her shoulder. Plaid PJ bottoms about a foot too long and washed so many times they were threadbare. Today's footwear of choice—Shrek slippers.

Yeah. She was ready for a Victoria's Secret catwalk.

She climbed off her bed and looked out the peephole. Dark, silky hair. Dark eyes. Navy sweatshirt. Sexy jeans. Damn it. *What was he doing here?*

"I can hear you breathing," Tanner said.

She stopped breathing and went utterly still.

"And now I can hear you panicking."

She let out the breath with a *whoosh* and backed away from the door, heart pounding. "Why are you here?" she asked the door.

"Because our table was already taken at the bakery."

"What? That's ridiculous. It's not our table."

"Felt like it," he said.

She thunked her forehead on the door. "Why are you really here?" she whispered.

"Because you didn't show."

She lifted her head and stared at the door. "Why did it matter to you?"

"Open the door, Callie."

"Tell me why, Tanner."

Was that a barely-there sigh she heard? "Because you're not an ostrich," he said.

She blinked. "Maybe I am. Maybe I hide all the time. Maybe I'm a master hider." *Oh my God, Callie, shut up.*

"I do know you," he said.

She shook her head even though he couldn't see her. "You don't."

"I know you're smart as hell, so smart that most of us football players paid you to do our homework."

"That was ten years ago," she said. "You don't know me now."

"You run a hugely popular website that you design and handle by yourself," he said. "I don't quite get the need for thirty bazillion shades of white satin, or why anyone would want doves to fly over their heads and possibly crap on them, but that's just me. You're here in Lucky Harbor checking on your grandma—a serious pain in every bachelor's ass in this town—but that aside, what you're doing makes you a pretty damn sweet and caring person. Oh, and I know you have a serious thing for doughnuts."

She stared at the door. He really had noticed her.

"Open up," he said into the silence. "I've got something for you."

"A doughnut?" she asked hopefully. "Because that's the only way I'm opening this door."

"Better," he said.

"There's nothing better."

"A baker's dozen," he said. "And coffee."

Momentarily forgetting what she looked like, she unlocked the door. Indeed, he was standing there with a big baker's box and a carrier of four coffees.

"Gimme." Mouth watering, she reached for the box, but he lifted it high and stepped inside, kicking the door shut behind him.

His eyes were dark, hooded by heavy lids and his thick lashes. His jaw was covered in a few days' growth of beard, longer than she'd ever seen it, making him look simultaneously dangerous and...vulnerable?

That couldn't be right. Tanner didn't do vulnerable.

But something was bothering him. She didn't get the sense that it had anything to do with her, which meant it was none of her business, but it didn't stop her from wondering.

And wondering about him made her feel like that silly teen again, with the even sillier crush. "You okay?" she asked softly.

"Was going to ask you the same."

"Me? I'm great."

He laughed softly, then moved in closer, his body brushing hers. For a beat she thought maybe he was going to kiss her on the cheek. It threw her in a startlingly good way and she stilled.

He did the same. His dark eyes softened and the laughter faded out of them. Then he shifted even closer so that her body brushed his.

She felt every inch of herself quiver because *holy cow*. Something was burning and she was pretty sure it was her. Time slowed and she realized she'd actually stopped breathing.

So had he. Then he took a slow, long, thorough tour at what she was wearing from her hair to the tips of her Shrek slippers, and smiled.

"You haven't disappointed yet," he said.

She held her head high. "I wasn't dressed to impress."

"I like it."

This deflected most of her self-righteousness. "You do?"

"Yeah."

"Why?" she asked suspiciously.

"Mostly because you're not wearing any underwear."

"Hey!" She crossed her arms over her breasts. "How do you know that?"

"God-given talent," he said. "And you're happy to see me."

Her self-righteousness was back in a flash. "For your information," she said, "I'm cold."

He smiled.

"I am!"

"I just find it funny that on your website you have an entire section dedicated to fancy lingerie, and you don't wear any," he said.

"Ohmigod." She stared at him, horrified. "Why are you reading my website?"

"Why not?"

"Why not?" She tossed up her hands and struggled for the obvious. "Are you terminally insane? Soon to be married? A woman?"

He was grinning at her now. "No."

"Then why?" She poked him in a hard pec. Her finger practically bounced off the wall of his chest. Damn, he was built. "Why are you on my website?"

"I'm curious about you."

That should not give her a little thrill. "Well, don't be. And stay off the site."

"What if I was a client?"

"That would be entirely different," she said. "Then I'd sell you the whole fantasy. But you and I both know that fantasy is expensive and also simply a balloon just waiting to burst."

Tanner offered her one of the coffees. It was a bribe, of course, but she wasn't above falling for it. She took a big gulp and closed her eyes in bliss. "God have mercy, how I missed you," she whispered to the cup.

"Aw," he said. "Sweet."

"I was talking to the coffee." When the caffeine hit her system, she opened her eyes.

Tanner had set everything on her counter and had moved to the wall of windows. He was hands in pockets, looking out at the water.

She knew there was no way he could miss the fact that she had a perfect view of his boat. And therefore him, when he was out there working.

Now she was sorry that she'd pretended otherwise that first day at the bakery.

He turned to face her, brows up.

She ignored him and eyed the box of doughnuts. She didn't want to be rude and dive in, but she could smell the sugar. It was calling to her.

Tanner came back into the kitchen and leaned against the counter next to her, comfortable as you please in her space. He didn't appear to be in any hurry to get to the doughnuts so she tried to control herself.

He nodded to a stack of travel brochures for faraway, exotic places like Bora Bora and Anguilla.

"You planning on running off?" he asked.

"Just keeping up on the latest hot locales for honeymoons. Brides are usually incredibly picky about the location, thinking that's the most important part of the honeymoon."

"And it's not?" he asked.

"Let's just say that I tend to cash my checks fast, before reality sets in and they realize they've made a mistake."

"Ouch," he said.

"We both know relationships are one big ouch."

"True enough," he agreed. "They're messy and complicated, and screw everything up." He limped over to the drink carrier and pulled out a second coffee. When he caught her looking at him, he shrugged. "It's a double espresso kind of morning."

She nodded toward his leg. "It's bothering you."

Another shrug, one that said it always bothered him, he lived with it.

"Isn't there anything that can be done about the pain?" she asked.

"I don't like pain meds."

She could understand that. But she found she wanted to understand so much more. They weren't supposed to be doing this, getting to know each other, and yet she couldn't help herself. "So how is it you went from the navy to the oil rigs?" she asked. "Was it like once-an-adrenaline-junkie, always-an-adrenaline-junkie sort of thing?"

"After my tour of duty, I knew I didn't want to be career navy. But my college scholarship was long gone and I needed money."

"To support your family," she said.

"What there was left of it," he said. "My mom needed some help. I needed a good-paying job fast so I followed the guys to the rigs. They were working above-water but the money was far better below, planting explosives. I was the resident expert."

Yeah, he was definitely a long way from that wild kid he'd once been. He'd grown up hard and fast, molded by circumstance into a strong, capable man who was focused. Determined. And, apparently, fearless. "Dangerous," she said.

He shrugged. "I had the expertise. Why not use it? And yeah, maybe I can see how people thought the job appealed to the adrenaline junkie in me, but that's not what drew me. I was going to partner with the guys in Lucky Harbor Charters and I wanted to bring my fair share to the table. The job fulfilled all my needs." He gestured to the empty cup in her hands. "Feeling human yet?"

"Getting there," she said. "Thank you."

He opened the box of doughnuts and held it out. "Nothing with powdered sugar."

"Where's the fun in that?" She picked out a maple bar. Tanner did the same, and they ate there, standing up facing each other in her kitchen.

A kitchen that suddenly felt a lot smaller than usual. She licked her thumb to get the last of the glaze, sucking it into her mouth.

Tanner's eyes dilated black.

She went still, letting her thumb slip free with a little suction sound. "Sorry," she whispered.

"For?"

"The porn-star noises."

He flashed a grin. "That was my favorite part." He held out the box. "Another?"

"I think maybe I should stop at one."

"Not on my account," he said, and took a second doughnut for himself.

Callie blew out a sigh and did the same. "I won't be able to button my jeans."

"There's always your PJs."

They both looked down at them and for a moment she wished that she'd listened to her own advice from her site and was wearing some really sexy lingerie.

From the countertop her phone buzzed an incoming text. With maple glaze all over her fingers, she carefully swiped the screen with her thumb. "Siri, read my text."

"Text from Best Grandma Ever," Siri said. "Darling, the word on the street is that you keep going out into the wild wearing strange combinations of clothing. You're not going to catch a man like Tanner Riggs in sweatpants. Put on some of them fancy skinny jeans they sell nowadays. Show him what you've got."

Callie closed her eyes. "Thank you, Siri."

"Yes," Tanner said, smiling. "Thank you, Siri."

"You're going to forget you heard that," she said.

"I'm pretty sure I'm not," Tanner said. "And for the record, you could totally catch me in your sweats."

"Stop," she said, and blew out a breath. "Not that I'm not grateful or anything, but tell me again why you're here?"

"Because you didn't show at the bakery," he said. "You let your asshole ex scare you off."

"You think he's an asshole?"

"I know he's an asshole."

She took another big bite of the maple bar and let the sugar soothe her. "For all you know," she said, "I did something first that prompted him to leave me."

"Babe, even if that was true, the words are simple. I don't want to get married. That's all he had to say, preferably before the wedding day. Instead, he pussied out and screwed you over good."

"Why do guys say that when talking about weakness?" she asked.

"What, pussy?"

"Yeah," she said. "I mean, why isn't it that instead of acting like a pussy, he acted like a *man's ego*, because we all know there's nothing more fragile than that."

He grinned. "You're right. I stand corrected." His smile faded. "Is he the reason you left Lucky Harbor?"

"Maybe a little bit." Humiliated, angry, disillusioned, she'd stayed in San Francisco after graduation. She'd been finished with love, finished with forever-afters, and most definitely finished with men in general. But finding a job after graduation wasn't easy, and she'd fallen back on something she'd been good at—weddings.

And no, she hadn't missed the irony.

"Was yesterday the first time you've seen him since your wedding day?" Tanner asked.

"You know, usually people avoid talking to me about this. I think they're afraid I'm going to cry or something."

"Are you?"

"Hell no," she said. "Not over him."

He looked at her for a long moment. "Do you want to talk about it?"

"Definitely not," she said.

"Gotta talk shit out," he said. "Or it'll kill you."

"You don't seem like a big talker," she said.

"I pick my moments."

"And this is one of them?" she asked.

He slid her a look. "If I said yes, what would you want to know?"

Everything.

That thought was a little much for her to swallow, and she couldn't imagine how he'd feel, so she kept it to herself. "I saw you with your son on the boat yesterday," she said. "Things looked…tense."

"We're working on it," he said. "I've got about fifteen years of resentment to battle my way through."

"And his mom?"

"She's decided that she needs a mom break," he said. "I'm up at bat."

Callie took in the easily spoken words, which didn't match the pain in his eyes. "You're going to do great," she said quietly.

He met her gaze. "Yeah?"

"Yeah," she said. "You always do the right thing. It's who you are, it's hard-wired into you."

"And you got all that from our breakfasts?" he asked, holding her gaze. "Or from your grandma?"

She blew out a long breath and mentally debated whether to actually 'fess up. But she supposed it was time for the truth. "I had a huge crush on you in high school. I was basically your stalker and you didn't even know it. I could write your bio."

He arched a brow. "Let's hear it."

"Hear what?"

"My bio. The things you think you know about me."

"Oh, well…" She wasn't sure how they'd gotten on this road, but she couldn't back out now. He was watching her with those eyes that somehow always drew far too much of her truth from her brain and out her mouth. "I know you got Elisa pregnant at seventeen."

"Everyone knew that," he said.

"I know you had a promising football career with a scholarship on the line, but you gave it all up so that you could support her and the baby."

"Anyone would've done that."

"Actually," she said softly, "no, they wouldn't have. You made that choice for her and Troy's future, not for yourself. I know that Elisa ended up getting to go to the college you'd wanted to attend."

He took her coffee cup and set it on the counter. "Don't make me out to be any kind of martyr. That's not me."

"My point," she said, "is that you do whatever needs to be done. Even if it's not in your own best interests."

"Yeah, I gave up a scholarship," he said, "but I got something out of it. Troy. He's not all that into me at the moment and that's likely to get worse for a little while, but I don't regret any of the decisions I made. Because in the end they led me to him. I've screwed this daddy gig up more than a few times, but I plan on getting it right this time."

"How did you screw it up?"

He was quiet a moment, studying her. "I don't regret the navy," he finally said. "That's where I grew up. But I was away for long periods of time, and then the same on the rigs."

"But that's how you made the money you needed to support them," she said.

"True, but…" He shook his head and she thought that was it. He was done talking.

"I nearly died there," he said quietly, shocking her.

"And I'd have left my son without a dad and my mom without a son to take care of her." He met her gaze. "I set out to be a better man than I was a kid, and in doing so, I've learned that there are more important things than money."

Her throat was tight when she said, "And you don't see how good a man you are?"

"I've still got a lot to make up for."

He wanted redemption for the wildness of his youth. He wanted to make amends. He wanted to man up and be a dad.

She admired the hell out of that.

Tanner's phone buzzed and he read the text, his mouth going tight. "It's from Elisa. I've got to go."

She straightened and set down her coffee on the counter. "Is something wrong?"

"I've been summoned to the principal's office." His smile was grim. "Again. And here I thought those days were long gone." He moved to the door.

"Tanner?"

He turned back. "Yeah?"

"Don't doubt your ability to be a dad," she said softly. "You're a great one."

He stared at her for a few beats and then moved back to her, planting one hand on either side of her body, caging her against the counter.

"What are you doing?"

"Getting ready to kiss you," he said, voice low and…damn. Seductive as hell.

"You are?" she breathed. "Why?"

His mouth was at her ear but he lifted his head to look at her with a smile. "Because I want to."

"You want to kiss me?" she whispered, needing to hear it again. She couldn't help it; she'd dreamed of this for so long when she was younger.

"Yeah," he said. "I want to kiss you. To start."

Holy. Smokes. "But..." Her body quivered. Bad body. "But we talked about this. We're both way too screwed up, remember?"

"I don't feel screwed up right now."

She felt her stomach clench a little, in a good way, the kind of excitement humming through her veins that she usually associated with opening a gallon of ice cream or a new bag of chips. "But your text...you have to go."

"In a minute," he said, staring at her mouth.

Oh boy. He wasn't helping. In fact, he was making her want things. Lots of things, not a single one of them ice cream or chips. So she closed her eyes. This made him seem even closer. They weren't touching, not a single inch, but she felt completely surrounded by him. Intimately so.

She wanted more. "I'm off men, you know."

"Yeah. I know." He took his hands off the counter and pulled her in, hard against his body.

She took two handfuls of his shirt. For balance, she told herself.

But the truth was, she wanted to put her hands on him. His chest was warm and hard beneath her palms. It almost hurt to look at him, he was so damn good-looking. Those dark, dark eyes that held his secrets and emotions in check, that square jaw with a sexy amount of scruff.

Everything about him saying badass tough guy who didn't ever do soft and gentle.

And yet he did exactly that when his hands, strong and

warm, slid up her back and then down, pulling her in even closer.

Then he looked down on her face for another second, his brown eyes soft but full of intent as he slowly lowered his head.

"W-wait!"

He paused, eyes on hers.

She had her hands over his heart and could feel the beating beneath her palms. Slow. Steady.

The opposite of hers, of course.

"Callie?"

"I…can't remember what I was going to say."

His eyes were smiling into hers. "So I can continue?"

She cleared her throat and nodded. "Carry on," she whispered.

He started with a brush of his lips against one corner of her mouth, a butterfly touch. And then the other corner.

She heard a soft sound, an almost whimper, and realized it was her.

He slowly sank his fingers into her hair and she melted. No other word for it, her bones just melted clean away. And then he proceeded to kiss the living daylights out of her, a hot, wet, deep kiss that was good. So very good.

As it went on his fingers squeezed her hips, pulling her in closer. And then closer still, so that she could feel every inch of him. And, oh goodness, he had some really great inches.

She was lost, swirling in the sensations that would surely drown her if she let them. With a moan she leaned in, feeling his heart pounding at rocket speed now. Gratifying.

Tanner shifted and kissed his way over her jaw to the

shell of her ear, his lips closing around the lobe, sucking it into his mouth before his teeth scraped over it.

A rush seared through her belly and she gasped. She opened her eyes and found Tanner watching her with a look she couldn't quite place. "What was that?" she whispered, staring at his mouth.

"A test." His voice was husky, doing nothing to ease the need inside her.

"Did we pass?" she asked.

"No. We failed. Spectacularly," he said. And then he kissed her again—a hot, intense tangle of tongues and teeth that had her letting out that soft, needy sound again.

And again.

And again.

In fact, he didn't stop until she was completely and utterly one-hundred-percent upside down and inside out. She might have even been transported to infinity and beyond.

When he finally lifted his head, she had to take a second before she could open her eyes.

Or maybe it was an hour.

Or a lifetime.

But when she finally dragged her lids up and stared at him, he smiled an especially bad-boy smile. "We're going to do that again," he said.

"Oh," she whispered. "Okay."

He nipped lightly at her wet lower lip, flashed a grin, and then…

Left.

Chapter 11

♥

Tanner was halfway out of the building when Callie's front door whipped open. He turned to find her standing there, hands on hips.

Hair wild.

Sweatshirt slipping off one shoulder.

Nipples hard.

Lips plumped from their kiss.

"What the hell was that?" those lips asked.

His mind was still befuddled, enough that he shook his head. "What?"

"You kiss me and then just walk out of here like the hounds of hell are at your heels?"

Okay, so there'd been a little bit of that. But he'd gotten his hands on her, and her tongue in his mouth, and only one word had crossed his brain and locked into place.

Mine.

That's it, just that one syllable, going round and round in his head the entire time he was kissing her.

Mine.

There'd been a few other things, of course. The blood roaring through his veins like a locomotive on a downhill track, heading south to pool behind his zipper. Which meant that him thinking at all was somewhat of a miracle.

She was waiting for an answer and he didn't have one.

"Was there something in the coffee or doughnuts that made you feel ill?" she inquired politely.

"No."

"So it's me?"

"No." Yes. Jesus. He was unsettled as hell that he'd shared far more than he'd expected to. She was far too easy to be with.

He didn't understand why.

Or like it.

"I have a meeting," he reminded her.

"Right. At the principal's office. But if you didn't have a meeting…"

"But I do."

"Humor me," she said. "If you didn't have to leave right now, what would have happened in there?" She jabbed a finger over her shoulder at her apartment as if there could be any question about what she meant. She then crossed her arms, waiting not so patiently on his answer, and he realized she wasn't pushing him out of anger or even annoyance. She was unnerved.

"Anything you wanted," he said quietly. "As much as you would have let me."

She stared at him. Then she let out a low laugh and dropped her hands to her sides. She stared at her feet for a long beat and it hit him.

Anything she wanted would have been everything.

At his soft laugh, her head jerked up and her eyes narrowed. "Are you laughing at me?"

"At us." He rubbed a hand over his face. "Listen, I'm going to back off, okay? Nothing's going to happen unless you want it to."

A grimace crossed her face.

"You want it to," he said, liking that way too much.

She blew out a breath. "I'm not sure a nice guy would point that out."

"I'm not all that nice," he said.

She sighed again. "This is bad, Tanner."

Yes. Yes, it was bad. Very, very bad. It wasn't only a volatile situation but a dangerous one as well. More dangerous than being a SEAL. More dangerous than any rig job. Because this wasn't a threat to his body, which had time and time again proven itself able to withstand much more than he'd thought possible.

No, this time the danger was to his heart and soul.

And he didn't think either of them could take the hit.

"I'm not doing this," she said, gesturing to him and then herself. "Not happening. Been there, done that, bought the T-shirt, you know?"

"Yes," he said softly. "I know."

But apparently she wasn't sure because she kept talking. "I mean, I know what happens when you fall in love. You get stupid. Love's not enough."

"Callie, you're preaching to the choir here."

She still wasn't done. "Did you know that forty percent of the women who shop and plan their wedding on my website don't even have a groom? Forty percent, Tanner!"

"Jesus. Really?"

"Yes," she said, "and don't get me started on the other sixty percent." She shoved her fingers through her already crazy hair and shook her head. "Focus, Sharpe."

He smiled. "You talk to yourself a lot."

"Yes. Be scared. Be very, very scared. In fact, if you could be scared off, that would solve everything."

"Consider it done," he said.

"Good!" With that, she stormed back into her apartment and slammed the door.

The door next to hers opened and Olivia poked her head out. Above hers appeared Cole's.

Both grinning, of course.

"So are you really scared off?" Cole asked.

"Yep," he said. "I'm gone."

Cole laughed softly. "Liar."

Yep.

"I hear there's a girl," Tanner's mom said at her dinner table.

Both Troy and Tanner went still, eyes like deer in the headlights.

Tanner's mom smiled. "I hear everything."

Tanner turned his head and looked at his son.

Troy immediately lifted his hands in innocence and shook his head. "Hey, don't look at me. I got dumped when you and Mom made me move here. It's not me who has a girl."

All eyes locked on Tanner speculatively.

He kept his face even. It was his weekly dinner with his mom. She looked forward to grilling him all week and now that he had Troy to accompany him, she had *two* targets. Troy had tried to put up his usual sullen front, but Tanner's mom was hard to be sullen to. Plus it appeared the kid was starting to get into having his paternal grandma dote on him.

Or maybe it was the desserts.

Either way, Tanner hadn't had to drag the teen here tonight. Troy had actually remembered first and had to remind Tanner to get going so that they'd be on time.

"There is no girl," he told them both.

Beatriz studied her son. "I play bingo. I hear things."

"You can't believe everything you hear, Mom."

"I hear it from Lucille. The Oracle of Lucky Harbor."

Tanner laughed. "Ninety-nine percent of what she puts out there is B.S."

"Which means it's one percent spot on," she said calmly. "You're seeing her granddaughter Callie, a sweet, smart girl who nearly married the dentist. He's a good dentist but he's an idiot of a man. You'll do right by her." She looked smug. "How's that for one percent spot on?"

Troy grinned, enjoying this. "Is there dessert?"

"But of course," Beatriz said. "Soon as your father tells his mama about the woman."

"Hurry, Dad," Troy said. "Tell her."

Tanner went brows up on the "Dad." At least on the outside. On the inside his heart did an almost painful squeeze as pleasure flooded him so fast he got dizzy. When Troy had first come to Lucky Harbor, he'd refused to call him Dad, instead using Tanner's given name. Which had annoyed the hell out of him, but he'd hidden that because as he knew more than anyone, teenagers could see a weakness from a mile away. But he knew damn well that Troy knew how badly Tanner had wanted to be called Dad. "Now?" he asked the kid wryly. "Really?"

"Dessert," Troy explained.

Naturally. Forget the Hallmark moment, it was about dessert.

Beatriz was smiling at Tanner, her eyes sharp as tacks. She didn't miss a trick.

"Yes, it's Callie," Troy said. "They've had breakfasts together at the bakery. And one at her place."

Tanner stared at him.

"What? It's online. Don't blame me," Troy said. "Dessert?"

"You," Beatriz said to him. "Yes, you can have dessert, warm from the oven."

Troy flashed Tanner a smug look that turned into a grimace when Beatriz pulled him in and gave him a smacking kiss on the cheek.

Now Tanner sent Troy the smug look but after a moment took pity on his son. "Mom, he doesn't like to be hugged and kissed."

"No. This can't be true," Beatriz said, pretending to be aghast as she kissed Troy again and then again on his other cheek. "In our family, we like to kiss," she said. "It's the Brazilian blood."

Troy tried to be stoic while Beatriz kept at him, but seeing as Beatriz was in a wheelchair and she had Troy bent into a pretzel, Tanner couldn't help it. Eventually he started to laugh.

"There," Beatriz said, satisfied, finally letting go of her grandson. "That's much better. Why do you teenagers have to be all broody and sullen?"

"Because being a teenager sucks," Troy said. "You have no idea."

Tanner and Beatriz looked at each other and laughed.

Troy frowned. "You're not supposed to laugh. That wasn't funny. Why was that funny?"

"Baby," Beatriz said, "you have no idea. When I was your age, I was working in the banana fields twelve hours a day. When your dad was your age, he worked two jobs to help keep a roof over our heads, and then when you came along he had to go into the military to feed all of us."

Troy blinked. "I—I'm sorry."

"Oh, no, baby," she said. "It's okay, you didn't know. But now you do. Would you take Rio out for a walk around the block for your dear old grandma?"

Rio was Beatriz's aging toy poodle, the one sitting in her lap like he owned it, and he resembled a balding chicken.

"Don't move too fast now," Beatriz said. "He's got some troubles today. I think he ate a sock. Give him a moment to air out, you know what I'm saying?" She shoved Rio into Troy's arms, slapped the leash against his chest, and smiled sweetly.

Rio reached up and licked Troy's chin politely.

Troy looked down at the dog and then at Tanner.

Tanner kept his gaze on his mom, and a moment later the back door shut.

Beatriz grinned at him.

"Seriously," Tanner said, "you should bottle that skill."

"Which, darling?"

"How to be so evil and yet disarmingly sweet."

She laughed. "Oh, but you can't teach that. It comes naturally. Get the dessert, would you?"

Tonight it was fried cinnamon doughnut holes from Leah's bakery. His mom loved them, claiming they reminded her of bolinho de chuva from her childhood.

Tanner's dad had met her on spring break and brought her to the States. He'd stuck around long enough to see Tanner's fifth birthday party.

Ever since then it'd been just the two of them, as Beatriz hadn't been big on men after being dumped with a kid. She'd been an overworked, exhausted single mother working at the school cafeteria before rheumatoid arthritis had knocked her flat, forcing an early retirement.

He'd done his best to take care of her. And yeah, her body might have betrayed her, but her mind was still like a whip. She could read an eye twitch from a mile away, especially when it came to her son.

"Tell me," she said. "Tell me about the woman."

"There's nothing to tell."

"Look at you, lying to your own mother. My phone's been ringing off the hook. It's all true, what Troy said."

"You're going to believe the word of a fifteen-year-old whose sole mission in life is to eat his weight daily?"

"He eats like you. He also thinks like you. You've got a smart one there," she said fondly. "And don't blame him. You've been seen at the bakery."

Tanner sighed. "Forgot there for a moment that we live in Mayberry."

She laughed. "Might as well be. I remember Callie as a girl. I cleaned her parents' legal office at night for cash."

"I didn't know that," Tanner said.

"No one did. I didn't want charity, I wanted to work for what I earned. Her parents…" She shook her head. "They were good people, always made sure to give me a holiday and birthday bonus, but very self-involved. Scarcely noticed that they had a child." She went on for a little bit about that time and what she knew and then she turned her eagle eye on Tanner. "Tell me what Callie is like now. I remember her as sweet. And smart. Very smart."

"Still is," Tanner said. "She's running a site called TyingTheKnot.com, designing wedding websites and being a virtual wedding planner."

Beatriz's eyes lit up. "I heard this. A wedding site…"

He saw the stars in her eyes and laughed. "Don't get any ideas, Mom."

"Oh, I already have ideas. And they involve you not being on a dangerous job for once, killing yourself to make money for me, for Elisa, for Troy."

"I'm not in a dangerous job now."

"Hmm" was all she said.

"I'm not."

"You're still diving. When are you not going to need adrenaline rushes anymore? You're too old for that."

"I'm thirty-two, hardly old," he said on a laugh. "And diving doesn't bother my leg."

"A man hits his prime at age seventeen."

He was going to hope that wasn't quite true. "I've always been careful."

"No, you've always been hungry. You needed to support Elisa, even when she took advantage of you and lived in a way that was above her—and your—means. And then you felt the need to buy me this house…" She gestured to the two-bedroom townhouse he'd purchased for her after his second year on the rigs.

"You'd always wanted your own place," he murmured.

"And I love it. I love you. I just want it to be your turn to be happy." She smiled. "A wedding site."

"Mom."

"What? It sounds so romantic."

"It's not," Tanner said. "It's a paycheck, that's all."

She made a small *tsk*ing sound in her throat. "If she feels that way, then the two of you are well suited."

Tanner grinned at her.

"I don't find it funny, my only son refusing to let himself love."

He sighed, wrapped an arm around her shoulders, and pulled her in. "I love plenty. I love you, you meddling old woman."

"Hmph," she said, looking secretly pleased.

Tanner reached for another doughnut hole, freezing when he caught sight of his mom's mail. The top piece was a bank statement, opened. He zeroed in on the bottom line and the balance there. "Jesus. Did you win the lottery when I wasn't looking?"

"Don't take the Lord's name in vain," she said. "And yes, I did win the lottery. The son lottery."

He took his gaze off the statement and stared at her.

She stared back, a little smugly, he thought, and he narrowed his eyes. "You're scaring me," he said.

"Don't be silly. I scare no one."

"You scare everyone. The money, Mom. How did you get that much money?"

"It's yours."

"Mine." He looked at the balance again and shook his head. "What?"

"It's the money you've given me over the years. At first I used some of it, I had to. But then I caught up. I told you this but you wouldn't listen. Or stop giving me your hard-earned money. So I started saving it. Figured one day I could help you for a change."

"Mom," he said softly, staggered.

"I was waiting for a rainy day," she said. "That might be a rainy day called Troy's College Fund, I don't know. Maybe it's a rainy day called the Turks and Caicos. Whatever you want, baby."

He took her hands and looked into her eyes. "I told you that money was for you and I meant it."

"And I told you I didn't need it. But you always were stubborn as a jackass. Got that from your daddy because God knows I'm not like that."

"Yeah," he said dryly. "God knows."

"Listen." She set her hands on her cheeks. "I know and everyone else knows that you give to whoever's in need. You've always worked so hard. Then you started Lucky Harbor Charters with Sam and Cole and you still worked your buns off. You've always felt you had to be the hardest worker because you didn't start out with as much as everyone else. You cover your own burdens. It's what makes you special. But, baby, you can relax a little bit now. You have a cushion."

He was so moved he couldn't speak.

She smiled gently. "Now probably you're thinking, hmm, what can I do to pay back my mama? Well, let me tell you, son. You can give love a shot, a real shot. It won't always disappoint you, I promise."

Here was a woman who'd been disappointed by love herself, actually *deserted*, and yet she hadn't been destroyed by it. There wasn't an ounce of bitterness in her. He wished he could say the same. "You don't know that, Mom."

"And neither do you. Unless you try."

Chapter 12

♥

Callie dreamed about kissing. Not a surprise since all she could think about was how she'd felt in Tanner's arms, his mouth on hers. She'd known he was a reported master scuba diver and explosives expert, but turned out he was also a master kisser. Granted, it'd been a while for her, but she didn't remember nearly spontaneously combusting from just a kiss before.

It wasn't yet dawn when she gave up trying to sleep and went to work instead. There were plenty of emails and texts from brides to tide her over and take her mind off Tanner's sexy mouth.

How do I know I picked the right color for my palette? I mean, I think I'm a spring but my sister says I'm a summer.

What if both my mother and my mother-in-law-to-be want the same dress and neither will bend? In fact, my mother-in-law-to-be said she'd die if she can't have the dress she wants and my mother said that could be arranged.

How do I tactfully ask my fiancé to tell his bossy older sister to butt the hell out of my planning? I mean, she's still single so what does she even know about weddings, right?

Callie usually took these sort of questions in stride, but today she wanted to delete them all and tell each of them to get a life.

And then there was the email from her parents, doing their bimonthly check-in. Callie was sure they wanted to know her feelings on Lucille and her mental condition. It'd have been nicer, of course, to actually get a call, especially as she'd left them several voicemail messages over the past week. Since they hadn't called, she didn't have to admit that she had made absolutely no headway in her assessment of Lucille's mental condition.

Sometimes the woman seemed absolutely insane.

And sometimes she was perfectly tuned in, more so than any of the rest of them.

In either case, Callie wasn't ready to leave. And as she'd subletted her San Francisco apartment, she had no real reason to.

Well, except for the fact that her life was there.

Sort of.

Because it also felt like she was making a life here in Lucky Harbor and that maybe she was doing it better than she had the first time around.

By the time the sun came up and over the mountains and began to lighten the sky, she needed a walk. The dock looked deserted. Perfect. She hadn't had to Skype any of her brides this morning so she was in comfy clothes from head to toe, yoga pants and a big sweater. All she had to do was add boots and a jacket in deference to the winter storm blowing in and then hit the harbor.

She walked to the pier. She wasn't surprised to find the ice cream shop closed but was gravely disappointed. On the way back she found the dock showing signs of life now. Tanner's son Troy was on board the Lucky Harbor Charters boat, swabbing the deck. Grateful it wasn't Tanner—she wasn't sure she was ready to face him without begging for another kiss—she waved. "Hello," she called out.

The teen straightened and shielded his eyes. "Can I help you?" he asked.

So polite. Not at all the sullen kid she'd expected. "Is your dad here?" she asked. *Please say no...* She hadn't expected to run into anyone, and she suddenly realized that she should have thought this through because when it came to Tanner, she could bank on one thing: making a fool of herself.

Troy looked surprised. "You know who I am?"

"Sure," she said. "You look just like him."

"So you're the girlfriend."

Her heart stopped. "He has a girlfriend?"

"You Callie?" he asked.

"Yes," she said.

"Then it's you. You're the girlfriend."

She was both ridiculously relieved and horrified. "I'm going to ship my grandma off to a third-world country where there's no WiFi available," she muttered.

He grinned and looked so much like a young Tanner

that her heart panged. "Could you take my grandma too?" he asked.

She laughed. "Your grandma's perfectly normal and nice, so no, sorry. And for the record, I'm not your dad's girlfriend. I'm just his—" The memory of Tanner's mouth on hers made her trip over the word *friend*. That didn't fit any better than girlfriend did. "Neighbor," she finally said, and gave a mental grimace. Lame.

Troy arched his brow, another perfect imitation of his father.

"So he's not here, right?" she asked, desperately needing a subject change.

"He's up at the warehouse with Sam. But he'll be back any second to check on his slave labor."

That didn't sound like Tanner. "You're not getting paid?" she asked.

"Twelve bucks an hour," he said morosely.

She laughed. "I'll trade you jobs."

He leaned on the mop and shoved back his dark, wayward hair from his face. "Do you really do a wedding website?" he asked.

"Yep. I deal with demanding brides all day long, and trust me, they've got nothing on your dad."

Troy didn't look convinced.

"I also design wedding websites," she said. "And granted, that's a lot more fun but takes some IT knowledge."

"I know a lot about computers," he said.

"Then you're ahead of the game. Do you play football like your dad did?"

"How do you know he played football?" Troy asked. "He never talks about it."

"I went to school with him," Callie said, and caught the sudden interest in Troy's gaze. "He set a bunch of records that I think still stand to this day."

"His jersey and two trophies are displayed in a glass case outside the athletic department," Troy said. "They say he could've gone pro if he'd been able to go to college."

Callie heard the change in Troy's voice at that. Guilt. "There were more important things to your dad," she said.

Troy looked at her, for a moment nothing more than a very young, vulnerable, hurting kid.

"It's true," she said softly.

"They talk about him at school sometimes. About his football record and some of the stuff he used to do. I guess he was pretty wild and crazy." Now there was a note of awe in his voice, like he wanted to be that guy.

Only thing was, Callie was pretty sure Tanner didn't want Troy living up to his legacy in that way. "I don't think he's as proud of that stuff as he is proud of you," she said carefully.

Troy snorted.

"What?" she asked.

"I got dumped on him, you know. Here in Lucky Harbor."

"He's happy you're here, however that came to be," she said. "He's happy he gets to be a real dad to you."

Troy gave an indifferent shrug that didn't match the unmistakable yearning in his eyes and went back to working the mop. "So you really know how to design a website and stuff?"

"Yep."

"I'd like to know how to do that," he said. "But not for weddings."

"I could show you sometime," she said. "I recently did a wedding site for Sam and Becca, setting it up so people can RSVP for the wedding, see their registry, and chat about it on a message board, all in one place. In fact, the wedding is coming up. We're having the bachelor/bachelorette party here on the boat."

"I don't know why anyone would choose to have a party here, much less live here," he said. "There's nothing to do."

She laughed. "Are you kidding? You've got the mountains *and* the water. You can ski, hike, fish, scuba, or just relax in the beauty of it all."

He didn't look impressed by any of this.

"Trust me," she said. "I grew up here. There's a lot for you to do."

"So you live here because it's fun?"

"No, I live here because of my grandma."

"Lucille." He grinned. "She's a little crazy."

"Crazy nice?" Callie asked hopefully.

"Crazy crazy," Troy said. "She put my dad and Sam and Cole up on Instagram this morning in a Who's Hottest poll. They were pissed. There's also a pic of you."

Oh God. She hadn't looked yet today. Just as she thought that, her phone buzzed with an incoming text from the woman herself.

I put this up on Instagram. Thought I should mention it before someone else did. People agree that you and Tanner make a hot couple, and I agree—although it wouldn't kill you to put on mascara and blush when you go out.

The pic was from the other morning at the bakery. She looked flushed and rather…anticipatory, and the reason for that was clear. Tanner stood behind her, hand on her shoulder, leaning over her, his intent gaze on her face.

If Callie hadn't actually been there that day, if she didn't know firsthand that Tanner was in the middle of pounding her back as she choked on a doughnut, she'd have said that she looked like she was halfway to orgasm and that Tanner was about to give it to her.

"Oh my God," she muttered, and Troy looked over her shoulder.

"I guess you're close neighbors, huh?"

Callie gritted her teeth. "I was choking on a doughnut and your dad was literally pounding me on the back." She shook her head. "I'm going to have to hack into her account and set up some perimeters and blocks."

This caught Troy's interest. "You can do that too?"

She looked over at him. "Uh, no. No, that would be entirely unethical. And bad. Very, very bad."

That got a grin out of Troy, and she saw that he was going to be a lady-killer in no time at all, if he wasn't already.

"My grandma doesn't get online but she's pretty nosy too," Troy said.

"Yes, but she's a nice crazy," Callie said. "Mine's just crazy crazy. And I'm the one who sent her out into the world with my technology knowledge in the first place. I've created a monster."

"Did you see what she's been doing on Tumblr?"

"Oh, God," Callie said. "I'm afraid to ask."

"She's blogging daily naughty autocorrects."

Callie stared at him. "Okay, she clearly has way too

much time on her hands. Her art gallery's slow on week-day afternoons. I think that's where she gets bored because she goes to bed early." She tactfully left off the part of Lucille's day where she boinked Mr. Wykowski right after *Jeopardy*. "I guess she needs an afternoon babysitter."

"I babysit," Troy said.

She slid him a look. "Yeah?"

"For cash."

"Understood," Callie said. "You think you could put some time in and keep her on the straight and narrow?"

"I don't change diapers."

"She's old but not that old," Callie said. "Aren't you too busy for this with school and your work here on the boat?"

"I'm never too busy to make more cash."

"What do you need cash for?" she asked, curious.

He shrugged, but she could tell he was holding back.

"A girl?" she asked.

"Maybe. Maybe just a neighbor."

Smartass. She liked that. And him. She was still ribbing him when his dad showed up with Cole and Sam. Each moved in a way that commanded a woman's attention. That they were all smart and self-made had a lot to do with that, but there was no denying that they were each gorgeous in their own way. And yet Callie's gaze latched onto Tanner and held.

Around them the morning was gray, the weather was bordering on stormy. Temps hovered in the forties.

And yet the guys were in board shorts. In deference to the windchill, they also had on sweatshirts. Tanner's hood was up and he wore dark sunglasses and some dark stubble.

GQ does *Sports Illustrated.*

As Callie took in the sight of him, her heart kicked hard. Her gaze shifted over his body but stuttered to a halt when it came to his left leg and the scar revealed there from the hem of his board shorts to midshin.

From the rig fire.

The sight of it drove home just how lethal and scary his life had been and how close he'd come to not making it back, which would have left a big hole in a lot of lives, including her own.

Tanner had picked up the provisions for the cruise they were chartering later. He and the guys had walked down the dock to the boat together, but when Tanner saw Callie on the boat looking like she belonged there, laughing with his son, he forgot about Sam and Cole, forgot his job entirely. Just seeing Troy smile at all felt like a gift. Add Callie to the mix and it was a lot to take in.

They both seemed to catch sight of him at the same time and their amusement died. Callie's gaze held... affection? A lingering desire? Hell, that might be his imagination, but he'd like to think she was remembering the last time she'd seen him, when she'd had her tongue in his mouth.

Or maybe that was just him thinking about it.

A lot.

All the time.

Then her gaze drifted south. Way south. Past any good parts to his scarred-up leg, and Tanner didn't miss the flash of horror and pity.

And damn if he didn't wish he'd worn jeans.

Troy's expression didn't hold much but teenage pissiness. Not a surprise. All Tanner had to do was breathe and he irritated the kid.

He'd told himself that was the way of things. It was the rite of passage for a teenager to resent the hell out of his dad.

Tanner certainly had, sight unseen.

Sam and Cole greeted Callie warmly and Tanner met Troy's gaze. "How's it going? You get the floors belowdecks too?"

"Not yet," Troy said.

"I distracted him," Callie said, and smiled at Troy. "Sharp kid. He's interested in helping me handle Lucille and her antics, if that's okay with you."

"Of course."

"That's nice of you to help," Cole said to Troy.

"That's me," Troy said with more than a hint of irony. "Nice. A real chip off the old block."

Sam barked a quick laugh and reached out and snagged Troy with an arm around the neck, giving him a noogie. "Watch your mouth, kid. Your dad's dunked me for less."

"Dunked?" Troy asked.

Sam gestured to the water.

Troy looked over the edge of the boat at the dark, choppy water. "You'd get hypothermia today."

"Nah," Sam said. "He almost always rescues you in time."

Troy looked at Tanner. "He's kidding, right?"

"Nope," Cole broke in with a straight face. "You know he was a SEAL, yeah? If he doesn't get to you in time it's because he didn't want to."

Troy gulped audibly.

Cole grinned at Tanner. "We'll meet you at the hut."

And with that, Cole and Sam left the dock.

Tanner looked at Callie. He would've liked to pull her in close and see if she'd melt against him like she had yesterday, but they had a young, impressionable audience watching them with avid curiosity.

And then there was the fact that Tanner had walked away from what he and Callie had started. Which made him an idiot. "I need to unload these provisions," he said, and gestured to the bags in his hands.

"Don't mind me," she said. "I was just out for a walk. I'm headed back to do more work."

Tanner was standing in the boat's galley putting things away when he heard the voices.

"Just neighbors, huh?" Troy said.

"Yep," Callie replied, emphasis on the "p" sound.

"You didn't look at him like you were just neighbors," Troy said. "And you stared at his leg."

"I hadn't seen his scar before," Callie said.

"He got it in a fire on the oil rigs," Troy told her. "He nearly died."

There was no sullenness in the boy's voice, Tanner noted. No negativity at all, in fact.

"I'm glad he's not still working out there," Callie said.

"I'm not sure he can," Troy said. "You've seen him limp."

Tanner winced but it was fact. He limped. He probably always would. Realizing he was straining to eavesdrop, he attempted to ignore them and unloaded the bags.

"His limp isn't that noticeable," Callie said. "And the Tanner I know wouldn't let anything stop him from doing what he wanted to do—" She broke off at the sound of a text coming through. There was a beat of silence and then she snorted.

"What?" Troy asked.

"It's my work, from a bride. She says: My shoes are at least a shade off from my dress—exclamation point, exclamation point, exclamation point. The wedding's going to be ruined!" Callie sighed. "My poor, overwrought, overly emotional bride."

"You've got brides texting you?" Troy asked.

"It's my job to deal with them," she said. "I don't know why I do it."

"Why do you?"

"Well," she said thoughtfully. "We all do things we don't necessarily want to do."

"Yeah," Troy said, sounding mopey. "Like mopping a boat. But you're a grown-up. You get to do whatever you want."

Callie laughed. "That's so not true. There are consequences to everything, you must know that. And responsibilities, which only grow as you get older. We all end up doing things that we don't always want to."

"Like?" Troy asked.

"Like your dad didn't necessarily want to be out there on the rigs."

"Yeah, he did," Troy said. "Just like he'd rather be working in South America for the winter on some big diving job instead of here with me."

"I think you're wrong," Callie responded, her voice far more serious now. "He could've taken a job in South America but he's here because he wants to be. He wants to be with you."

Tanner strained to hear Troy's response, but if the teen

said anything more, he didn't catch it. A few minutes later he made his way above deck and found Troy alone, back at work mopping.

Callie was halfway up the dock.

Tanner called out to her and, feeling Troy's eyes on his back, headed her way. She'd stopped and was watching him.

Tanner rarely gave his leg much thought other than the fact that it ached like a sonofabitch, but in that moment he'd have paid big bucks to have a normal gait. "Hey," he said.

"Hey yourself. Your son's a great kid."

"He's got his moments."

"So you're okay with me hiring him to babysit Lucille?" she asked.

"If he wants, sure."

"He said he does." She tilted her head to the side. "You okay?"

The leg, she meant. "Fine. Are you going to brave the bakery for breakfast?"

She arched a brow.

"What?" he asked.

"Well, first of all, you're not okay. You're frowning. You're frustrated, and your leg is bothering you."

"What does that have to do with breakfast?" he asked, baffled.

"It doesn't. But I asked if you were okay and you said fine. When you're clearly not fine," she pointed out, sounding perturbed.

He paused. "I know you're speaking in English but—"

"Never mind." With a head shake, she started to walk off.

He stared after her, wondering when the hell they'd taken a turn into Crazy-Ville. "Callie."

"Gotta go." Halfway down the dock, she turned to him, still walking. "I'm having breakfast with Olivia and Becca. And then I'm getting a new coffeemaker. I'm going to be making my own coffee from now on."

Yeah, that didn't sound like it boded well for him. "How about the doughnuts?"

"I'm just giving them up."

"Cold turkey?"

"Cold turkey," she said. "They say that's how it's best done."

Something was off. *They* were off—which was his own doing. He opened his mouth to somehow try to fix things but she turned away again and walked off.

And he let her.

He walked back to the boat where Troy was leaning on the mop watching him, shaking his head.

"What?" Tanner asked.

"She's into you."

"We're…"

"Neighbors?" Troy asked, heavy on the dry.

"Yeah." Tanner rubbed a hand over his face. "Sort of."

Troy snorted. "Did you not see the way she looked at you? Jeez, even I know what that means."

Tanner had to shake his head. "You usually avoid talking to me and suddenly you're all chatty, and *this* is the conversation you want to have?"

Troy shrugged. "I like her."

"I do too."

"But you're screwing it up."

"No, I'm not," Tanner said. *Yes, you are…*

Troy just looked at him. "You know a lot about a lot of stuff," he finally said. Tanner didn't have the time to enjoy the compliment before Troy went on. "But I don't think you have much game."

He actually sounded pretty disappointed about this, and Tanner found himself coming to his own defense, ridiculous as it was. "I have plenty of game."

Troy didn't look impressed so Tanner repeated it, like he was fifteen too. "I do."

Or he used to anyway. He eyed the dock. The empty dock. Because Callie was long gone. And that's when he realized it was true.

He had absolutely no game.

Chapter 13

♥

In the good news department, Troy spent the next several afternoons with Callie's grandma and was earning his pay. The first day when she picked him up from the art gallery to drive him home, he came out to the car, slouched in his seat, and said, "Yeah, she's crazy. And also she's dating some guy who's older than dirt."

"Mr. Wykowski," she said. "He's nice."

"Yeah, he pulled me aside and said he'd double my salary if I sabotage her run for mayor."

"What?" Callie squeaked.

"Don't worry, I don't have to do anything illegal. Just go around and take down the posters she puts up, the ones that say 'Lucille for Mayor of Lucky Harbor and Beyond!'"

"Oh my God."

Troy grinned and for a moment he looked so much like his father that it had taken her breath.

She missed Tanner. Badly. Silly to miss a guy after three breakfasts and one kiss, but she missed him with an ache that suggested she'd put far too much importance on what had turned out to be just a renewal of her silly crush. "Did my grandma make you tell her all your secrets?" she asked Troy.

"Every single one," he said with a sigh.

"It takes practice to learn to resist her," Callie told him. "You'll do better as time goes on."

"What's going on?" Becca asked Callie at breakfast three mornings after she'd met Troy and scared Tanner off but good.

"Nothing," she said, and quickly dove into her pancakes.

Becca and Olivia exchanged a look that Callie chose to ignore. She'd learned that was her best tactic because if she gave an inch, her two new friends took a mile.

Or two.

"You sure?" Olivia asked.

"Mm-hmm," Callie said, nodding, shoving in another bite of pancakes. She was starving. This was what happened when you closed yourself in your apartment and worked for three straight days without coming up for air.

"You know we really like you, right?" Becca asked.

Callie chewed, swallowed, and nodded. "Yep. Sure."

"She doesn't know," Olivia told Becca.

Becca sighed. "Okay, Callie, I need you to listen to me. You've got all that really great strawberry blond hair with those natural curls that look effortless, and you have the kind of naturally fit body that doesn't require hours of torture in the gym, and you don't even need makeup, and women everywhere probably line up to hate you, but I can't do it. I can't hate you."

"Me either," Olivia said. "In fact, we kind of want to be you."

Becca nodded.

Callie stared at them both. "Did you both lace your orange juice with liquor?"

"You get to work from home with your PJs and Shrek slippers," Olivia said. "I'm so jealous of the slippers. But back to the point."

"Yes," Becca said. "The point. Let's start with the evidence, shall we?" She set her phone on the table so that both Olivia and Callie could see the screen. "Earlier in the week you managed to spill your coffee, your purse, and your pride all over the bakery floor and get onto Instagram as Lucky Harbor's cutest but most klutzy bachelorette."

"That pic was supposed to be taken down," Callie said.

Becca swiped her finger across the screen and brought up another picture, the one of Callie and Tanner.

"Okay," Callie said. "That's a little deceiving."

"And this one?" Becca accessed the next pic. It was of Eric and the blonde leaving the bakery. "It says he's your ex-fiancé, who left you at the altar."

Well, wasn't this fun. "I...didn't see that one."

"I'm glad," Becca said, her usually mild-tempered eyes hard. "He's an ass. A good dentist but a complete ass." Becca shook her head. "I'm sorry you had to run into him like that when you were alone. I'd have liked to be with you."

Callie shook her head. "It wasn't a big deal. He just... startled me."

At this Becca reached out and squeezed her hand. "I'd like to startle him into next week."

Callie smiled because it wasn't so far off from what Tanner had said. She couldn't deny that it felt good to have people care enough about her that they wanted to defend her honor. But she could handle herself. Probably. "Not necessary," she assured Becca. "It was all a long time ago."

"Good," Olivia said. "But that's not even the most interesting part."

Oh great, Callie thought, having a bad feeling that she knew what was coming next.

"True," Becca said. "That honor goes to the fact that it's rumored you're no longer going to the bakery because you're holing up with—" She looked at Olivia. "What did they call him?"

"Mr. Sex Walking," Olivia said helpfully.

Callie grimaced.

"Mr. Sex Walking," Becca repeated, and burst out laughing. "Tanner's going to love that."

Olivia grinned too. "No, he's not."

"No, he's not," Becca agreed.

Callie sighed and reached for the syrup. She was going to need a lot more sugar to get through this. "It's a very long, very boring story."

"I love long, boring stories," Olivia said.

Great. "Okay, well…I had a crush on him in high school," she admitted. "A big-time crush."

"Tanner's pretty crushable," Becca said, and when Olivia slid her a look, she shrugged. "What? I'm engaged, I'm not dead. Those dark eyes, that hard body." Becca sighed dreamily. "His body language always seems to say that he's been badass before and he has no problem being badass again if the need arises." She shook herself. "The man is hot."

"Yes, well," Callie said, "he's also out of my league."

"Don't make me set down my fork to smack you," Olivia said. "Because I don't want to stop eating but I'll totally do it."

"I mean it," Callie said. "Look, I was the nerd in school. You know, the girl that guys like him paid to do their homework. And I know it sounds stupid, but when I see him sometimes my tongue gets all tied up like it used to."

"Because he's hot," Becca said. "Not because he's out of your league. Honey, whatever you were, you're the equally hot girl now. Brains are in. Own it."

Callie smiled at her. "You're sweet."

"Yes," Becca said. "And I'm smart too, so believe me."

Callie did. Maybe she'd felt a little invisible at first, but that had been before Tanner had brought her doughnuts.

And kissed her.

She hadn't been invisible then. Tanner had been as gobsmacked by their chemistry as she. Nope. She no longer felt invisible at all.

Now she just felt…longing.

"Okay, so now that that's settled," Becca said. "Explain the bakery breakfasts."

Fine. This was easier anyway. "I was there first and Tanner came in and took the only empty seat." She paused. "Next to me."

"Three times?" Becca asked.

Hmm. Maybe not so easy. "Well, the first time any-way," she said, diving back into her pancakes. "Maybe the next two times I sort of saved a seat for him."

Becca and Olivia grinned at this, and Callie sighed. "We told each other we were sitting together in order to not have to socialize with anyone else."

"Interesting," Becca said slowly.

"Very," said Olivia. "Which do you find more so, the evasion technique or the out-and-out lie?"

Callie rolled her eyes. "It was stupid. Hanging out with him renewed my stupid high school crush. And then he saw the whole thing with Eric, which was mortifying. So I didn't go for coffee the next day. And…

"*And*?" Becca and Olivia asked in unison, leaning for-ward.

"And…" Callie grimaced. "Tanner showed up on my doorstep with coffee and doughnuts."

"What kind?" Becca asked.

"An entire baker's dozen. Assorted."

Her avid audience sighed dreamily.

"No," she said, pointing her fork at them. "Don't do that. No sighing like that. It wasn't cute."

"No," Becca said. "It was sexy."

"Sexy as all get-out," Olivia agreed. "I heard the whole thing as it happened."

Callie stared at her. "What? Then why did you ask me about it? And how? How did you know?"

"No insulation," Olivia said.

"Oh my God," Callie said. "I'm calling our landlord!"

"Good luck," Olivia said. "And I swear I wasn't trying to eavesdrop. At least not at first. Cole and I were in bed and then you two started talking, and before we knew it we were trying not to listen with our ears pressed against the wall."

Becca grinned.

Not Callie. "Cole heard?" she asked on a moan. "Oh, God." She dropped her head to the table and thunked it a few times, which didn't help whatsoever. "Okay, you know what? It doesn't matter. It's done. Seeing Eric reminded me that no good comes from crushes. Or relationships. And since Tanner agrees, subject closed."

Becca's expression went from amused to troubled. "He said that?"

"Didn't have to," Callie said. "He left in a pretty big hurry after the kiss."

"There was a *kiss*?" they both screeched together.

Callie went back to thunking her head on the table.

"It's okay. I know how to fix this," Olivia said.

Callie lifted her head. "We wipe Cole's memory?"

Olivia ignored that and turned to Becca. "I really thought out of the three of us, I was the most screwed up and that you took second place."

"Hey," Becca said. Then she sighed. "Okay, true."

"But it's her," Olivia said, and looked at Callie. "You're the most screwed up."

"Gee," Callie said. "Thanks?"

"Oh, no worries," Olivia said. "We can fix this."

Becca nodded.

"Fix what exactly?" Callie asked warily.

"Well, Tanner's in a bad head space," Becca said. "He's had a lot on his plate and it's all about the people he cares about. It's time for him to do something for himself for a change. And you're perfect as that something."

Callie opened her mouth but Becca kept talking. "And you. You work for crazy people and don't get out much. You need something for yourself too. Tanner's that perfect something. So together, it's all perfect, you see?"

Olivia was nodding her head. She saw.

Callie did not. "Listen, I don't think—"

"Go with that," Becca said. "Don't think. We'll do the thinking for you."

"And our plan is…?" Olivia asked Becca.

"Get Tanner to crush on Callie," she said like she'd just solved world hunger. She was beaming. "It's perfect."

"Not quite," Callie said. "He's not the type to crush. And I'm not—"

Olivia pointed her fork at her. "If you finish that sentence, I will totally stop eating to smack you. I swear it this time. You're totally crush-worthy. In fact, I have a crush on you. If I swung that way, we'd rock the hell out of a good mutual crush. Now just leave this to the masters."

Becca nodded. "That's us. The making-a-guy-crush-on-you masters."

Since Callie couldn't imagine anyone making Tanner do anything he didn't want to, she left breakfast secure in the knowledge that things would remain status quo.

The next day when she picked up Troy, he wasn't scowling. He looked a little proud of himself.

"Oh, crap," Callie said. "I know that look. She talked you into trouble. What did you two do?"

"Huh?" He shoved his hands into his pockets and slouched. "Nothing. I just helped her with a little camera work."

"Camera work for what?"

"Her new blog."

"For...the art gallery?" Callie asked.

"No, she said this was her personal blog." He paused. "It's a YouTube channel."

"Oh my God." Callie gave him a quick glare. "You were supposed to keep her out of trouble!"

"Hello, have you met her? No one person can control that old lady. And she moves fast!" He shrugged. "And anyway, you should be thanking me. I talked her out of her first idea."

"I'm afraid to ask," Callie said.

"She wanted to do *Live from the Gym*, where she planned on interviewing guys with their shirts off."

"Oh my God."

"But I talked her into doing a *Live from Bingo Night* thing instead."

Callie sighed. "Good. That was really good."

"Worth a raise good?" he asked.

Callie laughed. "No. You get her to close her Tumblr and Instagram, then we'll talk."

"She's pretty crafty," he said. "She'd probably just re-open them under a different name. Oh, and there was a little toaster ordeal."

She glanced over at him again. "A toaster ordeal?"

"She put four pieces of bread down even though she said her toaster could only do two at a time without catching fire."

"What?"

"Yeah," Troy said. "And then the fire alarm went off, but don't freak. There weren't any flames, just smoke. I unplugged it right away, but the firefighters and sheriff still came. She insisted."

"Not the pretend fire thing again," Callie muttered.

"Uh-huh. And a firefighter named Jack told your grandma that the next time she pulled another stunt like that, they might arrest her. And she said she hoped it was Sheriff Sawyer Thompson who arrested her because she had a thing for a man with handcuffs."

Callie groaned and decided she needed a doughnut. Maybe two. "And then what happened?"

"The sheriff came. He said that he was going to call you to tell you that you needed to get her hormone levels checked or he was going to be sorely tempted to arrest her."

"Did she behave after that?"

"Well, you'd have to define *behave*," Troy said. "But she did promise to try to be good. No one looked all that convinced though."

Tanner's day had been a shit pile. Troy had gotten in trouble for hacking into his teacher's computer to change a grade. The thing was, he hadn't been changing his own grade but someone else's. The principal wouldn't say whose, but she did admit that the teacher had entered the grade incorrectly in the first place.

Troy refused to discuss it. Shock.

Then Sam had made an offer on a second boat for Lucky Harbor Charters, a boat they'd been eyeing for a long time and wanted badly, but they'd been a day late and a dollar short—the boat had sold yesterday.

And then as a topper, Tanner had been halfway through a swim to clear his mind when a vicious leg cramp had nearly done him in.

When he'd limped out of the water and collapsed on

the rocky beach, gritting his teeth in pain, he discovered he had a witness.

Troy.

Most of the time Tanner didn't give a shit about his leg and the fact that it was only at about 50 percent. He only thought about it when it sent a stab of nerve pain through him. Or when Callie had noticed his scar. But rolling on the shore in the grip of that vicious cramp with Troy hovering over him asking "What can I do?" over and over again had been humiliating as hell.

Now Troy was with Elisa for the night. Her parents were in town and the kid was to help her make a good show. So Tanner, Cole, and Sam had walked to the Love Shack for a pitcher of beer.

"To Gil," they toasted at their first drink, as they always did, and though Tanner felt the usual familiar pang of grief, it wasn't accompanied by the also all-too-familiar pang of guilt.

For surviving when Gil hadn't.

"You okay?" Sam asked.

Was he? "I still expect to see him sitting here with us, every time."

Neither Sam nor Cole had to ask who. Sam blew out a breath. "He is here; he's always here."

Cole lifted his glass. "I'll drink to that."

They all drank to that, and turned to a game of darts.

"What are we betting?" Cole asked before starting the game.

"Ten bucks," Sam said.

Cole and Tanner both laughed.

"What?" Sam demanded.

"You're so tight you squeak when you walk," Cole

said. "Does Becca know this? Does she realize she's marrying a tightwad?"

"What's wrong with ten bucks?" Sam asked with a scowl.

To be fair, the guy couldn't help himself. He'd come from nothing, less than nothing. Tanner too, but at least he'd had his mom to share the reality of their rather grim situation.

Sam had patched things up with his dad now, but there'd been many, many years where his only home had been the one that Cole's mom had made for him in a spare room of her house.

But Sam had been money smart. He'd turned a dime into a dollar and then a dollar into many, many more. He'd been in charge of their rig earnings, and he'd done incredibly well for them all. They'd gotten off the rigs and were able to buy their boat and start Lucky Harbor Charters, all thanks to Sam pinching every penny.

"Fifty bucks," Cole said. "And the loser has to tell us why he hasn't told us he's seeing Callie." Sam and Cole stared at Tanner.

Tanner felt himself scowl. "Why do you assume I'm going to lose?"

"'Cause you always do," Sam said. "You suck at darts."

"Notice he didn't deny the Callie thing," Cole said, eyes still on Tanner.

"I'm not seeing Callie," Tanner said. *Because you're an idiot.*

"Then what was the other morning?" Cole asked. "Coming out of her place?"

"None of your business."

"Or…" Sam asked, brow arched.

And for some reason, Tanner felt himself lose his temper. Maybe it was knowing that tentative and rather precious beginning to whatever he and Callie had been doing was all past tense thanks to him fucking it up. "It was nothing," he said. Snapped. "She's a coffee companion. Just that, nothing more."

Cole was giving him the slicing the finger across the throat gesture but Tanner was on a roll now, so no, he wasn't going to cut it out. "Just because you're getting married doesn't mean love's in the air, so knock it off with the Callie shit and butt the fuck out."

"Excuse me," someone said from behind him.

A female someone.

An unbearably familiar female someone.

He turned and faced—yep—Callie.

She was dressed in a pretty skirt and those boots he loved. She smiled without a hint of teeth and gestured that she needed to get through. Behind her were Olivia and Becca, both giving him the hairy eyeball.

Feeling like a first-class jerk, Tanner tried a smile. "Hey." Shit. He was such an asshole. "You ladies want to join us?"

"No, thank you," Callie said with utter politeness, even though the underlying tone in her voice suggested that he could fuck himself. Sideways. She started to push past him but he slid a hand to her elbow to pull her back around. She stared down at his fingers on her until he let go.

"Callie," he said quietly, desperately wishing they didn't have an audience. "I'm sorry. I didn't know you were there."

"I got that," she said.

"I was trying to explain that we're just…"

"Nothing?" she asked.

He grimaced. A first-class asshole. "Callie—"

"Gotta go." She flashed another quick, tight-lipped smile to Cole and Tanner and walked off.

Olivia and Becca each glared at him. Becca moved, snuggled into Sam, and kissed his jaw. "I'll meet you back at home, 'kay?"

He tipped her face up and gave her a longer kiss, touched his forehead to hers, and nodded.

Wash and repeat for Cole and Olivia.

And then the women were gone.

A flash went off in Tanner's face and he blinked Lucille into focus.

"Sorry," she said, not looking sorry at all. "I just wanted to get a picture of the horse's patoot." Turning, she smiled very sweetly at Cole and Sam before once again glowering at Tanner. "You." She didn't even come up to the middle of his chest, but the way she was looking at him made him feel about two feet shorter than her. She put a bony finger in his face. "I thought you were a smart man. I thought wrong."

When she was gone, the three of them fell into silence. "Nicely done," Sam finally said to Tanner.

"You do realize you're going to be decimated within the hour now, right?" Cole asked. "Whether on Instagram or Twitter or whatever."

"I don't give a shit," Tanner said. He couldn't think about anything other than the look on Callie's face.

"I think you do give a shit," Sam said. "You give a shit about what Callie thinks, and that's the problem."

Tanner turned to the dartboard. "Drop it." Okay, yeah, he'd been too harsh, but other than that, he'd told the truth. Technically he'd done nothing wrong.

Damn it.

So why the hell did he feel like he'd lost his best friend?

Chapter 14

An hour and another round of beer later, Tanner was trying to maintain that he was the injured party, but all he could think about was the expression on Callie's face when he'd turned and faced her.

On top of that, he'd lost darts two out of three.

Tanner grabbed the darts. "New round. The two losers"—he pointed his darts at the both of them—"have to take Lucille and her gang out on that tour she commissioned for the senior center tomorrow."

"Shit, man," Cole said. "Now you're just being mean."

Tanner won. They bought another round of beer. He was glad for the win, but the truth was that he'd rather be tossing back a few in the company of someone soft and willing.

And naturally the face that came to mind was one he shouldn't be thinking about.

Callie.

Which meant that Sam was right, and shit, how Tanner

hated that. He'd opened his big, fat mouth and made a mess of things.

Especially since the truth was that he wanted to see her. He'd already had her in his arms. Her kisses had him nearly out of his mind. He couldn't imagine what it'd be like to have her in his bed, wrapped around him, panting his name.

Okay, he could imagine it. Truth was, he'd been fantasizing about it since he'd gotten his hands on her. In fact, he was thinking about it right now—

"So what happened in the water today?" Sam asked him, refilling everyone's beer.

"Nothing."

"That's not what Troy said."

Shit. A complete shit day from start to finish. At least he hoped it was nearly finished. He drank some more, stalling for time. But neither Sam nor Cole looked stalled. They were both looking right at him, waiting for an answer. "I got a cramp," he said. "It wasn't a big deal."

"Troy said you were in a lot of pain and that you couldn't even walk," Sam said.

"A cramp," Tanner repeated. "No one can walk with a cramp in their leg."

"But you were swimming," Cole said. "Alone. And we've seen you swim. You go miles."

"So?"

"So, if you hadn't been close to shore…"

Tanner narrowed his eyes. "I'd have been fine."

"I'll swim with you," Cole said. "Next time."

"Every day?" Tanner asked, trying not to get pissed off.

"Nope," Cole said, and clapped Sam on the back. "We'll switch off."

Sam looked less than thrilled at this. "I hate swimming with him," he said. "I'll take the boat and tail him."

"I'm fine!" Tanner said. "Jesus." He pointed to Sam. "I liked it a whole lot better when you were the one we were all worried about."

"Yeah, but you helped me straighten my shit out," Sam said calmly.

"What about Cole?" Tanner pointed out. "Only last month he was all sorts of fucked up."

Cole smiled. "I got over myself." His smile faded. "Your turn."

Tanner shook his head and finished his beer. "Whatever, man. I'm fine."

Sam's phone rang and he pulled it from his pocket. In the old days, he never answered his phone. But that was B.B. Before Becca. Suddenly the silent, brooding Sam was Mr. Chatty Cathy.

Sam slid his phone away and grinned. "Gotta go."

Undoubtedly he'd just gotten a booty call from Becca.

"Me too," Tanner said. He didn't know where, he just had to move.

"Where you going?" Cole asked.

Tanner narrowed his eyes. "Why, you writing a book?"

"Just answer the question."

"Not until you tell me why you want to know."

"You're so suspicious all the time."

"With you I have to be."

"You've been to war," Cole said. "You've nearly been killed in a rig fire. What could I possibly dream up that would be worse than either of those two things?"

Good point. "I'm going to walk around and clear my head. Okay with you, Mom?"

"Sure," Cole said. "I just didn't want you going after Callie and messing with her head."

"I wouldn't do that," Tanner said.

"Not on purpose," Cole agreed.

"Your concern for her is touching."

"Actually," Cole said, "my concern is for you. You gotta get your head screwed on tighter before you go for it with her. Hurry up and get that handled, and the two of you could really have something."

And with that confusing-as-shit—and wrong—assessment, Cole left.

Tanner said to his back, "I won. I want it on record that I won. I don't have to take the geriatrics out tomorrow. One of you two assholes has to."

"Fine," Cole called over his shoulder.

"Fine." Satisfied that he wasn't the only miserable one now, Tanner left on Cole's heels and stood in the chilly night air for a moment. He had a nice buzz going but it wasn't coming close to chasing away the look on Callie's face.

He'd hurt her. He hated that.

He crossed the street to the pier and stood at the entrance to the arcade, surveying the action.

There was very little.

It was a weeknight and cold as hell. There were a few teenagers huddled together in front of the dart booth and no one else.

Nope, scratch that. There was one more person at the far end, in front of the football-through-the-tire booth.

Callie.

She turned, frowned at him, and then shocked the hell out of him. "Well, hurry up then."

He craned his neck and looked behind him because surely she wasn't talking to him.

"Can you do this or not?" she wanted to know, pointing at the game in front of her.

Shoving his bare hands into his pockets, he strode over to her. Toe to toe, he stared down into her stormy eyes, noticing with some grim satisfaction that her breath hitched at his nearness.

"Do what?" he asked.

Her gaze dropped to his mouth and she drew her lower lip in between her teeth. "Um." She gave herself a visible shake and hoisted the football in her hands. "I've spent twenty-five bucks on this stupid game to win a stupid stuffed animal and I'm not leaving without one. Your throwing arm is legendary. Teach me how to throw."

He blinked but nope, she was still here, looking hauntingly beautiful and, better yet, speaking to his sorry ass. "Show me what you've got."

She wound up and tossed the football. It missed the target by a mile. In fact, it would've hit the lanky kid behind the counter if he hadn't thrown himself to the ground.

The kid got up, retrieved the ball, and handed it back to Callie.

Callie stared down at it. "What am I doing wrong?"

"Other than throwing like a girl?"

Eyes sparking, she thrust the football at him. "You've got two shots."

"Actually," the kid behind the counter said, "only one more shot."

Callie glared at him.

The kid lifted his hands. "Hey, lady, I don't make

the rules." He gave Tanner a good-luck look and backed away.

Tanner weighed the football in his hands. "I haven't thrown in a long time."

"I'm not leaving here without a stuffed animal, Tanner."

"Why don't you just buy it?" he asked.

"That's not the point!" she said, irritated. "I have to *win* it." She paused and then admitted, "And plus I've spent twenty-five bucks already. If I lose this round, I have to go back to my place for more money."

"Okay, *I'll* buy it for you."

This produced an icy glare that nearly froze his nuts off. "Don't you dare," she said. "You're a football star. You have a record a mile long. Haven't you seen the Nike commercials? Just do it."

He stared at her. "Have you been drinking?"

"Not yet."

He stared at her some more.

"I know," she said. "I'm a nut."

"A bossy nut," he agreed. "But a beautiful, bossy nut."

She rolled her eyes. "Hello, I run a bridal empire. Bossiness is a required trait. Throw the damn ball, Tanner. I want the purple unicorn. But you should know I'm still not speaking to you."

"Fair enough." He looked at the ugly purple unicorn sitting on the shelf with about fifty other ugly rainbow-colored unicorns but all he really saw was Callie's expression earlier. The hurt, the vulnerability. She was hiding it now, but it was still there just beneath the surface and he wanted to be the one to make it go away. "I've had a few drinks," he said.

She stared at him and then tried to grab the football

back. "Fine, give it to me if you don't think you can do it."

"I can do it," he said. "Of course I can do it." He really hoped that was true.

"Well, then." She slapped the football against his chest and stepped back, gesturing impatiently with her hand for him to go ahead.

"I will," he said, stepping closer. After he apologized. "Listen, about before at the bar—"

"Just the purple unicorn, please," she said stiffly.

"It's just that you came in at the tail end of a conversation that—"

"I know," she said. "Whatever. Forget it."

He wished he could. "Callie, I'm trying to say I'm sor—"

"Throw the damn ball, Riggs, or give it back."

He threw the ball.

And missed.

The kid sucked in a breath of shock. "Dude," he said, sounding hugely disappointed.

Not Callie. She tossed up her hands, muttered something about men not being worth jack shit, and started to walk off.

God damn it. Tanner grabbed her wrist and held tight with one hand while he shoved the other into his pocket, fishing for money. He came out with a five and slapped it on the counter.

"Never mind," Callie said.

Hell no. "Wait," he said, and gestured for the kid to bring him the football. When he did, Tanner bounced it in his hands a moment, familiarizing himself with the feel and weight of it after all this time.

"Seriously," Callie said. "This isn't necessary—"

He silenced her with a look and threw the ball. If it didn't make it through the tire, he was going to have to shoot himself.

Luckily, the ball sailed right through.

More than a little relieved, he started to turn to Callie, only to let out an *oomph* as something crashed into him.

Callie throwing herself at him.

"Thank you!" Cupping his jaw, she brought his face down and gave him a smacking kiss on the cheek. "Thank you." She kissed his other cheek. "Now I don't have to kill the kid who kept selling me tickets."

"Hey," the kid said.

"Just kidding," she told him.

He didn't look mollified. "I'm closing now."

"My prize first," she said.

"Which one?"

Callie didn't hesitate. She pointed to the purple unicorn with a hideously bright pink mane.

None of the prizes was great but she'd seriously chosen the least attractive of the bunch. "You sure you want that one?" Tanner asked as the kid handed it to her.

"Of course I'm sure." She hugged it to her chest like it was precious cargo. "Why not this one?"

"Because it's a purple unicorn?"

She stared down at the stuffed animal as if just realizing it was purple. "When we were in school, I'd come play my entire allowance away trying to win her." She paused and stroked the neon, eye-blinding pink mane. "I never did."

Tanner had seen her throw. He wasn't surprised. He kept that to himself, as he was in enough hot water.

"Should've gotten one of the football players who paid you to do their homework down here to win it for you," he said.

"I wasn't like you," she said, talking into the unicorn's plastic eyes. "I wasn't popular. I didn't have a lot of friends that I could've asked to do this." She paused and then grimaced. "Okay, I had no friends that could have done this…" She trailed off, looking as though she wished she hadn't said that.

But he'd already flashed on the image of the shy girl who'd paid a buck to send him a Valentine all those years ago.

And then he thought about her getting left at the altar. And every wedding she planned probably took another piece out of her, and she didn't even realize it. "Callie," he said softly.

She lifted her head to meet his gaze, her own carefully shuttered. He knew she'd learned how to do that the hard way, and a surge of emotion nearly choked him.

"Closing now," the kid said again, sounding worried that they'd never leave.

Yeah, they needed to take this shit somewhere private anyway. He took Callie's hand and led her out of the arcade and down the dark pier.

They stood alone there, the surf pounding the shore behind them, hitting up against the wood pylons beneath their feet so that the foundation shuddered with the power of it.

"I'm still mad at you," she said quietly, staring out at the water. "But thanks for winning the unicorn for me." She gave him a side glance. "I owe you."

"Do you?"

"Yes." She turned to face him and her gaze dropped to his mouth, telling him exactly where her mind was at.

His was already there.

She was leaning back against the railing now, beyond which was the dark night and churning waves, matching the storm in her eyes. Reaching out, he took the unicorn from where she had it clutched to her chest.

"Hey," she said.

He set the thing on a bench and turned back to her.

"What are you doing?" she asked, brow furrowed with great suspicion.

Setting a hand on either side of her so that he was gripping the railing at her hips, he leaned in. "I'm trying to say I'm sorry."

She stared up at him for a beat. "Why?"

"You know why."

"You're referring to when you said I was—and let me quote you here—'She's nothing.' Yes?"

Holding her gaze, he let her see his regret. "I said 'She's a coffee companion. Just that, nothing more.' And that was true—until the kiss."

She looked at him for a long beat. "And the rest?" she finally asked. "The knock-it-off-with-the-Callie-shit thing?"

"That was me being an idiot and saying the opposite of what I meant when I was backed into a corner."

Another long, searching look. "Okay." She crossed her arms and met his gaze. "Go on with your apology then."

"I shouldn't have said any of it," he said. "I certainly didn't mean it. You just…" He shook his head. "Christ, Callie. I feel a little out of my league with you and—" He broke off at her hard laugh. "What?"

"You feel out of your league with me?"

He couldn't tell by her expression if this was a good thing or not. "Yes," he said, going for broke.

When she only shook her head and muttered something he couldn't quite catch, he shoved his fingers in his hair.

"Frustrated?" she asked mildly.

"Getting there, yeah. This makes me nuts. You make me nuts, and I don't even know why."

"Oh, don't worry, I know," she said, turning away. "It's because I have that effect on men."

Shit. He was truly the world's biggest fuckup. "Callie, look at me."

"No."

Too bad. Hands on her hips, he turned her to face him. "I meant that you drive me nuts in the very best way."

She narrowed her eyes. "There's a best way for that?"

"Apparently. And you're it." Sliding his hands up her arms, he cupped her face, needing to make sure she heard what he was going to say. "I'm sorry I hurt you. It's important to me that you know that. Hurting you is the very last thing I would ever want to do."

She looked at him for a long beat—she didn't have much choice as he was holding her head—but then she slowly shook her head. "I don't want to talk about this anymore."

He opened his mouth and she made a sound of complete and utter annoyance, like he was driving her nuts as well, which was something to think about. "Okay, no talking," he agreed. Finally something he could get on board with.

"Good," she said.

"Good," he said. Like the dog grateful for the slightest bit of attention, he stilled, not wanting to scare her off.

She was staring into his eyes and then her fingers were tight in his hair. "Not a single word," she breathed against his mouth.

"Not one."

She nodded and licked her lips, and then it was game over. Wrapping his hand around the back of her neck, he pulled her to him and covered her mouth with his in what started out as a soft exploration and ended up in two point zero seconds as a hard, demanding kiss that she met with equal fervor.

Chapter 15

Tanner heard the sweet sound of Callie's moan as she wrapped her arms around him and kissed him back. Music to his ears. They were both breathing raggedly when he pressed his forehead to hers.

"Not here," he said.

"No," she murmured, and grabbed her unicorn before heading off the pier at warp speed.

He followed. Not that she looked back at him. He knew that she had no doubt he'd follow her to the moon and back.

When they hit the street, he took her hand and the lead, pulling her along with him.

Still no talking.

Just heat.

So much heat he could barely think straight.

"Where?" she gasped half a block later.

Her apartment was closer but his was more private by far. "My place," he said.

"Too far."

They practically ran the last block to the warehouse. In the hallway, he waited, half expecting for her to go inside alone. In fact, if she was smart, that's exactly what she would do.

And she did slam the door. But she yanked him inside first. She hit the lock and then turned to him.

"Callie—"

"Still not talking," she said, and shoved him up against the door, her sweet, soft, curvy bod pressed up against his. He could feel her breasts, her thighs, and wanted to think he could feel the heat between them. "Callie—"

"Not one word."

Since her mouth was now at his throat, her busy little hands at his shirt working the buttons as fast as she could, he couldn't have talked if his life depended on it. He huffed out a low laugh and the little minx bit him. "Jesus."

"You're not paying attention," she said.

"Trust me, you have one hundred and fifty percent of my attention."

Had he ever been so hard? He couldn't remember. Hell, at the moment he couldn't remember his own name. Fisting his hands in her hair, he pulled her back to him and kissed her until he was damn sure she couldn't possibly remember her name either.

When they surfaced for air he had one hand under her sweater cupping a perfect breast, the other gliding up the back of her thigh, bunching up her skirt as it went. And then he was beneath it, palming her very sweet ass. Her panties didn't cover much and he squeezed an ass cheek, letting his fingers slip beneath the cotton.

"Wait," she gasped. "Stop."

He went utterly still, not even breathing. He'd known it was too good to be true, that she would change her mind. He was going to take it like a man. He was absolutely not going to cry—

She pushed him away and then ran around the room. She yanked open a drawer, pulled out an armload of... socks?

Yeah, socks.

He watched in disbelief as she continued racing around, shoving a pair or two of socks into each heat vent. There were four.

"There," she said, straightening after blocking off the last vent. She dusted off her hands and came back to him. "Now."

"Now what?"

"Now I don't have to remember to be quiet."

He stared at her.

"The vents," she said. "There's no insulation in this place. Becca, Olivia, and I can hear each other breathing. Or..." She grimaced. "You know."

He felt himself grin. "You're afraid you'll be noisy."

"No." She went red. "Well, maybe. It's been a while. I mean, I don't want to be concentrating and forget to be quiet."

He yanked her into him and nuzzled at the soft spot just beneath her ear. "Callie?"

"Yeah?"

"You're not going to have to worry about concentrating."

"I'm not?"

"No," he promised.

With another sexy-as-hell breathy moan, she finished unbuttoning his shirt and shoved it off his shoulders. She took a very satisfying long look at his chest and abs and actually licked her lips as she reached for the button on his jeans.

"I still don't want a relationship with you," she said, and unzipped him. Before he could suck in some desperately needed air, her hand slid inside and took a hold of him.

"Works for me," he managed to say. "Me either. Take off your clothes, Callie."

"I mean it, Tanner. This changes nothing."

"I hear you. I get you. In fact…" He tugged off her sweater and found a white tank top beneath it that revealed her nipples pressing hard against the thin fabric. Picking her up, he dropped her onto her bed and followed her down. "I not only get you, I got you."

She squirmed and struggled, but only a little, and it was more like jockeying for the top position. He allowed her to have it for a moment, let her roll him to his back and hold him down and kiss him.

He couldn't get enough of that. Her hair was in his face and he loved the scent of it, of her. He listened to her ragged breathing as her breasts pressed into his chest, her thighs snug to the outside of his. Tightening his hold on her, he pulled her in even closer.

Her body soft and eager, she whispered his name. With a groan he rolled, tucking her beneath him before he could lose his head again. "Still too many clothes," he said, and began to strip her. It was like unwrapping the last, big, best present left under the Christmas tree. In a beat the tank was gone and so was her skirt, leaving her in just a plain white bra and panties, both skimpy on fabric, leaving his mouth dry, his body hard and aching.

"Pretty," he said, and stroked the pad of his thumb over the tip of a breast. Lowering his head, he kissed her neck, then made his way to her shoulder, her collarbone, then dipped beneath the cotton to flick his tongue over a puckered nipple.

She gasped and arched up into him. He rocked his hips into hers, pressing her back down into the bed. Writhing beneath him, she made soft, sweet sounds that wreaked havoc on his tenuous control.

Stopping, he looked down at her. Her face was upturned, her lips parted, her eyes closed. She was a man's greatest fantasy.

She was his greatest fantasy.

With Tanner's mouth and hands on her, Callie couldn't breathe—she simply couldn't get enough air into her lungs—and she made a sound that must have resembled the one she made when choking on a doughnut because he lifted his head.

"Okay?" he asked.

She tightened her fingers in his hair. "Don't stop!"

Flashing her a heated, wicked smile, he braced up on one forearm as he unhooked and slowly pulled her bra free, tossing it over his shoulder.

"So pretty," he whispered again, and lowered his head.

Her fingernails dug into his shoulders now, sliding their way down his back to grip his very fine butt as she made a sound of dissatisfaction, pushing at his jeans.

When he didn't stop kissing her to assist, she attempted to use her toes to shove his pants down.

Laughing at her, he kicked them aside and kept his mouth on her like he couldn't get enough either.

She opened her eyes and looked at him. Lifting his head, he met her gaze and her heart clenched at the emotion there, raw and stark and unspoken but as apparent as the beat of her heart.

She started to say something, she had no idea what, but instead she touched. She had to. She rocked up to spread kisses over his broad shoulders, his throat, needing to get closer still, wanting to eat him up. But he was holding her down to do the same to her. Unable to get enough, she growled in frustration.

"You first," he said. He brushed his lips across hers and though she tried to hold him close, he evaded her.

"Tanner—"

"I know. Christ, I know, but I've been dreaming of this. You're not going to rush me, babe, not tonight—" His hands slid down her body, igniting fires along the way. Her head arched back as his fingers traced the edge of her panties, teasing, slipping between her legs. Then his thumbs hooked into the sides and he dragged the cotton slowly down.

She met his gaze, his eyes dark and heavy lidded with desire. She was riding a fine line here between wanting him to hurry and letting him make the most of the moment. But again he took the matter out of her hands by lowering his head.

Making the most of the moment then.

And that was the last thought she had for a good long time because he replaced his fingers with his tongue. She cried out and shamelessly ground her hips up toward his mouth.

Stilling her movements with his hands, he used his lips and tongue to whip her into submission.

And into coming.

Which she did, faster and harder than she could re-member ever happening before. When she could breathe again, she tackled and straddled him like a rodeo star.

He grinned up at her. "You liked that," he said.

"I did. And now you're going to like this."

"Whatcha got?" He broke off with a hiss of breath through his teeth when she nipped at his lower lip and ran her hands down his chest, savoring the feel and taste and scent of him.

Heady stuff.

Her heart was pounding so hard she could feel it echo in every part of her body as she trailed kisses on his skin. His collarbone. A pec. Ribs…His stomach. Oh, how she loved his abs. They quivered as she dragged her lips over them, continuing southbound until finally she was at eye level with the part of him she'd been craving.

"Callie—"

She took him into her mouth.

He gripped the bedding in fists and groaned. Lifting his head, he watched her from dark, heated eyes, his fin-gers sliding into her hair to hold it back for her. He let her have her way with him for a few minutes, until his hips were moving with her every stroke. Then without warning he pushed her back on the bed and covered her. She could feel him, hard and heavy between her legs, and she'd never wanted anything more. "Now, Tanner. Oh, please, now."

But he didn't move. In fact, he remained so carefully still that she forced her eyes open and stared up at him, hungry and desperate. "Why aren't you oh-please-nowing me?" she murmured.

"No condom." He said this from between his teeth, as if he couldn't quite believe it himself.

She blinked and then, as the words sank in, shuddered in disappointment. "Damn it!"

"I'm sorry," he murmured, and brushed his mouth along her temple.

"Don't guys carry them in their wallets just in case?" she asked.

He let out a low laugh. "Not this guy. I haven't had a just-in-case situation in a while."

"But this is so unfair! I wanted a one-night stand! I—" She broke off and brightened as she remembered she had a small box of condoms in the bathroom among the stuff she'd brought with her from San Francisco. "Don't move," she said, and pushed him off of her to run to the bathroom. Naked and not caring, she dug through the drawers. "Here!" In triumph, she raced back to the bed wielding the box. "Don't ask," she said, and jumped back on the bed.

A quick study, Tanner snatched a condom, protected them both, and then, kneeling on the bed, pulled her to him so that she was straddling his thighs.

Guiding her hips, he slid in. Deep. Deliciously deep. "Oh," she said in wondrous surprise, clutching his shoulders. He felt good, so good.

He rocked into her so that she was taking all of him now, his gaze never leaving hers as both their worlds came apart and then back together again, face to face, skin to skin, heart to heart.

When he could move, Tanner rolled to his side and pulled Callie in tight, stroking her still-trembling, damp body. "You still with me?"

"Mm-hmm." She was practically purring, her face pressed into his throat, her breathing still erratic. "Loved that," she murmured.

"Good. Because we're going to do it again."

"Was hoping you would say that," she said.

Chapter 16

♥

Somewhere in those dark, erotic hours, Callie fell back on the bed, gasping for air.

Next to her Tanner did the same.

"Holy cow," she whispered. "We're going to kill each other."

Laughing low in his throat, he entwined their fingers and brought hers to his mouth. "Not a bad way to go."

Agreed, she thought, and her smile faded in the dark. "And I meant it before. This changes nothing."

"I'm not worried," he said.

"Good." She was no longer upset about what he'd said at the bar. She got it. She really did. After all, she didn't want this to mean anything either.

But she knew better. And even though she really had meant it—that this changed nothing—she knew better there too.

A worry for the morning, she decided. And luckily morning was still hours away. With great effort and a moan she sat up and pulled on the first piece of clothing she came to—Tanner's shirt—and together they hit her kitchen for sustenance.

In the harsh fluorescent lighting she ran a hand down her hair, fully aware that she must look like a complete train wreck.

Tanner caught her hand. "You're beautiful."

She let out a soft, self-conscious laugh.

"I mean it," he said. "I like you like this." He lightly tugged at a strand of her hair. "Hair wild." He ran his fingers along her jaw. "Relaxed…" He met her gaze. "When your walls are down," he said, "that's when I can't take my eyes off you."

She shook her head but he cupped her face, held her gaze, and said her name in that voice that would've melted her panties off—if she'd been wearing any. "Callie."

"Still don't want to talk," she whispered, and then she made them a snack of apple slices, cheese, and crackers.

And warm chocolate milk.

Tanner looked at the milk. "TyingTheKnot.com says a romantic late-night snack should include liquor."

She sighed. "What did I tell you about reading my site?"

He flashed a grin that made her want him again. "You're not practicing what you preach," he said. "I find that fascinating."

"It all leads to heartache and annoyance," she said, and then winced when his smile faded. "Don't listen to me," she said. "I always end up saying things to you that I don't mean to."

He stopped her when she would've walked by him. Taking the plate from her hands, he set it down and then drew her in, eyes dark and serious. "I'm sorry I didn't pay you the attention you deserved in high school," he said. "I was an asshole."

"No, you weren't." She moved to grab the plate again but he stopped her.

Stroking a finger along her temple, her ear, and then her jaw, watching the movement of his touch, he said, "You have a lot to offer, Callie. I don't like thinking you aren't going to ever try again to find the right guy."

She shook her head, even as something deep inside her quivered. She didn't know if it was because he clearly meant every word or because she understood he wasn't talking about himself. Or maybe she was just hungry. "Why does it matter to you?"

He was quiet a moment. "You matter to me."

The words were a little thrill, but they came with some of that pain he'd not wanted to cause her. "Let me get this straight," she said slowly. "You want me to find a guy. The right guy."

"Yeah."

"Now?" she asked. "Because I should probably change out of your shirt first."

He took her in from head to toe, slowly. "At the risk of sending mixed messages," he finally said, yanking her into him, "you're not going anywhere." He slid his hands beneath the shirt, cupped a cheek in each hand, and hoisted her up until she wrapped her arms and legs around him. He carried her to the bed, which was now minus most of its bedding thanks to their extracurricular activities.

And oh, holy cow, they'd had some serious extracurricular activities. Like the most amazing extracurricular activities she'd ever had. The night was a bright one, a million stars and a near-full moon bathed them in a light blue glow.

Tanner went back for the snack plate. When he sat at her side, he set the plate down and pulled the shirt over her head, tossing it to the floor so that they were both once again naked.

"Hey," she said, and lifted a hand to cover herself.

He took that hand in his and brought it to his mouth, his eyes dark as he studied her. "Snacks consumed after midnight have to be consumed naked. It's a rule."

"Where?" she asked. "Where is that a rule?"

"In the rule book. Damn, Callie," he said softly, reaching out to feed her a bite of cheese, "you look good in nothing but moonlight."

He ran a finger along a red spot at her throat, where he'd buried his face as he'd come. "I marked you."

"Oh." She covered the spot. "It's okay, I—"

"You what?"

"You know exactly how much I liked what we did," she said, picking up a piece of apple and cheese and stuffing it in her mouth. "I didn't think I needed to stroke your ego by saying it out loud."

He laughed and when he did, his eyes lit, his mouth curved, and he let her see everything he was feeling in that moment. It was even more intimate than being naked. As she stared at him, soaking him up, she…choked.

Still laughing, he pulled her closer and gently patted her on the back. "Sorry," he said.

"Not your fault," she said. "You look good laughing."

She picked up the plate and busied herself making a selection. She'd never eaten naked before. It felt incredi-

bly revealing and yet somehow freeing at the same time.
Still, she was pretty sure she wasn't ever going to be a
nudist. How did one cook nude anyway? She'd have to
give up bacon. And fried chicken. She really liked bacon
and fried chicken—

"You're talking to yourself because?" Tanner asked,
relaxed and sprawled out for her viewing pleasure like
he'd forgotten he was butt-ass naked. And why shouldn't
he? He looked amazing.

"I'm not talking to myself," she said.

Looking amused, he grabbed the plate and returned it
to the kitchen. Coming back to the edge of the bed, he
was limping more than he had earlier in the night. She
waited, holding her breath. Was he going to stay? Go?
"Your leg's bothering you," she said softly.

He didn't answer. Which was the same thing in
testosterone-guy-speak as yeah, his leg was bothering
him. And then she realized that he was waiting for her to
make a decision on the rest of the night. Holding his gaze,
she lifted up the covers in an open invitation.

He slid in and pulled her in close, his big body warm
and solid against her.

"Can I get you something?" she asked, shivering in delight when he buried his face in her neck. "Advil? A hot
pack? A massage?"

She felt him smile against her skin. "You want to give
me a rubdown?" he asked, voice husky.

"Would it make you feel better?"

"Yes," he said without hesitation. "A beautiful woman
touching my body would make me feel a lot better."

"Do you always make everything dirty?"

"Yes—" He broke off with a groan when she went for

the tight muscles of his thigh and began to dig in, finding a lot of knots.

He didn't say a word, just gripped the sheets in his fists, and unlike before, this clearly wasn't in pleasure.

"Try to relax," she murmured, and kept at the torture, doing her best to find every single millimeter of his leg that hurt.

"Jesus Christ," he gasped as she kneaded a particularly hard knot until it seemed to finally ease somewhat.

Once it did, she lightened her touch and finally he began to relax. Her hands got sore but she kept at it, feeling her heart squeeze at the pain he must feel all the time. "Is it always this bad?" she asked.

"It's good now, at least compared to how it was."

She was quiet a moment, hating how he'd suffered. "The story goes that you nearly died."

"Nearly doesn't count except for in horseshoes and hand grenades," he said. "And I was the lucky one, remember."

She stroked his leg again, running her finger along the scar. "He was a good friend?"

"Gil? Yeah. Really good."

"Can you tell me what happened?"

"A tank caught fire," he said. "There was an explosion. We both landed in the water and I got pulled out first. By the time they went back for Gil, it was too late."

His eyes were hooded from her now. She couldn't imagine the pain of what he'd been through. "I'm so sorry."

He reached for her hand, brought it up to his mouth, and kissed her palm.

"Is that why you came back to Lucky Harbor?" she asked. "To recover?"

He scrubbed a hand over his face and sighed. "The four of us were always going to come here sooner or later. We were saving up for a boat to start the charter business. But that night after I hit the water, pretty sure I'd just bought the farm, all I could think was that I'd be leaving my mom to fend for herself in her old age and Troy would have to grow up without knowing his dad. So we came sooner rather than later. Of course he's not always thrilled now that he is getting to know me." He smiled wryly. "He's been a tough nut to crack. Apparently he's also a whole lot like me."

Callie let out a low laugh. "Yeah, he is." She cocked her head and smiled. "I like him, though."

He met her gaze, his own heating again. "Yeah?"

"Yeah," she said.

"You like me too?"

She smiled. "Maybe." Her smile faded. "But I'm trying really hard not to."

He nodded. "You should stick with that," he said softly.

Right. Because neither of them wanted this. "Don't worry," she said just as softly. "I plan to."

Tanner woke to a soft, warm woman pressed up to his side like a second skin as she tried to slide out of the bed.

The woman who'd not blinked or flinched when, after tearing up the sheets, they'd reminded each other that this wasn't going to become a real relationship.

He cracked an eye and watched as Callie moved with exaggerated care, attempting to separate their entangled limbs and—at least going off her expression—sneak away.

It wasn't an easy escape. She had a leg between his, her arm tucked up into his armpit, and her breasts pressed inside his side.

She started with her leg.

He simply tightened his.

Her gaze flew up to his face and she squeaked when she saw him eyeing her.

"Oh," she said, all casual-like, in complete opposition to the look of panic on her face. "Didn't mean to wake you."

"Where you going?"

"Um…" She tried to free her hand that she had tucked in his pit but he tightened his arm on it. "Yeah, see, I need that to…"

He waited, but she just bit her lower lip and stared at his mouth.

This made him grin.

"Stop that," she said, pushing at him. "Stop distracting me. Let me go."

"This first." He leaned in to kiss her but she slapped a hand on his chest.

"I have to…you know," she said. "Do stuff. *Morning* stuff."

He blew out a sigh, rolled to his back, and let her go.

She scrambled out of the bed before she seemed to realize she was naked. To his great enjoyment, she whirled around, clearly looking for clothes. Apparently nothing came to her immediate vision because she gave up and ran totally, gloriously nude for the bathroom, slamming the door on his laugh.

Damn.

That was a sight he could get used to waking up to. All

those sweet, hot curves bouncing around. He'd be dreaming about it for a good long time to come. Then his gaze landed on the ugly purple stuffed unicorn on her dresser and his smile faded. He thought of the fragile, vulnerable look she'd had on her face standing in front of that game, wanting the prize.

And the reason behind her wanting the prize.

He'd wanted to make things better, wanted to make her smile, and he'd done that.

But he'd done more too, and he couldn't help but think that even with her reassurances about what this was and what it wasn't between them, he'd done the wrong thing by her yet again.

When she came out a moment later, he was sorely disappointed to find her wrapped in a towel.

Still the hottest thing he'd ever seen. He watched every move she made, wanting to fully take in this moment. Just in case he never got another moment like it with her.

Carefully not meeting his gaze, she strode to her dresser and pulled out some undies. Then she made his day even better by attempting to pull them on without revealing herself to him.

Sitting up to better see the show, he shoved a pillow behind his head and made himself comfortable.

When the towel dropped for the second time, he grinned from ear to ear. "So is there any fancy lingerie at all?" he asked. "That stuff you claim is such a crucial part of keeping the romance alive between the sheets—and out of them."

"What did I tell you about reading my site?" she demanded.

He grinned.

"I mean it," she said, pointing at him. "It's all crap. Don't read my crap."

Laughing, he reached out and tugged her back down onto the bed, pinning her beneath him. When she struggled and sputtered, he grabbed her wrists and pulled them above her head.

She blew a strand of hair from her face. "What's with all the *Fifty Shades* moves?"

He made himself at home between her thighs. "Did you do your…morning stuff?"

She blushed. "Yes."

"All good?"

"Yes. But you're cuffing my hands."

"It's so you won't distract me from doing my stuff," he said.

And then he proceeded to show her exactly what that stuff was.

In slow, great detail.

Twice.

Chapter 17

Tanner got to the harbor at the same time as Sam, who took one look at his face and nodded. "Good, you finally got laid. I hope to hell it was good enough to keep you in a better mood for a while."

"I'm always in a good mood," Tanner said.

"Yeah, you're a regular ray of fucking sunshine." Sam rolled his eyes. "I assume you groveled and made up for your bone-headed move from last night at the bar, right? Oh, and you might want to stay off Tumblr. Lucille's got a new poll up. She's asking who'd be a good match for Callie other than you, since you proved yourself unworthy last night."

"Shit," Tanner muttered.

Sam laughed.

"Thanks for the sympathy," Tanner said.

Sam's grin never faltered. "Is that what you felt for me when I was so screwed up over Becca? Sympathy?"

"Yeah, well, you were an idiot."

.

"Uh-huh," Sam said.

"You saying I'm an idiot?" Tanner asked.

"No, I'm saying you're a fucking idiot." Sam pulled out his keys to let himself into their warehouse. "My dad here yet?"

"He just got here too," Tanner said. "How is he?" Mark was fighting liver disease and hopefully doing a good job of it.

"Stubborn as hell," Sam said.

"He's sticking around," Tanner said. "That's something."

"He's got nothing better to do."

They both stopped when a car pulled into the lot. It was Elisa and Troy.

"How's the kid?" Sam asked.

"Stubborn as hell."

Sam laughed again. "He's sticking around," he said, mirroring Tanner's words. "That's something."

"He has to stick," Tanner said. "He's fifteen. And maybe he's not bleeding me dry like Mark does to you, but he's got a way of sucking the soul right out of a room."

"Yeah," Sam said. "It's called being a teenager."

As if proving the point, Troy slammed out of his mother's car and started to walk right by Sam and Tanner.

Tanner stopped him. "Hey. Morning."

Troy grunted.

"How was last night with your grandparents?"

Another grunt.

Tanner remembered mornings with his mom when he'd been fifteen. But if he'd tried to ignore her with nothing more than an unintelligible caveman sound, she'd have smacked him right upside the head. "Problem?"

Elisa rolled down her window. "Did he tell you the good news?" she asked Tanner.

Feeling Troy shift to make his escape into the warehouse, Tanner took a handful of the back of the kid's sweatshirt and leaned down a little to meet Elisa's gaze. "We were just getting to it."

Elisa smiled. "He's thrilled."

"Yes," Tanner said with a side glance at Troy. "I can see that."

"Have a good time," she said, oblivious. "I'll see you next week."

And then she drove off.

Next week? Tanner and Sam exchanged WTF looks and then Tanner turned to Troy. "What's going on?"

"She's dumped me on you for another week."

"Works for me," Tanner said. But if he was getting Troy for another week, it meant Elisa had some sort of ulterior motive. "How did this come about?"

Troy shrugged.

"Words," Tanner said. "For the love of God, man, use your words. I'm out of practice with the emo shrugging shit."

"Her boyfriend wants her to go to Catalina Island with him for a week," Troy said.

That'll do it.

Sam blew out a breath, looking ticked off into the direction where Elisa's car had just vanished.

Tanner was ticked off too. Not because he'd have to spend time with the kid. He wanted that. He wanted that more than he wanted his next breath. What he didn't want was Elisa making Troy feel like an unwanted piece of luggage. He looked at the kid standing there, hands shoved in his pockets, shoulders hunched.

Pissed off at the world.

Yeah. Tanner got that. Hell, he'd been there, done that. He'd been younger when his own dad had walked away and not looked back, but he'd never forgotten that feeling. "You didn't get dumped on me," he told Troy.

"You just saw me get dumped here."

"It's not being dumped if I want you here." He looked at his watch.

Troy hunched deeper into his pockets. "I can walk to school."

"I was looking to see how much time we had. Come on." Tanner started off toward the dock.

Sam was already ahead of him and hopped on board, heading for the tie-downs.

When Tanner realized Troy wasn't following, he glanced back. "You coming or not?"

Troy stood there on the docks, jaw locked, face tight. The anger of a full-grown man, the defiance of a teen who needed some guidelines. "For what?" he asked, attitude snapping in each word.

"Two options," Tanner said. "Consider it a multiple choice. A, you can walk to school, or B, you can drive yourself."

"Or C," Sam added. "You can stand there and brood."

Tanner nodded his approval. True enough.

"Don't have my permit yet," Troy said.

"Don't need a permit for the boat," Tanner told him.

The kid's eyes went wide and he forgot to maintain his 'tude. "You're going to let me drive the boat to school?"

"I'm going to teach you how to drive the boat. It's not easy," he warned when Troy forgot to hold on to his bad attitude and whooped. "In fact, it can be dangerous as hell. And it's going to take a lot more than just this one lesson. It's going to take dedication and hard work." Tanner moved to the controls, gesturing Troy close.

When the kid leapt forward, Tanner pointed to all the gauges and levers. "Every single move you make behind the wheel needs to be well thought out and calculated because every move has an effect, one that can't always be changed—at least not in a timely fashion. You get me?"

Troy looked at the control panel and then out to the horizon in front of them. "You're telling me not to be hotheaded."

Tanner nodded. "That's what I'm telling you. So you in or out?"

"In," Troy said. "All the way in."

"Me too," Tanner said.

Troy turned his head and met his dad's gaze. A long beat went by, during which time it seemed that Troy was searching for the truth in Tanner's simple statement.

Tanner waited for it to sink in.

Finally Troy nodded. They were both all the way in. For better or worse.

It was nice but Tanner wasn't fooled. There would be worse. But they'd handle it. Together. And for the first time he actually believed that there'd be a chance to do just that.

Chapter 18

♥

Callie did her best to distract herself from memories of the most sensuous, erotic night of her life. It wasn't easy. She had questions. Such as did Tanner have regrets? Did he feel differently about her now that he'd had his merry way with her, several times over?

Work helped. She was on crazy bride alert for several clients and their upcoming weddings. She spent an entire day talking brides off the ledge. One lost her venue to a flood, and Callie had to find another with twenty-four hours' notice. Another lost her groom to cold feet. Callie had way too much experience there as well.

That night she fell into bed early and was fantasizing about Tanner showing up to strip her out of her PJs and show her some new "stuff" when a knock sounded at her door.

She peeked through the peephole and went still. Speaking of the devil.

When she pulled open the door, he was arms up on the doorjamb, head down.

"Hey," she said a little breathlessly.

He lifted his head. "Hey. You busy?"

She had a choice here. The safe choice—which was to say yes. It would keep her heart protected.

And there was the unsafe choice. The scary choice. The one that would keep her up all night and give her multiple orgasms. "Not busy at all," she said. "Where's Troy?"

"In bed. In his dark purple room."

"You left him alone?"

"He's fifteen. Plus Sam came over to play on our Xbox. I've got an hour. Or two." He stepped toward her, and she lifted her face, expecting a scorching-hot kiss to kick off their hour or two.

Instead he ran a hand down her hair and then just pulled her in and hugged her, pressing a kiss to her temple, letting out a long sigh.

He wasn't here just for a booty call, she realized. He was here for…comfort?

He'd certainly given her comfort, more than a few times now. But he'd never sought it from her before. Until now.

Her heart swelled and she pulled him in further so she could shut the door. "You okay?"

"Yeah," he said.

Liar. She could feel his exhaustion and worry. "You hungry?"

He lifted a shoulder. Just like a man. She took him by the hand to her kitchen and made them French toast.

He ate every bite.

"Tell me what's wrong, Tanner," she said softly, running a hand up his arm, past his rock-hard bicep to the nape of his neck. When her fingers glided into his hair, he let out a rough groan of pleasure and dropped his head forward to give her better access. "Is it Troy?" she asked quietly, massaging his scalp and neck.

"Something's up with him," he said. "Can't get him to 'fess up."

"Like father, like son," she said with a quiet smile.

He gave a low laugh. "You might be right."

"What can I do?" she asked.

Lifting his head, he met her gaze. "You're doing it."

She took him to her bed. She would give him the comfort he sought. She'd give him whatever she could.

Always.

That last thought was just a little too far outside her comfort zone so she shoved it to the dim recesses of her mind, to a compartment labeled "future worries."

A week later, Callie was exhausted from long days working on some new wedding site designs. And also, maybe, from deliciously long nights in Tanner's arms.

He usually showed up late, after Troy was in bed, and stayed a few hours. Long enough for a talk over a late snack and some laughs, and then…

She sighed dreamily. The "and thens" had been amazing. Her musings on this were disrupted by a Skype call from another distraught bride.

"It's black tie," she wailed. "And my mother-in-law wants to wear a pantsuit. You just know it'll be in some horrid shade of green that will clash with the chartreuse bridesmaid dresses."

Not for the first time, Callie reminded herself that most brides went off the rails at some point and she'd been there herself, so no judgment. "I'll call her for you," Callie said, fingers pounding away on her laptop. "I've got two bridal shops within five miles of her house. We'll get her in something off the rack that works, no worries."

When she disconnected, her stomach growled and she realized it was late afternoon and she'd skipped lunch. She texted her grandma: *Hungry?*

Starving.

Callie grabbed her purse and hit the road. She was on her way to her grandma's house when she saw Troy walking along the highway. She pulled over and rolled down her window. "Hey," she said. "No bus?"

"Missed it."

"Need a ride?"

He hesitated and then shook his head.

"What's up?" she asked.

"Nothing."

"Uh-huh," she said. "And I'm the Easter Bunny."

"The Easter Bunny carries candy."

"Well, you've got me there," she said. "I don't have any candy. And if I did, that would be highly frowned upon, me luring you into my car with candy."

He snorted.

"You getting in?" she asked. "Or am I going to get a ticket for loitering?"

Troy got in. He pulled on his seat belt and leaned his head back, closing his eyes with a sigh.

She texted her grandma that she was going to be a little

late and then started to drive him to the harbor where Tanner was working, but then on impulse parked at the pier.

Troy looked out. "This isn't home."

"It's the home of the ice cream."

She bought them both double cones from Lance and then they sat on the end of the pier and stared out at the water.

"Thought only creepers bought kids ice cream cones," Troy said.

"Or women who just really need a sugar fix. You made me hungry with the Easter candy thing. You going to tell me what's wrong?"

Silence.

"Okay, then. How about why you have a bruise on your jaw and you're limping?"

He shrugged.

"Ah, so you...ran into a door?" she asked.

More silence.

"You fell down some stairs?"

That got an almost smile out of him. "It's not a big deal. I tried out for the school play."

She glanced over at him. "And the part was to get beat up?"

"I got the part," he said, not answering her question. "But you can't tell anyone."

"Why not?" she asked.

"Because he'll think it's stupid. I didn't try out for football but I'm in a play."

"Troy, your dad wants you to be happy here. That doesn't mean you have to follow in his footsteps. You'll find your own path, and he'll understand that."

"No, he won't. He doesn't understand anything."

She couldn't help it—she laughed.

He scowled. "What's so funny?"

"Well, let's see. From the moment he knew you existed, he changed his life to protect you. Went into the navy to support you, continued on the oil rigs, and then worked with your mom to get joint custody and cleared out the office in his house to give you a bedroom. And then he let you paint it dark purple. Dark purple," she said, and laughed again. "He hates purple."

Troy's mouth twitched.

"What?"

"I hate it too." He scrubbed a hand over his face. "I was just trying to piss him off but instead he said sure, I could paint my room purple." He dropped his head and looked at Callie. "Who does that?"

"A dad who's human and has regrets, and loves you. Now tell me about the fight you had at school."

He sighed. "Some of the football players think being in a play is dumb. I disagreed."

With his fists, apparently. "Can't you just stay away from them?"

"Yeah. But they need to stay away from the drama kids and not pick on them."

She looked into his angry eyes. "You were protecting someone."

He shrugged.

"The other boy needs to tell a grown-up," she said. She broke off when his jaw only tightened. "It's not a boy," she said softly. "It's a girl."

He shrugged again.

Yeah. It was a girl. She sighed. "If this is an ongoing problem, you really need to talk to your dad."

"Why?"

"He could help," she said.

"No, he can't. The principal hates him even more than she hates me." He stood up. "Just forget it, forget all of it."

"Troy—"

"You can't tell him about the fight. Or the play. Not any of it."

"Then you have to," she said.

"Fine. I will."

She looked into his fiercely determined eyes. He was at that stage, half boy, half man, and her heart ached for him. "I'm trusting you to do that."

"I know," he said, and it wasn't until that night when Callie was in bed that she realized he hadn't said when he'd tell his dad.

Should she say something before Troy did? The last thing she needed was for him to think she'd tattled. Nor did she want Tanner to think she was butting into their lives. She wasn't. How could she? They were friends with benefits, and sometimes just benefits. Her own decree with the this-changes-nothing thing.

But then the matter was taken out of her hands when Tanner didn't come over that night.

Callie lay in bed missing him much more than she'd thought possible.

The next day Callie's phone beeped, reminding her to pick up Troy from his Lucille babysitting duty. She raced out the door and headed toward the art gallery. Halfway there, she was startled into a near heart attack when she saw blue lights flash in her rearview mirror.

Damn it!

She pulled over and was tearing through her purse for her driver's license when the police officer rapped politely on her window.

She jumped, hit her head on the visor, swore, and finally rolled down the window. "I'm sorry," she said, turning her purse upside down into the passenger seat. Where the hell was her wallet? "I didn't mean to be speeding. I'm just late to pick someone up." She tried a smile.

He didn't return it. He was mid-thirties and extremely good looking in a dark and brooding sort of way. She recognized him as a longtime Lucky Harbor resident, but she wasn't sure what his name was. "Your tag's expired," he said.

"No," she said, shaking her head. "This is my grandma's car and she put the tag on a few weeks ago."

"No tag."

"It's there," she insisted. "She got it in the mail."

"It's not there."

She stared up into his handsome but hard face. "Look," she said, "it's pretty cloudy. Maybe if you took off the dark glasses you'd be able to see the sticker."

His expression didn't change. It was still dialed to Badass Cop. "License and registration," he said.

Gritting her teeth, she gave up the search for her wallet. She knew exactly where it was.

On her kitchen countertop where she'd accidentally left it.

But the registration, that she could provide. She leaned over, opened the glove box, and pulled out the envelope from the DMV that her grandma had stuffed in there.

When she opened it, the registration tag fell out and into her lap.

She stared down at it. Blew out a sigh. And then held it up for the police officer. "Funny story," she said.

He didn't look amused.

"I found the tag." She waved it at him.

He took it. "Driver's license?" he asked, face deadpan.

Shit. "Yeah, about that. It's another funny story—"

She broke off at a knock on the passenger window. She craned her neck the other way and felt relief roll over her.

Tanner.

She powered that window down as well. "What are you—"

"Officer," he said, looking past her to the cop. "Is this woman giving you any trouble?"

The officer didn't even blink. "She's about to be taken in for questioning."

What? She gaped at the police officer. "Okay, listen, I'm sorry if I insinuated you couldn't see past the Dirty Harry glasses, but—"

The guy flashed a smile and she stared at him. Then she whipped around and looked at Tanner.

Also grinning.

"You do sort of look like Dirty Harry," Tanner said to the cop. "Hand me the registration sticker. I'll put it on for her."

The officer handed Tanner the sticker, and the two of them went to the rear of her car like she didn't even exist. They were talking and laughing, and she sat there grinding her teeth for a beat before she exited the car. "Excuse me."

They were still yucking it up.

"I said excuse me!" She crossed her arms and tapped a foot. "I'd like to know what exactly is so funny here. I get pulled over, nearly have a heart attack over Dirty Harry here, and then I find the two of you cackling like a pair of hens."

They looked at each other and were set off again. Finally Tanner got himself together and straightened, still smiling. "I got the sticker on for you."

"Thank you." She snatched the envelope from him. "I'm going to kill my grandma."

"I'd appreciate it if you refrained," the officer said. "Murder involves a hell of a lot of paperwork for me. Plus I'm not sure black stripes are your color."

"Callie, you probably never met Sheriff Sawyer Thompson," Tanner said. "In the old days he was on the other side of the law."

The sheriff grinned. "Long time ago."

She was not in the mood for this. "Are you giving me a ticket or not?" she asked.

"Not," he said. "But thanks for the entertainment of the day." He nodded to Tanner and was gone.

Tanner ran a finger over her shoulder. "Pretty," he said of her cashmere cardigan sweater. "Love the look."

Callie went still and then glanced down at herself.

Yep. Perfect.

She'd forgotten to change out of her ratty sweats and fake Uggs again.

"It's the new style," she said, nose in the air, ignoring his smile and the way it affected her. "Now if you'll excuse me—I'm late to pick up your son."

"I'll get him."

"Then I'm late for a meeting."

"You've got a meeting," he said, heavy on the *liar, liar*.

"Yep," she said. He didn't have to know that it was an emergency meeting with the bakery because she needed a doughnut.

"Well," he said. "Hope it's a good one."

"It will be."

And then, with as much dignity as she could find—which wasn't much—she got into her car and drove off.

Chapter 19

Tanner would have liked to follow after Callie. He'd kiss that annoyance right off her mouth, buy her dinner, and then take any and all crumbs of affection she was willing to throw his way.

But he couldn't. He needed to pick Troy up and grill him. The day before he'd come home with the obvious markings from a fight, and no amount of badgering had gotten him to spill his guts.

Today Tanner was trying a different tactic. He had an afternoon free from work and planned to take Troy out on the boat.

And yes, he was reduced to flat-out bribing the kid.

He pulled up to Lucille's, and Troy slunk out, walking toward the truck like he was heading toward his own execution. He shut the door, seat-belted up, and then slouched, staring straight ahead.

"Hey," Tanner said.

Troy grunted.

"You have an okay day?" Tanner asked. Jesus. Listen

to him. Ward Cleaver. Not that it mattered, all he got was another grunt. "Troy, look at me."

Troy huffed out a put-upon breath and looked at him. "What?"

"Just checking to see if you had any other new bruises," Tanner said.

"Funny."

"Not being funny," Tanner said. "I really wanted to see." He drove them to the harbor and parked. "Come on."

Troy followed without question. This was more out of sullenness than any sort of blind obedience. The kid didn't speak until they were on the boat and Tanner was pushing off and steering them away.

It was one of those startlingly gorgeous blue days. Skies so blue it hurt to look at them. White cotton-ball clouds scattered to the east. Choppy seas dotted with whitecaps, slapping against each other in a constant beat. Tanner felt at home here, maybe more than any other place. He wanted that for Troy.

The teen had come out of himself a little bit and was taking in his surroundings as well. Calm. Alert.

Which wasn't to say he was happy. He wasn't.

And Christ, Tanner hated that. He wanted to make it better more than he'd ever wanted anything else in his life. Out in the middle of the harbor, he handed over the wheel to Troy.

"Me?" Troy asked, straightening up.

"You," Tanner said. "You think you're ready to get us out of the harbor?"

"Yeah." Troy paused. "Why?"

"Why what? Why are you sometimes a butt-munch?" Tanner shrugged. "No idea."

Troy bit his lower lip, looking nervous.

"What?" Tanner said.

"Nothing."

"It's something. Just say it."

Troy sighed. "I'm not doing football."

"I know that."

"You know?" Troy asked. "Callie told you?"

Tanner blinked. "No, the coach told me. You told Callie?"

"Yeah."

Tanner stared at him, stuck between being grateful his son had been able to confide in Callie and jealous as hell that it hadn't been him.

And why hadn't Callie told him herself?

"It's not because of the stupid coach's kid," Troy said defensively. "It's because I don't want to."

"That's a relief," Tanner said.

Troy stared at him. "It's a relief? You were the football star. I thought you wanted me to follow in your footsteps."

"Hell no," Tanner said. "In fact, please don't follow in my footsteps. You going to tell me about the bruises?"

Troy looked out at the water, his stance natural, easily balancing himself on the choppy water like he'd been born to it. "You wouldn't get it."

Tanner let out a low laugh. "Right. Because I've never been fifteen."

"Because you owned that school." Troy looked at him. "I'm not that kid. I didn't grow up here. I'm not a star athlete. I'm the new kid. And I'm a little different."

"Different is good," Tanner said. "So is standing up for yourself."

"It's not like I'm alone," Troy said. "I have friends." He met Tanner's eyes, his own shadowed.

Tanner tried to read them but the kid was good. "You've been standing up for your friends."

Troy nodded once.

"Good," Tanner said. "One more thing."

Troy tensed. "Yeah?"

Tanner put his hand on the kid's shoulder. "The way you've got your friends' back? I want you to know that I have yours in the same way. And I expect you to let me know when you need me to do something more."

Troy seemed to grapple with that a moment and then nodded again.

Tanner helped him guide the boat out of the harbor. They then took the water exhilaratingly fast and hard, and both were grinning like fools when they finally returned to the docks two hours later.

Troy helped tie everything down and lock up without being asked, already knowing the drill.

When they were back in the truck heading home, Tanner said, "You did good."

"On the boat?"

"That too."

Troy stared straight ahead, but Tanner thought maybe he was smiling just a little bit.

Callie hung out at her grandma's that night. She told herself it was because she was worried for Lucille, but that wasn't it.

Callie wasn't worried about her grandma. Nope, she was pretty sure her grandma was saner than all of them put together. The truth is, Callie needed the comfort of being there. Period.

Just after dinner, Lucille squeezed Callie's hand. "Stay with me tonight?"

"Of course," Callie said, even as she knew it was a pity date. But a bunch of Lucille and Mr. Wykowski's friends came over, and they brought out the big guns—Kahlua and milk.

Which meant that *Jeopardy* was a rowdy affair, after which Callie fell asleep on her grandma's couch.

And woke up with a man with a jackhammer inside her head. She drove home and told herself it didn't matter if Tanner had come looking for her last night. They weren't a thing.

But still, as she walked into her building, she looked around as if she could possibly see signs of him having been by.

As she was unlocking her door, Becca peeked out and smiled. "I was just coming to see you," she said. "Two things. One, remember when we made a list of things to do for my wedding and I insisted on handling a lot it myself? Well, with the big bachelor/bachelorette party coming up this weekend, I forgot all about one of the things I said I'd do."

"What's that?" Callie asked.

"Booking the B&B for the weekend of the wedding for our out-of-town guests." She grimaced. "I know, it's a biggie. But I'm banking on the fact that this is really off season and the place will still have rooms. I also want to get my mom and cousin a day at the spa there. Do you think it's too late?"

"Let me handle it for you, okay?" Callie asked. "Consider it done."

"Thanks," Becca said gratefully. "And the second thing

is, I'm planning to sell my furniture since I'll be moving into Sam's soon. I wanted to see if there's anything you need before I sell it. A couch? Microwave? More socks for the vents?"

"Ha," Callie said. "No need for those, I don't think." She ignored Becca's frown. "And no furniture, thanks. I don't know how long I'll be staying so I don't want to acquire a bunch of new things."

Becca smiled.

"What?"

"Well, I said the very same thing when I first came to Lucky Harbor. And then I met Sam."

"Yes, but Sam's taken," Callie said.

"You never know who might turn into your Sam."

"Pretty sure I don't have a Sam in my near future," Callie said.

Becca chewed on her lower lip. "Are you sure? Because you might have already met him."

Callie ignored the little squish her heart did at this thought. "Nope."

"I was trying to be subtle here," Becca said. "But I'm just going to come right out and say it, okay?"

Callie sighed. "Could I stop you?"

"Definitely not. Look, we know Tanner's been sleeping here with you. And I'm real glad because other than his temporary assery at the Love Shack, I think he's an amazing guy."

She could deal with this, Callie told herself. Probably. All she had to do was a little gossip control. "It's not what it looks like."

"Really? Because what it looks like is that you finally decided to let your hair down and have a good time—

which after how hard you've been working, you totally deserve. And it looks like that good time came in the form one of extremely sexy ex–Navy SEAL."

"Okay," Callie said. "So maybe it's exactly what it looked like."

Becca laughed. "Yay!"

"But it's just a good time."

"Whatever you say," Becca said with a secret smile.

Callie shook her head. She gave up.

"I've gotta run," Becca said. "Breakfast tomorrow?"

"Yeah, sure," Callie said. "Um…that's it? You're not going to grill me for more info?"

"Yes, but I'm saving it for breakfast. Mostly because Olivia's much better at getting info than me." She flashed a grin when Callie groaned.

"I really don't have info on what's happening," Callie said. "Or not happening."

"Honey, that's the very best kind of story." Becca squeezed Callie's hand. "And don't worry. Sam mentioned a few days ago that Tanner's been wearing the same silly grin you're wearing. So there's got to be a bunch of good stuff to tell."

"Sam said what?"

Becca's grin widened. "I believe his exact words yesterday were 'Tanner's good for shit today. He's so relaxed I had to check him for a pulse.'"

Callie bit her inner cheek.

"Sam asked him if he'd just gotten a massage or something," Becca said, "and Tanner apparently said 'or something.' So then Sam told me he wants a massage."

No sense in denying it. She'd covered the vents but she

couldn't cover the truth; it was probably all over her face. "It's a temporary sort of thing. Very temporary."

"I don't believe that," Becca said. "You guys can't keep your eyes off each other, and the chemistry…it's like watching fireworks whenever you're together. I really thought this could turn into something more."

"I don't want more."

Becca didn't look convinced, so Callie took her hand. "It's true. I know you're new in love and think it's for everyone, but it's not. I've been there, I know."

"Then he wasn't the right one," Becca said.

"Definitely he wasn't," Callie agreed.

"But how will you know if Tanner's the right one if you don't give him a shot? What if he's the One, Callie?"

She brushed that off, but as she went about her day, the question stuck with her.

What if Tanner was the One?

Did she even believe in the One?

Once upon a time she had, but she'd changed. Hadn't she? The question stuck with her as she stopped by the B&B to book the place for Becca's wedding weekend. She met Maddie, the innkeeper, who took her reservations, and then Maddie introduced her sister Chloe, who ran the day spa.

"Heard you're seeing Tanner Riggs," Chloe said.

Callie blinked. "Is there a sign written on my forehead?"

Chloe laughed. "No. It's your grandma. She's on a mission to see you matched. She considers herself somewhat of a master on the subject."

"She's a master at the crazy," Callie muttered.

Chloe laughed. "That too." Her smile softened as

someone came into the room. Callie turned and found Sheriff Thompson standing there.

He wasn't dressed like a cop at the moment. Jeans, a University of Washington sweatshirt, and battered running shoes, and he wore them with the same authority that he'd worn his uniform. The gun at his hip might have helped there. He strode directly to Chloe, pulled her in, and laid a kiss on her that had the temperature in the room skyrocketing.

Callie studied the ceiling and then her toes, wondering if ridiculous displays of romance were in the water or something. Good Lord. Was everyone in this town starry-eyed?

A year later Sawyer pulled back, playfully tugged on a strand of Chloe's hair, and smiled into her face. "Later."

Then he winked at Callie and left.

"Sorry," Chloe said, sounding dreamy. "Where were we?"

When Callie left the B&B, she drove to her grandma's to relieve Troy of babysitting duty.

She found him playing poker with her grandma and Mr. Wykowski.

"Pay up," Troy said to Lucille, holding out his hand.

Lucille turned to Callie. "You going to let him cheat an old lady out of her social security?"

"You're the one who cheated," Mr. Wykowski said to her mildly.

"How much money are we talking?" Callie asked.

"Not money." Mr. Wykowski went to the counter and brought back a family-size bag of potato chips. "I believe you won these fair and square," he said, and presented the whole thing to Troy.

Lucille sighed. "I hope they go straight to your hips," she said to the kid.

Troy just grinned and shoved one in his mouth. "Mmmm."

"She's still crazy," Troy said when he and Callie were in the car, same as he always did. But he no longer looked like he meant it, and since she'd just watched him and her grandma do some complicated handshake in good-bye, she didn't take offense. She drove him home and, just before he got out of the car, turned to him. "Troy—"

"I told him. About what happened at school." He touched his bruised jaw. "I wanted you to know that."

"Good," she said relieved. "And the play?"

"I'm working up to that."

"And the girl?"

"That too."

"Work faster," she said.

She watched him vanish inside Tanner's house. He'd looked…better. Not exactly chipper, but not quite as unhappy as usual either.

Progress.

She wasn't sure why she felt so invested in him, but it wasn't just her feelings for Tanner, she knew that much. Troy had wormed his way into her heart all on his own.

She picked up Chinese take-out and drove back to her grandma's.

"I want you to know I exercised restraint in today's social media posts," Lucille said as they ate.

Mr. Wykowski laughed, but when Lucille looked at him, he turned it into a cough.

"Restraint?" Callie asked her grandma warily.

"Yep. I haven't posted about you or Tanner in days.

I'm leaving things alone." She beamed. "See? Restraint." She paused. "And maybe a little self-preservation. I didn't want you to pull the plug on me."

"I wouldn't do that," Callie said in horror.

"I meant cancel my WiFi." Lucille opened her fortune cookie. "Hmm. I think I got yours by mistake."

"Why, what does it say?"

"*You will get lucky.*" Lucille paused. "In bed."

"Grandma!" she said over Mr. Wykowski's hoot of laughter.

"What," Lucillle said. "I'm old, not dead. Don't you kids play that game anymore? Add the 'in bed' to the end of your fortunes?"

Callie chose not to answer, instead opening her own fortune cookie. She stared at it and shook her head, stuffing it into her bag.

"What does it say?" her grandma wanted to know.

She sighed. "I will get lucky."

Lucille stared at her and burst out laughing.

"Stupid mass-produced fortunes," Callie muttered.

"So you *do* believe in them," Mr. Wykowski said.

She ignored this.

"And why doesn't getting lucky suit you again?" her grandma asked. "I never really understood this."

"Love doesn't suit me," Callie corrected. Lust, however, suited her just fine.

"And why doesn't love suit you?" her grandma demanded.

"Grandma, I see how badly love turns out on a daily basis at work. And then there was my own misguided attempt at getting hitched. Let's not forget that one."

"How can we?" Lucille muttered.

"What?" Callie asked.

"Nothing. Love you," Lucille said.

Callie narrowed her eyes and opened her mouth but Mr. Wykowski spoke first.

"So you got unlucky once," he said. "So what? I was unlucky a bunch of times."

"That's right," her grandma said. "It only takes the one. The *right* one."

Callie gave them both a long look. "Have you guys been talking to Becca?"

"No, why?" Lucille asked. "Does she need advice? She's got that hottie all wrapped up so I thought she was good. Do I need to step in and smack some sense into Sam? Because I can do that. I'll have to stand on a foot-stool to do it but that doesn't matter. I'm there for her."

"No, Grandma," Callie said, unable to hold back her laugh at the picture of the diminutive Lucille trying to take down the tall, built Sam Brody. "She's good. And Sam's good."

"So why can't you be good?"

"I am good," Callie said. "There's nothing wrong with being alone, Grandma."

"Well, of course not." Lucille smiled when Mr. Wykowski squeezed her hand and gave her a kiss on her cheek before rising to make coffee.

Lucille leaned into Callie and whispered, "But as I've recently discovered, letting someone in brings unex-pected benefits. And I'm not just talking about the money that can be saved on batteries." She waggled her brows suggestively.

"*Grandma.*"

"Oh, relax," Lucille said. "I'm talking about the joy

of waking up to the person you love and seeing their face right away. Or going through hard times, such as the death of a friend, and having someone be there to hold your hand. Or when you're sick yourself and need help…I mean, sure, you could handle all that on your own and you always have. Again, I blame your shortsighted, selfish parents. But this is about you, honey, and sometimes, just once in a while, it's nice not to be all on your own."

"Says the woman who chose to be alone for five decades," Callie pointed out.

"Single," Lucille said. "Not alone." She wore a secret smile, one that turned not so secret when Mr. Wykowski turned and gave her a wink.

Callie stared at them, absorbing the clear, easy affection between them. The kind that came with *years* of knowing someone. "Just how old is this 'new' thing between you two?" she asked suspiciously.

Lucille laughed and slid Mr. Wykowski a sidelong look.

He shook his head at her but smiled and winked again.

Her grandma winked back. "Well, what does it really matter," she asked Callie, "when it feels new?"

Well, she had Callie there. And she was thrilled for her grandma. She was. But not everyone would be lucky enough to find such a relationship. In fact, the odds were stacked against it. "It's nice, what you've found, Grandma."

"Hey, I didn't 'find' it," her grandma said. "We worked our butts off for it. You think it's easy? It's the polar opposite. Men don't put the toilet seats down. They don't get the importance of putting the toothpaste cap back on.

And they certainly don't understand why it's disgusting to drink right out of the milk container. Some things you just gotta let go of."

"Ain't that the truth," Mr. Wykowski said, smiling as he brought them each a mug of coffee.

Lucille ignored him. "Look at your own parents," she said to Callie. "They've been together for forty years. Forty years of joy and selfish-but-genuine happiness. Which means that you yourself grew up in a house full of love. How did that not rub off on you? Have you forgotten?"

"No. I—" Callie broke off. "I'm sorry. I'm still processing. You and Mr. Wykowski?"

"Told you," she said. "I've had lots of love in my lifetime."

"You hid it well."

"I hid nothing." She smiled. "I kept waiting for you to read between the lines."

"You said he was just a friend."

"Yeah," her grandma said. "He's the kind of friend that you and Tanner are, apparently."

Callie rubbed her eyes with the heels of her hand, but nope, the images were stuck in her brain. "Grandma, tell me the truth. Are you okay?"

"If I tell you yes, are you going to use that as an excuse to leave town?"

Callie stared at her. "Please, just answer the question."

"I maybe sometimes pretended to not be okay to keep you here," Lucille said. "Which I believe makes me wicked and deceitful, but not crazy. And if you're being honest with yourself, you already knew this."

True. To the bone true. "I've got to go."

"To San Francisco?"

"I should say yes," Callie said.

Lucille, confident, happy, grinned. "Take the leftover brownies, honey. They were made by Leah with love. Not as good as I made back in the seventies, but love wasn't the key ingredient in mine and they frown upon those nowadays. Anyway, these'll do nicely. Maybe some of that love will wear off on you by digestion."

Halfway back to her apartment, Callie took a detour and drove past her childhood home. It was a small row house, on a long street of others just like it.

Her parents had sold it a decade ago when Callie had gone off to college and they'd retired and moved to Palm Springs.

Another family lived in it now, and she had no idea why she was even here. Especially since not all the memories were good ones.

Lucille had been right, her parents had loved each other, and her. Still did. But they'd been much older than most of her classmates' parents, and not particularly active.

Without siblings, Callie had spent many lonely days and weeks, even months alone during the summer when her friends had been on vacay with their families.

Her parents, being as reserved as they were, had never questioned why Callie had spent so much time by herself. Nor had they ever encouraged her to engage in social activities, or play sports, or anything like that.

At the time, it'd simply been her life, and she hadn't given it much thought. But now, looking back, she wished they'd given her a push, at least a little one.

But it'd been Lucille who'd pushed her out of the nest and into the real world.

As Callie sat there lost in her past, two little girls came out of the house. They were clearly twins, with matching red hair and toothless grins as they raced each other across the grass. One was in all pink, the other in a variety of mismatched clothes, but together they let out peals of laughter as they ran.

Not quiet, not shy.

The sight made Callie smile. Thankfully history didn't always repeat itself.

From across the street, a boy about the same age as the girls joined them. The twins stopped cold a moment, looked at each other, and then seemed to have some sort of silent communication between them because they let the boy join them.

Callie thought about Eric. He'd been her boy across the street. She'd latched onto him from the day he'd moved in. He hadn't been a nerd like her, but he wasn't a jock either. They'd bonded quickly, and he'd been her first real boyfriend. He'd made her laugh, made her heart pound, and, best yet, he'd paid attention to her.

She'd really believed it was love, true love. The forever-after kind of love.

Looking back, she could admit it hadn't been. She'd fitted him into the mold that she'd needed, not worried about what would happen when he couldn't possibly live up to her expectations.

And he hadn't.

Now she no longer had expectations at all. And yet sitting there thinking too hard, she suddenly realized that wasn't any healthier.

The kids had started a game of tag and were having the time of their lives. Callie sat there watching and…aching.

She loved her parents, she really did. They'd given her a roof over her head, clothes and food, and they'd done their absolute best. She knew this. She didn't blame them for their shortcomings any more than they blamed her for hers. But she swore to herself right then and there that if she ever got lucky enough to have her own family, she'd do more for them. She'd be in her kids' lives every step of the way, and she'd give them guidance and—

Whoa.

Was she actually sitting here contemplating someday when she'd have a husband and kids? In just over three weeks of a renewed crush on Tanner, she was suddenly thinking this way? Good Lord. Of all people, she knew better.

Way better.

Most relationships didn't end up with a fairy-tale ending. She saw that every single day at work. She needed to remember it.

Damn, she really needed a doughnut. Or anything chocolate, she thought, and jumped when someone opened her passenger door and slid into her car.

A tall, built, gorgeous someone.

Tanner Riggs, of course, showing up when she was feeling especially vulnerable and uncertain, as only he could unerringly do.

Chapter 20

♥

T anner sat comfortable as you please, even though Callie's car felt way too small for him. He leaned forward a little, making a show of looking at the house she'd been staring at as he handed her over a to-go mug of hot chocolate.

She took a sip and smiled. "Are you magic?" she asked. "Can you read minds?"

"Neither," he said. "In the span of five minutes I took multiple calls that you were sitting in your car on the street where you used to live, looking sad."

This snapped her spine straight. Ah, there she was, his proud, stubborn Callie. "I'm not sad," she said. "And who called you?"

"I promised not to say."

"My grandma," she guessed. "That damn Find Friends app. Honestly, what was I thinking when I bought her that smartphone for Christmas last year?"

Figuring silence was best here, he just sipped his hot chocolate.

"And then…either Becca or Olivia," she guessed. "Although I have no idea how they'd know."

"One of them is marrying a guy with an eagle eye and a natural nose for details, who just happened to be driving through and saw you," he said.

"Yeah, well, people in this town need to get a life."

"People care about you," he said.

She turned her head and met his gaze. "People?"

"People."

She looked at him for a long beat. "You?"

"Little bit."

"We're not even friends," she said. "You don't have to worry about me. Scratch that, you don't get to worry about me."

Did she really believe they weren't friends? Who the hell was she fooling? Clearly herself, which was irritating as shit.

"It's time to rethink our relationship," he said.

She stared at him like he'd lost his marbles. And he probably had.

"No," she said. "No rethinking. Rethinking is a dangerous sport. Rethinking gets people hurt."

People as in her. Her voice had risen slightly, and though she was doing her best to keep her cool, she was a little panicked. Her eyes gave her away. He reached out for her hand, entwining his fingers with hers, squeezing gently. "You grew up in that house?" he asked quietly.

"Yes."

"I knew your parents," he said. "My mom cleaned your parents' legal office at night for extra cash."

Her only movement was to rub her thumb over his. "I had no idea," she finally said.

"No one did. It was in her verbal contract with them. My mom's pride was at stake, and she has a lot of it. She didn't want anyone to see her as a struggling single mom. Your dad always gave her a bonus at the end of the year and for her birthday. My mom said that he was a fair man. Real fair. She also said he hardly even realized he had a kid, and all he ever had time for was work and his wife."

Callie kept her hand in his but she was staring at the house now. As intently as Tanner was watching her, he caught the exact second her eyes watered. She tried to blink the moisture away but it didn't help.

"She worried about you," Tanner went on. "Because you were an only child. You would come to the office and be told by your dad to sit still and keep quiet, and you would. You'd mess around some with the equipment, but so quietly that it was like you weren't even there. You followed directions to the letter. Like you were afraid to do anything else."

She shook her head. "No," she said, but her voice wobbled and she had to clear her throat. "I wasn't afraid of him, not like that. Never like that. He was just happiest if it was quiet and calm, so my mom made sure that we both gave him that."

"Kids aren't supposed to be quiet, Callie. Or calm."

"I was," she said.

Tanner brought their joined hands to his chest, waiting until she met his gaze to speak. "You loved your dad."

"Yes. Still do."

"You wanted to please him. That's what you'd been taught by your mother's example."

She met his gaze. "You think I set a life pattern, trying to please the men in my life?" She saw something in his eyes, something more, and she stared at him. "Or worse, you think I aim for the unapproachable man," she said slowly. "I set myself up to be hurt."

"Don't you?" he asked quietly.

"Oh my God." She pulled her hand free to press it against her own suddenly aching heart. "You really do think that. Then how do you explain you? Wait—" She pointed at him when he opened his mouth. "Don't you dare answer that. You think I've done it yet again, set myself up to fall for a man who won't fall back. You already told me you wouldn't fall, that this wasn't going to be a relationship. So yes. Yes, that's exactly what you think. Get out of my car."

"Callie."

"I mean it, Tanner."

"In a minute." He reached out and turned her face back to his. "I'm just calling it like I see it, but hell, what do I know? I grew up without a dad at all so don't listen to me. Listen to your gut. Follow your instincts. Live however you want. Just make sure you do it, Callie. Make sure that you live."

She stared into his eyes. "You don't know me," she said. "You don't get to make snap judgments about my life."

"I'm not making snap judgments. And I thought we established that I know you pretty damn well."

"No, you don't," she said. "This"—she gestured between them—"this thing we do, it isn't getting to know each other. We're not even friends with benefits. We're just the benefits."

He looked at her for a long beat. The only clue to his thoughts was the muscle twitching in his square jaw. "Fine," he finally said. "If that's how you want it."

Not trusting her voice, she nodded.

"Callie—"

"I'd really like you to get out of my car now," she said, hating that her voice wavered. She leaned across him and shoved open the car door in blatant invitation for him to get the hell out.

He did. But before he shut the door, he rested his arms on the roof and looked into her eyes. "Ignoring this doesn't change anything."

"Maybe not but it's worth a shot," she said, and started her car. She revved the engine and he took the hint, shutting the door and leaving her alone, just as she'd wanted.

She did her best to remember that when later she was by herself in bed.

But damn. Her pillow smelled like Tanner, and lying there in the bed all by herself, she had to remind herself that being alone had been a choice. *Her* choice.

It took forever to fall asleep, and it was only a few minutes later when she was woken by her phone. She answered without reading the screen because she couldn't focus yet. "'lo?"

"I need a ride."

"Troy?" she asked, coming more awake.

"Yeah."

She sat up. "Okay, no problem. Where are you?"

"You can't tell anyone."

Oh boy. Callie inhaled a deep breath. "What's going on?"

"Promise me."

It was hard to hear him because there was a lot of background noise. Wind? The ocean? There was a quality to his voice that said he was shaken, and she didn't want to waste another second getting to him. "I promise," she said, getting out of bed and shoving her legs into sweats right on top of her PJs. "Just tell me where you are."

Ten minutes later she was parked at the far north end of the harbor, where the rocky beaches were accessible only by a long, steep, rocky trail. Rock climbers loved this area because they could rock climb with the ocean at their back, the Olympic Mountains at their front. It was a stunning locale, shown off tonight by a full moon and a sky littered with stars like diamonds on black velvet. Gorgeous, and deadly dangerous, especially at night.

And Troy had come out here alone to…what? Swim? Her heart had been pounding the entire drive over here as she debated with herself whether to call Tanner. Or the police.

Promise me.

That had held her back, the soft and rather desperate tone of a teenager who knew he was in over his head and needed her help.

He'd told her to walk on the beach for about a hundred yards and then turn to the cliffs.

Using her Maglite even though she didn't need it with the moon casting a shocking amount of light, she made her way, counting paces, and then turned to the cliffs.

And gasped.

Lit by the moon and a gazillion stars was a lone lanky figure halfway up the cliff. The figure waved to her. And then her phone rang.

"Oh my God," she said to him before he could speak.

"I'm okay," he said. "Just…stuck."

"Stuck," she repeated numbly. Shielding her eyes from the moon's glow, she tried desperately to get a better view. He appeared to be sitting on a ledge of some sort, though she couldn't for the life of her understand how he'd gotten up there. "Are you injured?"

"No."

She drew a deep breath. "Okay, good. Now what the hell?"

"I drew something in the sand for someone and left them a note to come see, but then I wasn't sure if it looked right so I climbed up here to check. And now I'm stuck."

"Stuck," she repeated.

"As in I can't get down."

She took another deep breath. "You free-climbed up the rocks sixty feet to see if your picture was any good…" She whirled around and stared at the rocky sand, and realized she was indeed standing in the middle of a…heart. "Aw."

"No," he said. "No aw. It's not straight."

"Where is she?" Callie asked.

"I texted her and told her not to come, that I couldn't get out of work."

"So you lied," she said. "Because…?"

"The heart's crooked."

Being a teenager had been the most difficult time of her life. Stood to reason that Troy was feeling the same. "And now you're stuck," she said.

He sighed.

"I'll call your dad. He'll know what to do—"

"No!" he said urgently. "You can't call him. I'm supposed to be working on a research paper for English. I sneaked out."

She stared up at him.

"I know," he said. "You can yell at me later."

"Troy, I have no climbing skills. I can create a website and I can worry a lot. Those are my two skills."

"You have more skills than that," he said. "You make my dad happy. That's a real talent."

"Let's call him," she said softly.

"I'll get in trouble."

"But you'll be alive."

No answer.

"Troy. It'll be okay."

"We're finally sorta getting along," Troy said. "What if he sends me back to my mom's?"

There was such naked pain in the question that it stabbed right through Callie's heart. "Oh, honey, don't you get it yet? He'd never do that. He'd never walk away from you. He's not like that." Even as she said the words, she realized she really believed them.

Tanner didn't walk away.

Not from his son.

And not from her…

She could trust him, she knew this to her very soul. Which of course made him more dangerous than ever because she could fall. She could really fall for him, and he would catch her. "Let me call him," she said quietly into the phone. "He'll know what to do."

Troy didn't say anything, and she could feel his fear and hesitation through the phone. "Trust me," she said. "I'm going to disconnect. Hang tight—literally. I'm not going to move from this spot and I'll call you right back." She hit END, then sucked in a breath and called Tanner.

He arrived in three minutes, in navy running pants with a white stripe down the outline of each long leg, a skin-tight long-sleeved dry-fit tee and a backward baseball cap as he jogged across the beach toward her. "You okay?" he asked immediately, reaching for her.

Damn, he was a good man. "I am, yes," she said. "Listen, I was hoping you could make me a promise."

"Anything."

She gaped at him. Anything? *Anything?* And he'd answered so quickly too. But she'd have to marvel over that later because Troy was waiting. In fact, he was still on her cell phone listening to every word. "I want you to promise not to get mad."

Tanner studied her for a beat. "Have you ever seen me lose my temper?"

"Yes. When you lost your very last senior football game by one touchdown. You trashed the locker room and got taken to the police station where your mother promised the sheriff that she'd punish you far worse than he ever could just so he'd let you go into her custody."

He stared at her. "Let me rephrase. Have you seen me lose my temper lately? Say in the last decade?"

"A little bit, at the bar that night you told Sam and Cole to butt out."

"That wasn't me losing my temper. That was me telling my two nosy-ass friends to butt out."

Okay, yeah. And in truth, Callie couldn't really imagine him completely losing it. This Tanner, the man who'd been a SEAL and on the oil rigs, wasn't a loose cannon. He was careful, pragmatic, tough, and absolutely stoic. He was also hardheaded and opinionated, but he was right, she hadn't seen him lose his temper in a long time.

Giving up on waiting on her, he scanned their surroundings and she knew the exact moment he found Troy because he went still. "Give me your phone," he said to Callie without taking his gaze off his son.

"Um—"

He simply took it out of her hand and held it up to his ear. "Talk to me."

She had no idea what Troy said, but Tanner whipped around and eyed the crooked heart. She wasn't sure but she thought maybe the very corners of his mouth quirked slightly.

"Hold tight," he said into the phone, then handed it back to Callie.

"We need ropes, right?" she asked worriedly. "Maybe call search and rescue? Or I can call Matt Bowers—he's an old friend. He's a forest ranger now, but he's also a rock climber. He'd help."

"I know Matt, but I don't need him." And with that, Tanner strode across the rocky terrain, got to the cliff, and started climbing.

Callie sucked in a breath and held it, watching Tanner shimmy up the rocks toward his son, his movements sure and strong despite his leg injury.

When he reached Troy, there was some discussion and then they both began a descent. Tanner went first, remaining within touching distance of his son, clearly dictating his every move.

When father and son finally hit the beach, Callie let out a long shaky breath and hugged Troy hard.

He went still as stone for a beat and then awkwardly patted her back.

"I told you it would be okay," she whispered in his ear.

"I'm probably grounded for life," he whispered back.

"Not life," Tanner, said and cupped the nape of Troy's

neck, giving him an affectionate but none-too-gentle shove toward the way they'd come. "Just your foreseeable future. But hey, look on the bright side, you've got a dark purple room to sit in."

Troy sighed.

Tanner pointed to his truck and Troy got in.

Tanner walked past the vehicle and opened Callie's driver-side door for her, waiting until she sat before crouching down and looking into her face.

"Are you mad?" she asked worriedly.

He ran a finger along her temple. "My son got into trouble and he called you for help. I'm not mad. I'm fucking grateful. Now I have to go have a very long, very detailed discussion with my knuckle-headed son."

"You can't get mad at him," she said. "I promised him that you wouldn't."

"Not a smart promise, babe."

"Tanner, I'm serious."

"Me too," he said. "He screwed up. There's got to be consequences for that."

"You can't," she said. "You said you weren't mad."

"At you. I'm not mad at you."

"Tanner—"

"Callie, he's getting a D in English and he was supposed to be working on a research paper to help his grade. Instead he sneaked out of the house," he said with calm steel. "He put himself and nearly a teenage girl at risk. I have to deal with that."

"And in doing so, you're making me go back on my word."

"You shouldn't have promised him anything that had to do with him and me."

She heard him, heard the logic and accepted that he was right, but it didn't make it any easier for her to take. Nor did the fact that she had no idea why she was so fired up about this. Maybe because she could still see the fear on Troy's face, and how desperately he'd wanted to keep this screwup from his father. "He kept it from you not because he didn't want to get in trouble," she said, "but because he was afraid you'd send him away."

"I'll never send him away," Tanner said with such utter conviction that it brought tears to Callie's eyes. Great, and now she was envious of a father/son relationship. "Please move," she said, and when he did, she shut her door and drove off.

Callie was awoken yet again, this time to a knock at her door.

Becca, she thought. For breakfast. Damn, she'd overslept. No wonder, since it'd taken her hours to fall asleep after she'd gotten home.

At the thought of what had happened the night before, she sighed. She'd overstepped a line and tried to tell Tanner how to parent. She, who had no idea how.

What had she been thinking?

And even then, Tanner had followed her home to make sure she'd gotten there okay. Well, that or he was making sure she wasn't going to his house to yell at him some more. In either case, she'd seen him pull into the warehouse lot and wait until she'd let herself in.

A good guy to the end.

And it was the end. She'd let herself get in too deep. It was time to swim for shore and call it a day.

The knock came again.

She cracked a lid open. Muted, gray daylight poured in the windows. Rain slashed against the glass, drumming against the roof noisily.

A storm had rolled in.

And there went the third knock. "Coming!" she called out, and rubbed her eyes as she ran to the door. "I'm sorry," she said as she pulled it open, shivering at the chill that hit her. "I'm going to need a few minutes to—"

But she broke off because it wasn't Becca.

Nope.

Not even close.

It was the last person on earth she'd expected to see.

Okay, maybe not the last person. That honor certainly would've gone to Perfect Eric and his Perfect Wife with her freakishly straight white teeth...

Instead, it was Tanner, clearly having just come in from the rain, his clothes plastered to him, looking hotter and more awake than any man should look, holding—oh God, how was she supposed to resist this—coffees and a bag that smelled even more delicious than he did.

Chapter 21

Tanner had done a lot of crazy shit in his lifetime, often taking his life in his hands while he was at it: playing football without a healthy respect for the danger of the sport, going into the navy and then into Special Forces from there—talk about a not-guaranteed happy ending. And it hadn't gotten any better on the rigs.

So yeah, he'd say he was pretty good at danger, at adrenaline rushes, at living in the moment—knowing the next moment might never come.

What he wasn't so good at was doubt. He'd long ago learned to squelch that emotion deep and ignore it, pretending it didn't exist.

And yet a lifetime of lessons of doing just that flew out of the window as he stood there drenched from the pounding rain in Callie's doorway, never having felt less sure of himself.

He couldn't even bank on her opening the door.

But then she did. Hair wild, not a lick of makeup,

wearing…well, he wasn't sure what that was. Either really, really big sweats or a potato sack.

And it didn't matter.

She looked beautiful.

Her first expression was a flash of things. Relief. Happiness. A welcome heat.

But all that was quickly buried behind an expression of calm indifference.

He didn't even try to reason with her. He stepped into her, forcing her back a step if she wanted to avoid a collision.

Which clearly she did. Whether it was because he was wetter than the ocean or because she was still mad at him remained to be seen.

He took the liberty of shutting and bolting the door and handed her a coffee.

"Tanner—"

"Drink," he said firmly.

He waited until she'd taken a few sips, until her eyes cleared and focused, and then he braced for the real battle. "About last night," he said.

"I don't want to talk about it," she said stiffly.

"Tough shit."

She set down her coffee and went hands on hips. "Excuse me?"

"You heard me." He took her hand and led her to the couch, deciding that her passiveness was more due to the fact that she'd not yet fully absorbed the caffeine than actual submissiveness.

He gave her a gentle shove, and she plopped backward onto the cushions and sputtered.

Before she could bounce up again, he sat at her side

and faced her, planting a hand on the couch at either side of her hips.

Caging her in.

"You're all wet and cold," she complained.

"If that was what was bothering you, you'd not have let me in," he said.

"I didn't let you in, you just helped yourself."

"You could've stopped me."

She lifted a shoulder and turned her head away. "I don't care for the caveman treatment."

"And I don't care for being shut out."

"Shut out?" She shoved at his shoulders, but instead of moving, he caught her hands in his. "You can't be shut out when you're not in," she said.

"Oh, I'm in," he said, shifting closer so that he still wasn't touching her, wasn't getting her wet, but there was scarcely a breath separating them either. "I'm in and that's the problem, isn't it? You're not happy about that."

She didn't have a response. At least not one she was willing to share.

"You said we were friends with benefits," he reminded her.

"You're getting my couch wet. And I said we were friends with benefits without the friends part."

"You're wrong," he said. "We've become friends in spite of ourselves."

"We…" She frowned as she gave that some thought.

"You saved me a seat at the bakery," he said. "That was a *friendly* thing to do."

"I was saving the seat for you so that I wouldn't have to be *friendly* to anyone else," she said.

"And I brought you coffee here so you wouldn't have

to go back after you had your meltdown over Dickhead," he said. "Also a friendly gesture."

"Hey," she said. "I didn't have a meltdown."

He went brows up.

"Okay, it was a little bit of a meltdown." She covered her face.

He pulled her hands from her face. "You're there for Troy," he said. "Like last night. And more than anything, I love that."

"That's not for you," she said stiffly, still pissy. "That's for me. And him."

"It means a lot to him," he said. "And me."

Her gaze flew up to his and held, and then softened. "I'd do just about anything for him."

Her eyes said she'd do anything for Tanner as well.

"He reminds me of you," she murmured.

Grateful to see her warming up to him, he smiled. "Answer this," he said quietly. "Why are you really here?"

"Because I live here. And the only reason you're here is because you woke me up and made me let you in."

"Smartass," he said. "In Lucky Harbor."

"You know why. For my grandma. I came to make sure she wasn't losing it. She means a lot to me."

"I get that," he said. "But at least admit that it's not all about her. Because we both know Lucille's not losing it. She's saner than the rest of us. She is, however, bored and nosy as hell. Separate issues. So other than the guise of making sure she's okay, why are you here?"

"The guise of making sure my grandma's okay?" she repeated. "What's that supposed to mean?"

"You tell me," he said.

She stared at him. "You think I'm here for something

else. Maybe to figure my shit out. But I've got my shit figured out."

"Then why haven't you been in a real relationship in the years since you were engaged?" he asked.

"Besides the fact that my job's made me more than a little cynical? Hello, ditched at the altar," she reminded him.

"So?"

She snorted. "Spoken by a man who's never been left at the altar."

"I was left by my wife," he said dryly. "I think that counts."

"But Elisa didn't publicly embarrass you. I was *ditched at the altar*. Which makes me look pretty stupid. It means I can't discern the difference between a bad-idea crush and being in love."

He stared into her eyes. She actually believed that, as well as that she wasn't meant for love. Which was bullshit. He'd never met anyone more meant for love—to both receive it and give it. "Callie, everyone's allowed mistakes in the love game."

She turned away. "Yeah, but I didn't learn from mine."

His hands settled on her shoulders and slid down to hold her hands. "What was that?"

"Nothing."

He turned her to face him. "You said you didn't learn from yours," he said.

She blew out an exasperated sigh. "If you heard me, then why did you want me to repeat it?"

"Explain," he said, not giving an inch.

"I fall in crush," she said. "Not love. And then I try to make the crush something it's not."

"Eric not loving you back the way you deserved, that's on him," he said. "Not you."

"It doesn't matter," she said. "I'm sticking with low-key relationships."

"So you'll at least concede that what we're doing here *is* a relationship," he said.

She stared at him. "Maybe. But it's not love, and it's not going to be."

He stared back, not sure how to argue that one.

"Is it enough for you?" she asked softly.

No. Hell, no. But because that made him feel like he'd just been hit by an M-60, he didn't answer. Instead he pulled her close and did what they seemed to do best. He kissed her. He kissed her long and deep, doing his best to silence that little voice in his head that kept saying the right thing to do here was walk away...

But for the first time in his life he didn't know if he could do the right thing, not even to save himself.

Callie couldn't get enough of Tanner's mouth or his hands and especially couldn't get enough of his low groan of frustration just before he wrenched her sweatshirt over her head, taking her PJ top with it. Her bottoms went next, PJs, sweats, and panties all yanked down her legs in one hard tug. When she was bare-ass naked, he leaned over her and smiled a very naughty, very determined smile. Then his teeth closed over her nipple and a hand slid between her legs, and she gasped.

"Cold!" she said of his chilled fingers as they shifted, stroking the bare skin of her back now, sliding down to cup and squeeze her bottom, pulling her in against his wet self.

She sucked in a breath but couldn't deny she was thrillingly aroused. Being naked against his fully clothed, unyielding body was incredibly erotic, and she clung to him as if he were her next breath of air, winding her fingers through his hair, forgetting about everything but this.

"Shower," he said against her mouth. "I've made you cold, let's go warm you up."

Before she could say a word he stood, taking her with him. In the bathroom, he let her slide slowly down his body, eyes hot as he once again took charge, starting the shower, kicking off his shoes.

When he caught her staring, his eyes darkened even more and he yanked her into him while they waited for the water to heat. "What?" he murmured.

"I just like to look at you."

"Right back at you, babe."

She smiled, continuing to gaze up at him, memorizing each line on his face because this was going to be it. She knew that she couldn't keep doing this and not lose her heart. God, she loved the way he looked at her, his gaze so fierce and intense, like she was the only woman for him. She loved the way his mouth twitched when he wanted to smile but was trying not to. And she especially loved the way his voice got all low and husky whenever he said her name.

She didn't need to feel his body against her, hard, strong, rippling with power, to remember how much she loved it.

Or how she felt in his arms. Feminine. Desired.

Important...

The steam from the shower filled the bathroom and she moved to unzip his Lucky Harbor Charters wind jacket.

Before she could push it off his shoulders, he reached into the pocket, pulled out two condoms, and tossed them onto the bathroom counter.

Then his jacket hit the floor. She peeled his wet running shirt upward, her fingers tracing his abs, his pecs, every inch that she revealed until she couldn't reach any farther and he took over, tossing the shirt aside.

His pants were the next thing to go as he stripped in quick, economical movements, exposing his mouth-watering body to her in all its glory.

And there was a lot of glory.

He tipped her head up and then his mouth came down over hers, his tongue flicking out, tracing her bottom lip, seeking entrance and getting it when she gasped in pleasure.

His hands slid down her back and over the cheeks of her ass, lifting her off the ground and firmly into him. "Still cold?" he asked.

No. She was burning up. She could feel every single inch of his very hot body. He was hard and thick against her, straining between them ready for action, and she was just as ready. Hell, she'd been ready since the moment he'd walked through her door. "Not cold," she said, and his lips curved against hers.

"What are you then?" he asked.

"Desperate."

"How desperate?"

"Terrifyingly desperate."

He lifted his head, stared into her eyes, and then stepped into the shower with her. The hot water hit her and only fueled the fire. Pushing him to the back wall, she plastered her body against his, rubbing against him, tasting every inch she could reach. It wasn't enough so she dropped to her knees and continued her very important work of licking and nibbling.

The sound of his approving groan bounced off the walls as she ran her tongue along the length of him and then sucked him into her mouth. As the water hit them she kept the pace tortuously slow and controlled, much as he'd done with her so many times now, quivering with anticipation for the moment when he'd lose his composure, thread his fingers into her hair, grab a fistful, and take over.

And indeed his hands went into her hair, but not to get a little rough or guide her. Instead, he pulled her away from him, lifted her up, and put his mouth to the soft spot beneath her ear, his lips applying pressure, his tongue reminding her of the wicked things she knew he could with his mouth. Then that mouth slid up to graze his teeth along her earlobe and down again to gently bite into the crook of her neck before laving the spot with his tongue.

Impatient with need, she pushed against him, dying to have him inside of her.

But he took his time, doing as she'd imagined, fisting a hand into her hair, tilting her head to nuzzle her throat.

His other hand teased her nipples before sliding south while his lips alternately nibbled and sucked, driving her crazy but not detracting from where that busy hand was headed.

Between her trembling thighs.

With one finger he traced her, gently rubbing up and down with work-roughened fingertips.

Her heart kicked hard. Her pulse was already racing,

racing, racing, and she heard her own voice, hoarse with desire. "Tanner, please."

But even as she begged, he teased. "You're wet," he murmured in her ear, a naughty accusation. "And not from the shower."

She moaned, and then again when he reversed their positions and firmly pressed her against the shower wall and slipped a finger inside her.

"*Tanner.*"

"Tell me," he said, voice thick. "Tell me what you want. Anything."

His lips and tongue traced against her jawbone and made their way to her lips, but when she leaned in for the kiss, he allowed the connection for only the barest of seconds before he withdrew from her, making her suck in a breath of sheer frustration.

"You," she gasped. "I want you. Here. Now," she whispered against his lips, sliding her leg up his hip so that he'd have better access.

He let go of her only to reach for one of the condoms and then he was back, his mouth ravaging hers, his tongue pushing, stroking, reminding her of what he was going to do once he got inside of her. Her entire body felt tight, needy, desperate—until finally he slid home with one sure push of his hips and groaned her name.

She cried out at the same time, arching against him, close, so close to orgasm she couldn't talk, couldn't breathe, couldn't do anything but hold on. Knowing her body as well as he did, he angled her hips to his, purposely maximizing her pleasure. One stroke, she thought. That was all she needed.

But he held back. "Callie."

Blinking away the water, she did her best to focus in on him, taking in the carnal heat in his eyes, his need for her, and, maybe best of all, affection. Unable to control herself, wanting more, she ground her hips into his.

With one arm wrapped around her back, his other hand tangled in her hair, he said her name again, his voice low, guttural. Raw. And took her where she needed to go. When she came, he rode out the waves right along with her, gasping her name as he sagged against her, pressing her into the wall. After a moment he slid with her to the shower floor.

They lay there entangled, spent, unable to speak or move a single muscle as the water rained down on them.

After a beat Tanner pulled her into him, pressed his mouth to her temple, and murmured something. It was inaudible but his tone was protective, possessive, and so sexy she shivered.

Nearly a month ago now, he'd asked her if she believed in love and her knee-jerk reaction had been hell no, she didn't believe in love.

But the truth was, deep, deep, deep down, she desperately wanted to believe. She wanted to get it right.

She just didn't know if she could.

But until that defining moment there on her shower floor in Tanner's arms, she'd never really known that she wanted to. She felt warm and…sated for the first time in so long. Sated, but also afraid because she wasn't going to ever get enough of this.

Of him.

"This changes nothing," she whispered. And she had no idea if she was reminding him or herself.

Chapter 22

♥

When Tanner left Callie's place, he headed to the warehouse. He and the guys weren't going to be on the water today. They were on their way to Seattle to look at a boat for sale.

Tanner managed to keep his thoughts to himself during the drive up there and boarding the boat. "It's got one more room belowdecks than we have now," he noted.

"Uh-huh, and you could use it," Cole said. "So you don't have to remember to shove something into the vents at Callie's place."

Well, shit. This morning when he'd shown up at Callie's and taken her against the shower wall, he'd forgotten about putting socks in the vents. "How do you know who it was?" he asked. "Maybe it was Sam, you ever think of that?"

"You two sound different," Cole said. He grimaced and closed his eyes, scrubbing his hands over his face as he swore beneath his breath. "I'm not super thrilled that I know what you guys sound like mid-throes. Jesus. Can we change the subject?"

They decided against buying the boat and then spent the late afternoon working out how to reconfigure theirs to better work for them. They were still at it when Tanner got a call from Troy.

"You might get a call from someone," the kid said.

"Someone?"

"A mom. Not mine."

Tanner wasn't going to like this conversation; he could tell. "Talk."

"I got caught where I wasn't supposed to be."

"Like?"

Troy sighed. "Like sneaking out of a girl's bedroom window."

Jesus. "Are you kidding me?"

"It's not what you think."

"Good," Tanner said. "Because what I think is that I told you to straighten your ass out, and it seems like you're not even close to doing that."

"I also need a ride," Troy said, sounding unhappy.

The kid could join Tanner's club. And Elisa was on pickup duty today. "Where are you?"

"The art gallery."

"Be right there," Tanner said.

"Problem?" Cole asked when Tanner had disconnected.

"Several," Tanner said. "He got caught sneaking out of a girl's bedroom."

Cole grimaced.

"What?"

"You wouldn't have gotten caught."

Tanner blew out a breath at the not-so-gentle reminder that, if Troy was trouble, he was a chip off the old block. "Shit. I have to go get him. I'm going to do my best not to strangle him on sight."

"Thought Elisa was getting him today," Cole said.

"I thought so too," Tanner said. "I mean, she hasn't seen him all week so I thought she'd be on it."

The situation was odd enough that Tanner called his mom on the way to the art gallery. "You hear from Elisa?"

"No," his mom said, and then hesitated. "But she's been seen celebrating something at the Love Shack."

Tanner's gut clenched. "You know what that something might be?"

"My gut guess?" she asked. "That she's going to go back to Florida soon."

"She can't have him," Tanner said immediately. Hell no. The kid was giving him gray hair, testing him.

Troy could push all he wanted, Tanner wasn't going to walk away. He might have a stroke but he wouldn't give up.

"I don't think she's planning on taking him with her, honey," his mom said.

Tanner blew out a breath. This was not good. This would seriously fuck with Troy's head, being ditched by a parent.

As he knew all too well.

"Bring him here for dinner," his mom said. "You're both too thin. I'll fatten you up."

"He's not going to be in the mood."

"Baby, everyone's in the mood for my pot roast, trust me."

Tanner drove past the Love Shack, then decided the

hell with it and did a U-turn and parked in the lot. He took the extra minute to call Lucille, eyes on the bar. "You still got him?" he asked.

"Of course," Lucille said.

"Can you hold him five more minutes?"

"Honey, you can leave him here with me until I go to the big bingo game in the sky," Lucille said, forever earning a spot of gratitude in Tanner's heart.

"Five minutes," he said, and hung up. And then he walked into the Love Shack.

Elisa was belly up to the bar with Dan. They were toasting each other with a shot of something. Once upon a time, Elisa had been the hottest thing Tanner had ever seen with her wild blond hair and curvy figure and that way she had of smiling at a man like he was the only man alive.

She tossed her head back and laughed heartily, and her boyfriend hung on her every move.

She was still hot, Tanner could admit. But she no longer stirred his blood.

Catching sight of him, she straightened, sending him a much more muted smile than she'd given her boyfriend. "Hey," she said. "What's up?"

"We need to talk," Tanner said.

"Sure," she said, and glanced at Dan. "Go ahead."

"Here?" Tanner asked, giving her an are-you-sure look, wanting to give her the chance to make this private.

"Yes," she said. "Here."

Fine. Here it was. "You going back to Florida?"

There was a quick flash of an emotion he recognized all too well, because it'd been what he'd spent a whole lot of years feeling over her.

Guilt.

His guilt had been directly related to ruining her life with a pregnancy at age seventeen. He'd never regretted Troy, not once, but he did regret forcing Elisa to grow up fast. And though he'd done his best by her, the simple truth was that she'd been just a girl to him, never the love of his life.

And there was only one reason she'd ever flash guilt back at him. "You are," he said flatly. "And Troy?"

"He'll be happier here with you."

True statement. But she didn't want Troy. "Jesus, Elisa. You can't just walk away from him."

"Don't you judge me," she said, pointing a finger in his face. "Don't you dare judge me!"

At the tone of distress and fury in her voice, others around them quieted and started to take notice of their conversation. "Let's take this outside," Tanner said.

"Happy to," Dan said, slipping a proprietary arm around Elisa.

"Not you," Tanner said. "Me and Elisa."

Dan scowled. "Anywhere she goes, I go."

Perfect. Tanner gave Elisa a long, hard look and she turned to face the guy. "I've got this, baby." She leaned in closer and put her lips to the corner of Dan's. "He's an ex–Navy SEAL," she whispered, "so stop it."

"I'm not afraid of him," Dan said.

Elisa patted him on the chest, softening her voice. "Wait here, okay? I'll be right back."

Dan flicked her a glance. "You sure?"

"Yes." She went up on tiptoes and brushed a kiss across his lips.

Tanner turned on his heel and walked outside. Elisa

followed and then stood there, arms crossed over her chest in a defensive posture.

"What the hell, Elisa?"

"I'm getting married," she said.

Belatedly he noticed the rock sparkling on her finger. "What does that have to do with deserting Troy?"

"Deserting him?" she repeated in disbelief. "More like I'm giving you your turn. You deserted us, for years and years."

"If you're referring to when I went into the navy because I was a teenager with no other means to support the three of us—"

"Bullshit!"

"Elisa." He shoved his hands through his hair. "I gave up college for you. I went into the navy so you wouldn't have to give up college too. I sent you every penny I could—"

"I didn't want your money!" she yelled at him.

He raised a brow. To his knowledge, she'd cashed every single check.

"And I didn't want you to give up college! I wanted you!" She gave him a push to the chest.

He held his ground with ease and tried to process. "Is that why you took off for Florida and sent me divorce papers?" he asked. "Because you wanted me?"

"Yes. No." She blew out a heavy sigh. "It just got so messed up. And I was so young. And stupid." She closed her eyes. "It started out just me wanting to go to the same college as you."

He'd known that. But she hadn't gotten accepted. "In the end, it didn't matter," he said quietly. "You got pregnant and I didn't end up going."

"Yes, but I didn't know that when—" She tightened her mouth and he went still.

"When what, Elisa?"

She sighed. "When I pretended to be on the pill."

His world tilted a little bit, like he was off his axis. "Say that again."

She closed her eyes. "I got pregnant on purpose so you'd go to a junior college near home and stay with me forever."

He backed to the concrete wall lining the parking lot and sat. Had to, because his legs were like rubber.

Elisa came and sat next to him, quiet, staring down at her boots. "Of course you never did anything I wanted you to do," she said eventually. She reached for his hand and brought it to her heart. "I'm sorry, Tanner. I'm so sorry I lied to you, about everything."

He met her gaze, surprised to find her eyes shiny with tears and real regret. He was torn between being furious at her fifteen-year deception and being terrified for Troy to lose his mom. "He needs both of us, Elisa. Don't do this."

"I've given him everything I have," she said. "I need something for myself."

"And Dan is that something?"

"Yes. I love him, and I love Florida."

He thought of what Troy had gotten in trouble for today, and all the trouble he probably still had to find, and he knew that the kid needed two parents. At the very least. "Troy needs—"

"You," Elisa said softly. "He needs you, Tanner. You two will be okay. And he can come see me whenever he wants." She sucked in a breath. "Don't hate me."

He wanted to, badly. But he shook his head. "I can't." He squeezed her fingers back. "You gave me my son."

She hugged him and he let her for a moment. "I still think you're doing the wrong thing," he said, rising to his feet.

"You said you didn't hate me."

"I don't, but I'm still pissed as hell. Troy deserves better than this from his mom."

She shook her head, her expression stubborn and closed, and he knew he couldn't talk her into staying. Hell, he was just lucky that she didn't want to take Troy along with her because then there'd have been a real battle.

She stood too and tried to smile but sucked in a half sob. "You'll take care of—"

"Yes," he said. "I'll take care of him."

"And you," she whispered. "Take care of you too."

Tanner opened his mouth, but she spoke first, quickly. "I know I have no right to tell you what to do," she said. "But it's your turn, Tanner. You always take care of everyone even when it's at a high cost to yourself. So promise me you'll take care of you."

Chapter 23

♥

Tanner picked Troy up at Lucille's art gallery. The teen walked out to the truck, moving so slowly he might as well have been walking backward.

"So Mom finally bailed, huh?" Troy asked when he finally got close enough to be heard.

"You know?" Tanner asked.

"Yeah. I overheard her talking on the phone a week ago."

Shit. No wonder the kid had been attitude-ridden and pissed at the world. "You'll still see her," Tanner told him. "You can fly back there whenever you want and—"

"I don't care." Troy tossed his backpack into the back, slid into the truck, and buckled up.

"Troy—"

"I don't wanna talk about it."

Tanner wanted to say tough shit because they needed to talk about it, but that battle could wait until they weren't in the truck. So could the talk about getting caught in a girl's bedroom. "School okay?"

He got a barely lifted shoulder.

"You turn in your research paper for English that was due today?"

Another shoulder lift.

"Help me out here," Tanner said. "Is that yes, no, or go to hell?"

Troy let out a breath. Like maybe Tanner was a colossal pain in his ass. "I turned the paper in," he said.

"And?" Tanner asked.

"And what?"

"Did you get a passing grade?"

"Dunno yet."

Tanner started to pull away from the curb and then realized Lucille had come out of her gallery. She headed around the truck toward the driver side. Tanner slid Troy a look. "Anything you want to tell me?"

Troy apparently pleaded the fifth because he remained silent.

With no other choice except to remain parked or run Lucille over—which was a little too tempting—Tanner waited until she'd cleared the front of the truck to roll his window down.

She was so short that he could barely see her.

"Hi there!" she chirped, going up on her tiptoes to look into the cab. She winked at Troy. "You tell him?"

Tanner slid a look at Troy. "Tell me what?"

The kid shook his head.

"Eh?" Lucille cupped a hand around her ear. "Speak up, boy. You know I'm old as dirt."

"I didn't tell him," Troy mumbled.

"Well, why not?" Lucille turned to Tanner. "He got himself a part in the school play. The lead in *Romeo and Juliet*."

Tanner went brows up. "You tried out for the school play?" he asked Troy.

Troy slouched in his seat.

Lucille laughed. "He did it because Brittney's going to be Juliet. Tell him, Troy."

Troy closed his eyes.

"He needed help catching the girl," Lucille said. "My specialty." She peered up at Tanner. "You're next."

"What?"

"You're due," she said.

"Due for what?" he asked warily.

"To get the girl." She grinned. "You need a lot of help but you're not ready to ask. No worries, I'm invested in this one since it's my granddaughter we're talking about."

Tanner opened his mouth—to say what, he hadn't the foggiest clue—but Lucille tapped the side of the truck. "Whelp, have a great evening, boys."

And then she walked off.

Tanner turned to eyeball Troy. "Romeo?"

"I don't want to talk about it."

"Is Brittney the girl you made the heart in the sand for?"

Nothing.

"Is she the girl whose mother is going to call me about your visit?"

A very weighted, very loaded silence.

The list of things the kid didn't want to talk about was getting longer by the minute. And the tension in the truck cab was ratcheting up.

"It's not what you think," Troy said tightly in a tone that suggested he didn't expect to be believed but desperately wanted just that.

Tanner knew that was Troy feeling backed into a corner—a bad place for a teenager. Trying to lighten the mood, he said, "You get to kiss the girl in the play, right?"

Troy blinked and then…grinned. The kid actually grinned.

Tanner soaked up the beautiful sight and put the truck in gear. Some things were worth waiting for, he supposed. He drove them home and turned to Troy. "We still have something to discuss."

Troy sank into his seat again, crossing his arms. He couldn't have looked more defensive if he'd tried. "Nothing to talk about. People get disappointed all the time, it's just a fact. Grandma's disappointed I'm not a little kid that she can dote on. Mom's disappointed she had me. The color purple sucks. Life goes on."

Tanner stared at him. "What are you talking about?"

"Didn't you want to discuss being disappointed in me for being in the play over football? Or getting caught sneaking around?"

"Okay, now wait a minute—" But Tanner was talking to air because the kid was already half out the door. Tanner snagged him by the back of his sweatshirt. "Not so fast."

"I've got homework."

"Which you don't give a shit about," Tanner said. "Talk to me. Grandma loves you from your head to your fifteen-year-old punk smartass. Your mom loves you. I love you—and for the record, I always have, always will. And what the hell does the color purple have to do with anything?"

Troy sighed and let his head fall back against the seat. "Don't try to tell me that the football thing didn't hurt."

"We already discussed this." Tanner looked around to see if he'd stepped into some weird time warp, but nope, it was just him and the kid. And the kid was…well, it was a little bit like looking in a mirror circa his high school years. Still, he was definitely missing a couple of pieces to this puzzle. "Okay," he said, "because I'm feeling a little out of the loop and a whole lot behind, we're going to do this slowly. Football first. Go."

"I suck at it. Okay? Is that what you want to know? I'm not Tanner Riggs, and I never will be."

"Well, thank God for that," Tanner said fervently, then let out a mirthless laugh when Troy just stared at him. "Jesus. Do you really think I want you to be me?" he asked. "I made a boatload of mistakes, Troy. I hope to God you don't follow my path and make as many as I did."

"Like get your girl knocked up?" Troy asked.

Well, yeah. That. Tanner was pretty sure he shouldn't be craving a drink just to have this discussion with his teenager, but again, more proof he was about as far from a perfect dad as a guy could get. The most important thing he had to do here was walk slowly through the minefield, and not just because Elisa had never really been his girl but because he'd grown up knowing *his* dad had been able to walk away from him. And that shit…that had done a number on his head for a lot of years.

No way was he going to ever let Troy go through the same thing. "My actions were the mistake," Tanner said carefully. "Sleeping with a girl before I understood the ramifications enough to protect us both was the mistake. You're not a mistake. Never you, Troy." He felt his throat tighten and his eyes burn. "In fact, you're the very best part of my life."

Troy stared at him, obviously a little blown back by Tanner's vehemence.

"Now if we're straight in that department," Tanner finally said, "let's move on to the other points. Are you sexually active with this girl? Are you using protection?"

Troy blinked. "I told you it's not what you think."

"I don't know what that means, Troy."

Troy looked out the window, jaw tight.

"Okay," Tanner said, knowing pushing right now wasn't the answer. "Next point. No one, and I mean no one, wants or expects you to live up to whatever dubious distinction the name Tanner Riggs brings."

Troy snorted. "Everyone here expects me to live up to you, Dad."

Tanner went still. Troy had used the word "dad" several times now, but it was never going to get old. He wanted to treasure it, wanted to demand Troy say it again. "Well, then," he said instead, "what I really want you to know is that you shouldn't give a shit what anyone thinks."

"Easy for the football star to say. You're not going to put on a pair of tights and get on stage."

Tanner hid his grimace. "But you get to kiss the girl."

The kid tried to hold back a smile and failed. "Yeah. And I get to die. It's awesome."

"So see, it's what you think that matters," Troy said. "Not anyone else."

Troy nodded. "That's what Callie said you'd say."

"You discussed this with Callie?"

"Yeah, and I don't know what's up with girls but they have a way of making you talk."

Troy sounded so baffled that Tanner nearly laughed.

"Get used to it," he muttered, but a part of his brain was back on Callie. Was he actually jealous of what she and Troy had?

Yeah, he decided. He was.

"You can't be mad at her," Troy said, reading his mind with startling ease.

Since this was sounding like a repeat of a conversation he'd had with Callie in reverse, when she'd told him he couldn't be mad at Troy, Tanner shook off his annoyance. "And the color purple?" he asked. "You hate it since before or after you painted your entire room purple?"

Troy winced.

"Since before then," Tanner muttered. He leaned back. "Jesus. It's really true."

"What's true?"

"We're a lot alike."

Troy did not look any more thrilled at this knowledge than Tanner felt. He shook his head. "Think we can have a cease-fire?" he asked the kid.

Troy went wary. "What would that involve?"

Tanner slid him a look. "You talking more than you have, for one."

Troy made a face.

"You continuing to make yourself at home here in Lucky Harbor with things like doing the play for another," Tanner said.

Troy just stared at him.

"And most especially," Tanner added, "you picking out a color for your walls that you like."

"And what about you?" Troy asked.

"What about me?"

"Well, if I have to do all this stuff like talk and crap," Troy said, "seems like you should have to do something."

"Like…?"

"Like—" Troy broke off.

"Oh, don't chicken out now," Tanner said. "Talk to me."

"Callie."

Tanner paused. "What about her?"

Troy looked down at his feet. "If you're holding back with her 'cause of me…"

"No. I'm not."

Troy looked up. "So you two are a thing?"

"No."

Troy blinked. "I don't get it."

"It's complicated."

"Complicated, like you don't like her enough?" Troy asked, both disappointment and anger crossing his face. "Because that sucks. She's totally into you. Like, really into you. If you don't like her, you're leading her on."

Tanner let out a long breath. "It's not like that. We decided we're…friends."

Troy stared at him. "She put you in the friend zone?"

Why did everyone in his life think that this was all Callie's doing? *Because besides your son, she's the best thing that's ever happened to you, and everyone but you, the resident jackass, knows it…*

"What did you do?" Troy asked. "Did you forget your one-month anniversary? Or accidentally bring up another girl? Or tell her that you think any Nicholas Sparks movie is dumb? Girls don't like any of that stuff."

Tanner scrubbed his hands over his face. "We agreed to be friends. The *two* of us agreed."

With benefits…

And how's that working out for ya? a voice inside his head asked.

Troy shook his head. "That was dumb."

"Yeah." Tanner blew out another breath. "It was."

"So…"

Tanner looked at him. "So…what?"

"God, Dad. Even I know you go after the girl when you do something dumb."

Tanner stared at him and Troy laughed. Laughed. The sound was precious. "I love you," Tanner said.

Troy's smiled faded.

"I've been trying to give you your space before I said that too much," Tanner said. "I wanted you to get to know me, but that doesn't seem to be working out so well for us and I don't want to waste any more time. I love you, Troy. And like I said, that's never going to change. You need to know that."

Troy broke eye contact and stared out the window. "I do know it."

"Well…good."

Troy eyed him warily. "So do we have to, like, hug now or something?"

"Yeah," Tanner said, and snagged Troy with an arm around the neck and pulled him in, giving him a knuckle rub on the head first for good measure.

With another of those precious laughs, Troy shoved free. "Hope you got that out of your system."

"I probably didn't," Tanner said. "I might feel the need to tell you that. A lot."

"And the hugging?" Troy asked, the wary look on his face just a front now.

"I don't know, man," Tanner said. "I kinda liked it."

Troy stared at him, a new light in his eyes, one that Tanner had never seen before.

Not love, not exactly, but affection.

He'd take it.

Chapter 24

♥

One week later—seven deliciously sexy, erotic nights in Tanner's arms—it was finally Becca and Sam's bachelorette/bachelor party. Mother Nature cooperated with mild temps, but as night fell they combated the chill with carefully placed outdoor heaters along the dock and on the boat. The decorations were up and the boat was rollicking with friends and family when Callie took her first deep breath.

Her phone buzzed with an incoming text from one of her brides. The "litter" bride.

Everything was perfect, Callie. I know I panicked a lot leading up to the wedding. And I also know the odds are good I'll panic occasionally throughout this marriage as well. But the wedding was worth every bit of angst and so is my husband. Thank you for believing in love and teaching me to believe as well.

Callie stared at the text for a long moment. An epiphany probably shouldn't be inspired by a text from a bride she didn't even know all that well, but there was no denying that she felt something loosen in her chest as she let the words sink in.

The wedding was worth every bit of angst and so is my husband...

Thank you for believing in love...

Was it true? Had she slowly come to believe in love?

"You did well, honey." Lucille came up beside her and slipped a hand in hers. "Look at them. So happy."

Callie took in the sight of Becca standing in the bow, wearing a gorgeous dress and boots, both of which Olivia had gifted her from the vintage shop. Becca was glowing with happiness—as she had been since early that morning when she'd peed on a stick, turned it blue, and pounded on Callie's and Olivia's doors at the crack of dawn to tell them she was pregnant. Now Becca was greeting a group of friends as they arrived. Sam came up to his soon-to-be bride and, clearly not caring one whit that they had an audience, pulled her in close and laid a hell of a kiss on her.

Something tightened deep inside Callie. A yearning, she realized. An ache. Each of her friends here was part of a couple, and she was so happy for them. She truly was.

But something clicked in place and she realized...she wanted that too. She wanted what Sam and Becca had. What Olivia and Cole had. She wanted to wake up next to the same person every morning and have him see her Wild Man of Borneo hair and be okay with that and whatever their future brought. She wanted to let a man all the way in, wanted him to know her crazy grandma and understand those were her genes and have him still want her.

She wanted to know that the man she loved felt the same about her and always would.

This yearning went against everything she'd been telling herself for years. After all, she'd been down that road before and had purposely veered off, taken a different path.

But she could admit something now—she'd never really let herself love all the way. Not once. Seeing Becca and Olivia so open and loving with Sam and Cole, she knew she'd always held back, always kept a part of herself safe. Just in case.

But love wasn't safe. You had to take the plunge and hope for the best.

Sam pulled back from Becca just far enough to curl an arm around her, keeping her close as possible as they greeted people. He was as big and bad and tough as they came, but he kept looking down at Becca with undeniable and unapologetic love, like she was his entire world.

It actually made Callie's chest hurt. Cole and Olivia looked at each other like that too. And a part of Callie suspected that she looked at Tanner that way. And she thought maybe he looked at her the same. And even as she thought it, a little seed of warmth burst from deep inside her, soothing her ache of a moment before.

She could have that, she realized. In fact, it felt like she and Tanner were working their way up to exactly that. He was such a good man. He'd stepped up for his mom, for his son, for everyone in his life. It was what he did. For perhaps the first time in her life, she thought maybe she could really let herself believe. Believe in him.

Ironic, given that he'd been her first real crush.

And now he was her first real love.

Still at her side, Lucille sighed dreamily at Sam and Becca. "These two might be my favorite so far."

Callie looked at her. "Your favorite so far?"

"Well, it used to be Chloe and Sawyer, but then Sawyer told me he was going to have my driver's license taken away if I kept driving. Scratched him off the fave list pronto, I can tell you that. I mean, he's hot, but I'm an excellent driver. My next favorite was Dr. Josh Scott because, well, if you met him you'd understand. But he insists on bugging me about my diet and high blood pressure, blah-blah. And then there was Ben." Lucille smiled fondly. "Ben was the hardest match because trust me, Aubrey wasn't the obvious choice for him. Nearly everyone in town disagreed with me. But from day one I knew it'd work between them. I've never met two people more suited for each other. But then Becca moved to town and I could see her with Sam. So yeah, they're my current fave, but they won't be my last." She slid Callie a look. "That'll be you, by the way. In case you're not keeping up."

Callie had a feeling that she wasn't only not keeping up, she wasn't even in the same time zone.

Lucille sighed. "I swear, I'm starting to think you were adopted. You," she said slowly, pointing at Callie. "You're going to be my absolute fave, my darling, and my last."

Callie stared at her as a new fear gripped her deep inside. "Your last? Why, are you sick?"

"No, I'm not sick. I'm going to outlive all of you. I'm just going to retire."

"From the art gallery?"

"Oh, hell no. What would I do with myself? No, I'm going to retire from matchmaking. After you get your happily-ever-after, of course." She beamed. "With Tanner."

Callie's heart executed a little somersault right there in her chest as someone came up behind her, slid his arms around her waist, and pressed his mouth to her temple in a sweet kiss.

She did her best not to melt as Tanner's low voice sounded in her ear. "Hey, you," he said, and then lifted his head and smiled at Lucille. "You look like you're up to no good."

Lucille smiled innocently. "Mischief managed." She sent Callie a wink and moved off.

Tanner pulled Callie in even closer to him and dropped his head to kiss her neck. "Miss you."

"Hmm," she said. "I can feel exactly how much you seem to miss me." She nudged her backside into the part of him that missed her most.

He chuckled low in his throat. "I want you," he said. "Hard for a man to hide that."

Hard indeed.

She turned in the circle of his arms and felt her breath catch at just the sight of him. She smiled, cupped his face, and went up on tiptoe to press her lips to his.

He smiled against her.

And her heart sighed again. "I trust you," she whispered without realizing she was speaking the words out loud.

He bent and pressed his lips to hers. "Good to know. What is it you trust me with?"

Everything.

He laughed softly, a little wickedly, and kissed her once more. "You can tell me later. Better yet, you can show me later."

Cole came and snagged Tanner for something boat-and-equipment related. Olivia started up things with a wedding scavenger hunt, and Callie ended up winning a set of penis shot glasses—a gag gift Olivia slipped into the mix.

She stared down at them and thought she'd need to make sure Becca won those at Callie's own bachelorette party someday, and then laughed at herself. Second time she'd thought about her future wedding plans. Like before, it brought equal parts terror and...excitement. No, she didn't want a big wedding with all the glitz and glam she'd planned once upon a time. In fact, when—if, she reminded herself sternly—*if* she got to plan her wedding again, she wanted it to be a very small affair.

Just her and Tanner. And Lucille and Troy, of course.

The thought made her knees a little weak.

"Hey."

Speaking of. She turned and faced Troy. Tanner was paying him to work the party. His job was to watch the perimeters in case anyone got close to falling into the water, in which case he was equipped with a radio that he'd proudly hooked on his belt. If he spoke into it, he'd get his dad or Cole.

His secondary job, which Callie had hired him for, was to keep Lucille from the open bar if at all possible.

In fact, ever diligent, his eyes were on Lucille, who was on the arm of Mr. Wykowski. "I feel a little bit like I'm stealing money from you," he said.

"What happened to you resenting having to babysit the old lady?"

"She's not that old," he said. "And she's smarter than most of my friends."

Wow. High praise. "You look different," she said, narrowing her eyes at him.

"Me?"

"Yeah." She studied his face for a long moment. "You look happy. I know, I'm not supposed to say that to a teenager, right?"

He flashed a grin. "Promise you won't tell?"

Oh boy. "I'm not keeping any more secrets," she said.

"Oh, not like that. Mr. Wykowski's paying me today too."

"Whatever for?" she asked.

"To distract your grandma at the end of the party while he gets ready."

"For…?"

Troy leaned in. "His proposal," he whispered.

She blinked. "Are you serious?"

"Yep." Tanner laughed. "You might be getting a new grandpa. But don't worry. He doesn't approve of her use of social media. I'm starving, how's the food?"

"Amazing." She moved with him to the food table, where they bumped into Tanner with a group of people she didn't know along with Cole, Olivia, Sam, and Becca.

Clients, Callie realized as Cole introduced Olivia as his "girl," which made Olivia—and Callie—melt. Sam, of course, introduced Becca as his "wife-to-be."

More melting.

Tanner was up. He pulled Troy in with an arm hooked around his neck in a quick, easy, affectionate gesture. "This is my son, Troy," he said, and met Callie's gaze with the same easy smile. "And this is—"

Callie held her breath and time slowed. What would he say? Girlfriend? Was it too soon for significant other? Yes. Yes, of course it was. Girlfriend. It was an old-fashioned word but it fit. They weren't just friends with benefits, and the truth was they never had been. They were so much more than friends. And benefits. She was already smiling as time sped back up to normal and Tanner finished his sentence.

"—Callie." He smiled at her.

She stared at him. Everyone had gotten a label but her. She was aware of the conversation going on without her, but her brain wasn't participating. She wasn't a significant other. She wasn't a girlfriend. She was…just Callie.

Tanner leaned in and kissed her on the jaw. "Be right back, wait here for me?"

She tuned in and realized he was waiting for a response before moving off with Cole and Sam. She managed what she hoped was a smile and a nod.

And it must have translated because he squeezed her hand and was gone.

Barraged by unwelcome emotions, she stood there, trembling. The truth was, she'd created a fantasy—a relationship with Tanner. But it wasn't real. They weren't a couple at all. And the very thing she'd promised herself wouldn't happen—that she'd go into this thing with her eyes wide open and not get hurt—had come to be.

Because she was hurt. To her heart and soul.

Chapter 25

♥

Tanner didn't expect to enjoy himself at the party. In fact, he'd approached it like he would a root canal or paying bills. A chore he had to get through, no more, no less.

Not that he didn't want Sam to be happy with Becca. He wanted that very much. Sam deserved happiness, maybe more than anyone else he knew.

But being social wasn't really Tanner's thing. Not in big groups. He'd rather be out on the water. Or in the water, far beneath the surface with nothing but the steady thump of his own heartbeat and the hollow, beautiful sound of the world below in his ear. Or with Troy, who was probably teaching his grandma how to Instagram or something equally horrifying.

Or best yet, he'd rather be in bed.

With Callie beneath him.

Or on top of him.

Or however she'd have him. He'd take her any way he could get her. Especially since he was having trouble getting any time with her here tonight at all. Every time he sought her out, she was busy.

Mr. Wykowski stood up and toasted Becca and Sam, and then turned to Lucille. He thanked her for "loving him since the last ice age" and then took her hand.

"I can't get down on my knee," he said. "It don't bend that way anymore. But, Lucille, I want you to make an honest man out of me."

Then he shocked everyone by producing a ring.

"You old dog," Lucille said, and cackled. "Yes. Hell yes."

And for the first time in Tanner's memory, the gossip manager of Lucky Harbor became the gossipee.

The party really kicked into gear then. At midnight he sent Troy and Beatriz home with Lucille and Mr. Wykowski. The last part of the evening became a blur. The night was a dark one, but they'd strung a million lights along the dock and on the boat and they were both lit up like Christmas. Someone had cranked up the music, and everyone was dancing like loons.

Cole and Olivia were out there. Cole was doing his white boy thing, one arm straight up in the air, waggling his hips back and forth, but it was working for him because Olivia was all over it.

And though the beat was fast, Sam and Becca were slow-dancing, plastered up against each other like white on rice, staring into each other's eyes as if no one else existed.

Tanner's gaze ran over the crowd and locked onto Callie. For over the past two hours now she'd been wherever he wasn't, and if he hadn't known better he'd have sworn she was avoiding him. He smiled at her.

She smiled back but it was short her usual wattage.

And maybe it was an ego thing, but damn, he loved the way she usually looked at him. Like he was the best thing she'd seen all day. Like maybe he made her world a better place to be. Like she couldn't imagine not having him to look at.

But she didn't give him any of those looks now. In fact, she turned away.

And then vanished into the crowd.

What the hell?

He caught up with her in the parking lot just as she slid in behind the wheel of her car and started to shut the door. Holding it open, he crouched at her side. "Hey."

"Hey," she said, busy doing something in her purse.

"You're leaving?" he asked.

"Um, yeah...I just need to—" She tossed her purse into the passenger seat. "Yeah. It's just about over and I have to get up early and I'm pretty tired, and...yeah."

She was rambling. Which she did only when nervous or upset, and since he hadn't made her nervous since that first morning at the coffee shop, he had his answer. "You're upset."

She finally looked at him, her expression dialed to Give the Man an A+.

He wracked his brain but couldn't come up with a reason. "What's the matter?"

"Nothing." She tried to shut her door but he was in the way. "Excuse me," she said in that tone she reserved for her most annoying clients.

"Callie." He cupped her face and turned it to him. For the briefest of beats he'd have sworn there was hurt in those beautiful green eyes, but then they were twin pools of...nothing. Nothing at all. It was a defense mechanism, and one he knew well since it was his own. "Tell me what's wrong."

She shook her head.

Batting zero. "Give me a minute to say my good-byes," he said. "And then I'll go with you."

"Not necessary," she said. "I know the way."

"I'll meet you there then."

"No," she said quickly. Too quickly. "Um, I painted. The fumes are bad."

"You painted."

"Yes." But she didn't attempt to hold eye contact.

His heart sank to his stomach like a ball of lead. What the hell? "Then come to my place."

"Troy—"

"He's spending the night with my mom. Please, Callie," he said quietly when she started to shake her head.

"Fine." She tugged at the car door again. "I'll come over later."

Relieved, he rose and took a step back, standing there while she pulled out of the lot and vanished into the dark night.

Back at the dock, Cole met up with Tanner as they stood together watching Sam and Becca dancing like there was no one else in their orbit.

"They grow up so fast," Cole said.

Tanner found a laugh. "Yeah. He did good." He gestured with his chin toward Olivia dancing with Sam's dad. "So did you."

"And so did you," Cole said. "Callie's perfect for you. She loves Troy and, better yet, she appears to like your sorry ass too."

"Callie and I aren't a thing," he said, and even as the words came out automatically, he felt his heart ache in protest. Because goddamn, he wanted them to be a thing.

When had that happened?

Cole swiveled his head and stared at Tanner, and then he laughed. "Yeah, right."

"We're not. We're just…" Shit. He couldn't do it, he couldn't use the word "friends."

Because they were more, damn it. No matter what she wanted to believe.

Cole was staring at him. "What are you talking about? I've seen the way she looks at you."

"Yeah? And how's that?"

"Like she can't take her eyes off of you," Cole said.

Tanner let out a low, slow exhale.

Cole shook his head. "You're an idiot."

Damn, he was tired of people saying that. "Fuck you."

Cole laughed. "You've seen who I sleep with at night, right? Nothing personal, but she's a lot sweeter and softer than you."

Okay, that was it. He was out. Tanner pushed away from the railing and started to walk off.

Cole grabbed his arm.

Tanner went still and stared down at the hand on him. "You want to let go."

Cole let go. "Jesus. Touchy, much?" He stared into Tanner's eyes. "What did you do? How did you screw it all up?"

"I didn't do anything. And why do people keep assuming I screwed it up? I don't screw things up. I'm careful not to."

"When it comes to anything but yourself, yeah," Cole

said. "You're real good at taking care of the people in your life. You'd give them the shirt off your damn back. Hell, you'd give them your heart and soul—as long as you don't have to be responsible for theirs."

Tanner stared at him. "What are you talking about?"

"You're the rescuer," Cole said. "Never the rescuee."

WTF. "I don't need rescuing."

Cole's smile was sad. "Man, we all need a good save now and then."

Tanner thought about that his entire drive home. It was true that he'd done his best to be there for the people in his life. Elisa. Troy. His mom. Cole and Sam. So what? They meant everything to him—even Elisa with all her craziness because she'd given him his son.

But he didn't have a rescue complex. Nor did he need rescuing. Not in the damn slightest. He took care of himself. He sure as hell didn't need anyone. Need and want were two entirely different things and—

And the thought scattered on the night's light wind as he pulled up to his house and saw Callie's car in his driveway.

She was waiting on him.

His heart, which had been sitting uncomfortably in his gut all damn night, fluttered like a virgin's. He got out of his truck and jogged up the front walk, stopping at the sight of her sitting on his top step.

She rose, dusted her hands on her thighs, and met his gaze. Her eyes weren't as bright as they normally were. There were smudges of exhaustion beneath them. Her smile wasn't quite right either, and his heart squeezed. It was one of those moments where time stood still as something hit him.

He was willing to take whatever she would give him, and if that meant friends with benefits, or just friends, or just benefits, he'd take those crumbs. But if she walked away from him, he would be decimated. Apparently there was a point of no return, and he'd crossed it. Not just strolled over it but steamrolled past it.

"You're a sight for sore eyes," he said. "Want a drink? Or we could make something to eat, or—"

She shook her head. "I shouldn't stay long. I've got work."

"It's past midnight."

She shrugged. "Brides don't notice the time unless their groom is late."

He unlocked the front door and waited while she moved in ahead of him. Expecting her to stop in his living room and possibly remark on the fact that he had several cans of paint stacked up near Troy's room, he was surprised when he blinked and she was gone.

He followed her down the hall to his bedroom.

She was kicking off her shoes.

"You sure you don't want—" His words and breath escaped him in a whoosh when she pushed him onto his bed. "I—"

She climbed on top of him. "No time for a chat," she said, and then pulled off her sweater.

Beneath she wore a black and nude lace bra that pushed her up and nearly out of the tiny cups. His mouth went dry, even as a part of him recognized that she was wearing pretty lingerie. For him.

When she shoved up his shirt and bent low, putting her mouth on him, a rough groan escaped him. His hands slid into her hair as she took that mouth of hers on a tour south.

Jesus.

She had one hand in pants and him halfway to the finish line before he could draw another breath. "Callie."

Another stroke with her warm fingers and his eyes crossed. "Callie, wait—"

She shoved his pants down farther.

He moved fast. He had to, or he was going to lose it like a quick-on-the-trigger teenager. Rolling, he pinned her beneath him and held her down on the bed.

She struggled a moment, not to escape but to keep her hands on him, so he collected both of hers in one of his and yanked them up over her head.

"Now," he said. "What's going on?"

She blew a strand of hair from her face and said, "Well, I thought we were getting busy."

"You were," he said.

She rocked into him with her hips, nudging the hottest—and wettest—part of her over the undeniably hardest part of him. "You too," she murmured. Her motion hadn't stopped and her undulating hips were driving him wild. She fought to free her hands, only to clench a handful of his hair, holding his head to hers.

He obliged, kissing her for long, intoxicating moments before shifting to the hollow at the base of her throat and then that spot just beneath her ear that always seemed to make her crazy. He waited for it and wasn't disappointed to feel her quiver beneath him. Then he nibbled her earlobe before sliding his mouth to hers, feeling yet another tremor course through her as their lips collided.

Her fingers tightened in his hair enough to sting and the contrasting sensations of pleasure and pain had him throbbing painfully. He needed more, now, and going off the sweet sounds she was making, she felt the same. Dipping his head, he caught her lower lip between his teeth.

Her hands held his head close as his tongue slid against hers in a sensual dance that mirrored what he wanted to be doing with the rest of their bodies. A shuddering groan rumbled out of him and he tightened his hold on her, feeling her bare breasts, so perfect and beautiful, rubbing against his chest.

"Please," she whispered, her mouth traveling across his jaw to his ear, her breath hot and moist.

As if he could deny her a single thing. He fumbled in the top drawer by his bed for a condom but in the end it took the both of them to roll it down his length.

As he slid into her, he dropped his forehead to hers. "Home," he whispered. "You're like coming home."

This statement nearly startled Callie out of the haze of erotic, sensual desire, but she was too far gone. Tanner was inside her, filling her up like no one else ever had, and it seemed as though her body disconnected from her brain and was on its own mission.

The bottom line was that she couldn't get enough of him and even though she hated herself at the moment, she wanted this. She wanted any part of him she could get.

And right now she had one of her very favorite parts of him and she felt herself tightening, pushing toward the edge of orgasm as he moved deep inside her. He slid his hand along the underside of her thigh, holding her leg against his hip so he could thrust deep, sending her spiraling out of control. Staring up into his face, she thought that she'd never seen that look before, like he was completely lost in her. That, and lust, a sheer, unadulterated lust that took her over with one final thrust. He kept moving until they were both spent, unable to move a single muscle.

"Callie," he finally whispered, his voice filled with a wealth of affection that was like an onslaught, a battering ram against the wall she'd built around her heart.

He slid one arm around her back and pulled her in even closer while he cradled her head with the other. Then he lowered his mouth and kissed her with a tenderness that she wasn't prepared for. Not even close.

Playful and lust filled, yes.

But gentle and meaningful? God. God, she couldn't.

He briefly left the bed and then came back, pulling up the covers before sliding beneath them.

"What are you—*oh*," she breathed, and then held on as he spent a good long time exploring every inch of her body with his tongue and his hands. By the time he entered her again, she'd had another orgasm and was well on her way to yet another. Any thought of holding a part of herself back was gone because the only thing she could concentrate on was the feeling of Tanner on top of her and inside her.

How she felt in that moment was beyond any words she could have come up with. During the party, and especially after he'd let her and the world know she was just Callie to him, she'd been able to keep her emotional connection to him in check. She'd even told herself she'd cut that emotional connection entirely. Severed it clean.

A big, fat lie.

Tanner stirred when Callie slipped out of the bed. She gave him no lingering touch, not a good-bye, nothing. It was like their first time all over again.

He hadn't realized he'd become so dependent on the time they spent time in each other's arms, laughing, talking…It'd become almost as important as the sex itself.

Except this, with her, wasn't just sex. Not even close, not to him. "Where's the fire?" he asked.

She didn't answer right away, just moved about his room in the dark, picking up her clothes, righting them, putting them back on.

"I need to get home, I've got a thing," she said. Lightly. Carefully so.

And he got his second warning niggle. It hadn't occurred to him until now that she'd come here just for this. "Got all you needed?" he asked.

She glanced at him. "Yes. As did you."

"No question," he said. "I just didn't realize it was a booty call."

Her mouth tightened. "Well, what did you think we've been doing?"

"Actually," he said, "once you took your clothes off, I stopped thinking entirely."

She picked up her purse and fished out her keys.

"Can't the 'thing' wait?" he asked.

She looked at him for a long beat. "No. The thing can't wait."

Call him slow, but he was finally getting that something was truly, seriously wrong. He sat up. "Did I hurt you?"

"Just now?"

He'd missed something. Something big. He got out of the bed. "Or ever," he said. "Let's start with that."

She shook her head. "Definitely don't have time for this."

He caught her wrist. "Make time."

"I have to go."

He was getting that loud and clear. He was also getting that he'd fucked something up big time. "It's important," he said.

"I have to go," she repeated.

"Later then. Today. We've got to take a group out for deep sea fishing, but I'll be back by three. I'll take you out on the water for sunset and then dinner."

"A date?" she asked in a surprised voice, and regret hit him like a one-two punch to the solar plexus. Because of their work schedules and caring for Troy, most of his and Callie's time together had been late at night in bed. "Yes," he said, promising himself he was going to convince her that they could do better. That on top of that, they could actually work. "A date. I'll pick you up by five the latest."

She didn't look impressed, but he couldn't tell if that was disinterest or something else in her eyes.

"Please," he said.

Another long assessing gaze and he did his best to look like something she couldn't live without.

"I'll meet you on the docks," she finally said. "At five."

And then she was gone.

Chapter 26

♥

That afternoon Callie sat at her grandma's kitchen table. She was simultaneously inhaling the cookies her grandma had gotten from the bakery earlier and watching the clock.

"You late for something?" Lucille asked.

"Nope."

"You have a date with your hottie?"

"I refuse to answer that question on the grounds that if I do, everything I say will be used against me on a social media platform," Callie said.

Lucille grinned. "You do have a date." She clapped her hands together, clearly pleased as punch. "You two have decided to make a go of it. Am I right? Tell me I'm right!"

"Not entirely, you nosy woman. I'm merely meeting him at the dock at five."

"For a date."

"A *small* date," Callie corrected.

"To make a go of it?" Lucille repeated.

"I don't know." Callie hesitated. "I want to, but—"

"No but! That sentence should start and end with 'I want to.'"

"He doesn't think of me in that way," Callie said.

"Bullshit."

"Grandma!"

"I'm serious, Callie," Lucille said, and to prove it she even put down her cookie and leaned in, eyes solemn. "I've seen the way he looks at you."

"Like I'm an amusement?"

"Like the sun rises and sets in your eyes."

Callie blew out a breath. "He introduced me as Callie."

"Well, honey, last I checked that was your name."

Callie closed her eyes. She knew this sounded dumb. "Sam introduced Becca as his wife-to-be. Cole introduced Olivia as his girlfriend. Tanner then introduced me as just Callie."

Lucille looked at her for a long beat. "Do you think you're the only one who's afraid of getting hurt? Do you think you're the only one who's uncertain about the future and letting someone in?"

"No," Callie said. "Of course not, but Tanner—"

"—is just a man. A man who came back to Lucky Harbor to provide a steady family life for the people he loves. He doesn't turn his back on anyone, ever, and I've seen how he looks at you. If he didn't slap a label on your forehead, it's simply because he didn't know what that label was. That doesn't mean he doesn't feel anything for you. It just means that maybe he doesn't know what you feel for him."

Callie stared at her grandma. How many times had she told Tanner that their sleeping together "wouldn't change a thing"?

A lot.

She'd never once let on that she had growing feelings for him. Which meant her grandma was right, she had no one to blame but herself.

"Honey." Lucille took Callie's hands in hers. "What is it you want from him?"

"I don't know." A lie. She wanted him, all of him.

"I'm going to ask you again," Lucille said gently. "What is it you really want from him? Nothing? A good time? Everything?"

"Everything," Callie whispered.

Lucille smiled and squeezed Callie's fingers. "Then tell him. Tell him tonight."

"You think?"

"I know."

Callie's heart leapt and bounced against her ribs some. In a terrifying but good way. Was she ready for this?

Yes. God, yes. And this time when she looked at the clock, she rose. "Here goes nothing."

"Or everything," Lucille said.

Or everything.

"Don't forget some lip gloss," Lucille called after her. "And it wouldn't hurt to tame the hair a little."

"Grandma!"

"Just sayin'…And you're going to put real clothes on, right?"

Callie glanced down at her yoga pants and sweatshirt. Shit. Yeah. She needed real clothes. Because tonight she was going to be her own client, and she would never let a client meet her future groom in sweats.

She stopped at home and put on her cutest pair of skinny jeans. She did have to lie flat on the bed to zip them up, but they looked good tucked into the boots Tanner liked.

She got to the docks at a quarter to five. Habit. Normally she prided herself on being early and prepared, but today she would have liked to have been the one being waited for.

The boat was moored but empty. The hut was closed. The warehouse, locked.

The guys weren't still out on the water but they weren't here either.

Telling herself not to look at her phone again, she sat to wait.

And wait.

But Tanner never came. He just…didn't show. And it was like standing at the altar all alone waiting for Eric all over again.

Waiting for someone to love her.

Chapter 27

♥

T anner sat in the principal's office next to his son, who was also sitting, holding an ice pack to his eye.

The principal was glaring at the both of them balefully. "I thought we agreed that this behavior couldn't continue," she said in that principal-to-errant-student tone that made Tanner feel fifteen all over again.

Troy said nothing.

Tanner had docked the boat half an hour ago and found messages waiting for him. One from the principal that merely said "Need to see you in my office ASAP."

One from Elisa saying "Got a message from the principal, need you to handle it."

Not surprisingly nothing from Troy, not one little peep.

Cole and Sam finished up with their clients as Tanner headed to the high school.

And here the three of them sat.

"I'm going to have to take more severe action this time," the principal said.

Tanner ignored this and turned to Troy. "What happened?"

"He hit a fellow student and started a fight," the principal said.

Tanner didn't take his eyes off Troy. "I'm asking my son."

Troy lifted his gaze to Tanner's, his eyes registering surprise that his dad would listen to him over the principal.

Tanner gave him a small, reassuring nod. He wanted the truth, and he wanted to hear it from Troy.

"After school a couple of the guys were picking on someone," Troy said. "Saying mean stuff, pushing. I told them to knock it off but that only made it worse." He paused. "And then when the person they were teasing was tripped and fell, spilling all their stuff, I stepped in and pushed back for them."

"The boy you pushed hit the railing and got a cut lip," the principal said.

Troy didn't look apologetic about this. In fact, there was a flash of fierce pride.

"How did you get the black eye?" Tanner asked him.

"The kid I pushed jumped up and punched me."

Tanner made a show of looking around the office. "And where is he?"

The principal folded her fingers together. "He's not here because he didn't start it."

"Yes, he did," Troy said. "And it's not the first time. Last week he stole stuff from someone. Important stuff."

"Like?"

Troy went mutinously silent.

"Troy," the principal said disapprovingly. "I have four witnesses who say you pushed Caden into that railing. Not a single witness said that you were stopping him from picking on someone. Or that something got stolen."

"Because you asked the guys that were with Caden. You didn't ask the person they were picking on," Troy said. "And anyway, I got their stuff back already so it doesn't matter."

"And who are we talking about?" she asked. "Who's the kid who's being picked on and stolen from?"

Troy went mum.

Tanner looked into the kid's stubborn brown eyes, which was more than a little bit like looking into a mirror. *I got their stuff back...*

Aw, shit. The day Troy had gotten caught climbing out of the girl's window. He'd gone there to return her stuff. "Juliet," he said quietly.

Troy's mouth went hard with determination.

Yeah, Tanner thought. It was the girl. He looked at the principal. "Look, I think it's clear to both of us that he was protecting someone. It's also clear you don't have the entire story."

The principal looked at Troy for a long beat, then nodded. "Yes, I believe you're right."

"What's going to be done?" Tanner asked.

"What's going to be done is I'll get to the bottom of this and then decide. Troy," she said, "who did you step in to help?"

Troy remained mum.

The principal folded her fingers together. "I can't help you unless you let me."

"She won't talk to you," Troy said. "She won't tell you because she's been in trouble before. But those guys bully her because her brother turned them in for cheating on a test. They've been just saying mean stuff but today they touched her, and scared her."

"Who, Troy?"

Troy shook his head.

The principal leaned in. "I want to help you out here, Troy. I want to help whoever it is you're protecting. But I can't if you won't trust me."

Troy didn't look impressed by this, and the principal leaned back and blew out a breath. "If what you're saying is the truth," she said, "the boys can be suspended, all of them. And if they pull anything like this again, I can expel them next time. Help me stop the cycle, Troy."

Ten minutes later Troy and Tanner stood on the sidewalk by Tanner's truck.

"Proud of you," Tanner said.

Troy looked startled, and Christ, Tanner hated that. Didn't Troy know by now that Tanner stood at his back no matter what? "So proud," he said, and willed Troy to believe it.

"For the fight?"

"For protecting your friend. For standing up for someone you care about. For doing the right thing, which is rarely the easy thing."

"I ratted out those guys."

"Like I said," Tanner told him. "You did the right thing. You protected the girl, once by being there for her and again just now by getting help for her so that it doesn't happen again. But you should have told me all of it, from the beginning."

"I know."

"Do you?"

"Yeah." Troy dropped the ice from his eye and looked at him. "You're really not mad about the fight?"

"Hell, no." They got into the truck and Tanner leaned toward Troy to check out the bruise. "Does it hurt?"

"Like a mother."

Tanner smiled grimly. "Other than that, how are you doing?"

Troy shrugged.

"Come on, man. Spit it out."

"Well, I am kinda starving."

Tanner stared at him and had to laugh. He'd been afraid Troy would be suffering some long-lasting emotional angst over everything he was going through. But no, he was just hungry.

A damn good outlook on life when it came right down to it.

So Tanner took him to the diner. He intended to get him a quick take-out, but Jane, the diner's owner, had heard about the fight and insisted they sit down and eat "on the house," because as it turned out it was her great-niece that Tanner had protected.

Troy was brought a huge tray of food fit for a king and then dessert. When he and Tanner rose to go, Jane hugged Troy tight. "You're a good boy," she said fiercely.

Back outside, Troy looked down at his phone in shock. "Kids from school are texting me. Like a bazillion texts. They're happy Caden finally got in trouble." He looked up at Tanner in surprise. "Some of these texts are from the kids that wouldn't give me the time of day 'cause I was the newbie."

"Welcome to the most ridiculous years of your life," Tanner said. "High school."

"But how did people hear?" Troy asked.

Tanner slung an arm around the teen's shoulders. "It's Lucky Harbor, son. It just is."

Troy shook his head in disbelief. "My mom was right. This place is crazy."

"You that unhappy here?" Tanner asked, keeping his voice even. "Because if you are, we could talk about it and visit our options."

Troy was boggled. "You mean...move?"

"Whatever it takes to make this work between us," Tanner said.

Troy stopped walking to stare at him. "You'd really do that? Move? For me?"

"Whatever it takes," Tanner said again, and was stunned when Troy leaned in for a hug. Tanner didn't hesitate, just wrapped his arms around his kid and held tight for the moment it was allowed, closing his eyes while his heart swelled until it squeezed against his ribs.

All too soon Troy pulled back and looked away, clearly uncomfortable with the need for physical touch. "I don't want to move."

"Good," Tanner said. "Because I'm getting tired of buying paint."

He took Troy home and was halfway up the walk when he realized what time it was—six-thirty—and went still as stone. "Shit!"

Troy glanced back at him. "What?"

Christ. He'd done some difficult things in his life, but being a dad took the cake. He was overwhelmed by the sheer emotional drain on his system and the fact that, without Elisa, it was entirely up to him to give Troy everything he needed.

And in doing that, he'd forgotten Callie. He'd fucking forgot her. He whipped out his phone and called her.

His call went right to voicemail. Not a good sign. "Callie," he said. "I'm sorry. I got held up, but I'm coming now." He wasn't about to use Troy as an excuse, but an uneasy anxiety curled in his gut. He'd left her waiting for him, which killed him. He looked at Troy. "I've got to go."

"You had a date?" Troy asked.

"Yeah."

Troy studied him. "A big date?"

"Pretty substantial."

"Like you were going to ask her to marry you substantial?"

The kid was a mind reader. "I've been thinking about it," he said. Thinking. Breathing. Eating. Fantasizing… "Would that be okay with you?"

Once again Troy was dumbstruck. "You're asking my opinion?"

"Well, yeah," Tanner said. "We're a package deal."

Troy stared at him from eyes that were suddenly a little shiny.

Tanner cupped the back of the kid's head and lowered his own to be at eye level with his son's. "Right?"

Troy nodded.

"Good. Go inside. Do your homework. Don't leave without being in contact with me."

"I won't," Troy said. "I'm sorry I made you late."

"Not your fault," he said, and when Troy just looked at him, expression uncertain and worried, Tanner reached out and clasped his shoulder. "Seriously. This isn't on you."

"Bring her flowers," Troy said earnestly. "That's what

her site says to do. You bring a girl flowers when you screw up."

Tanner was pretty certain flowers weren't going to do the trick. He drove to the docks, which were deserted. Of course she wouldn't still be waiting there an hour and a half hour later.

He went to her place next.

She didn't answer his knock.

He texted her: *Open up, it's me.*

No response.

He knocked again, and Becca poked her head out her door. She was wearing Sam's shirt, knee socks, and I've-been-thoroughly-fucked hair. "She's not home," she told him.

"Do you know where she went?"

Sam appeared behind Becca. He was wearing nothing but a pair of faded jeans slung low on his hips to reveal the waistband of pink boxers speckled with red lips. His feet were bare, his jaw rough, and his hair was as wild as Becca's. "Hey, man."

"Didn't mean to interrupt," Tanner said. "I'm just looking for Callie."

Sam and Becca exchanged a long look.

"What?" Tanner said.

"We saw her a little bit ago," Sam said. "She was leaving."

"Leaving?"

Becca sighed and came forward, putting a gentle hand on his arm. "She said she was going out for a little while, that she needed to clear her head."

He didn't like the look that crossed Becca's face. "What aren't you saying?" he asked.

"She looked like she'd been crying."

"Shit." Tanner slid his hands into his hair. "Fuck."

"Why does it matter to you so much?" Becca asked. "Considering that the two of you are just"—she paused—"friends."

His gaze snapped to her. "That's the way she wanted it from the beginning. She didn't want a relationship."

Becca looked at Sam and did an impressive eye roll.

"It's not his fault," Sam told her.

"What's not my fault?" Tanner asked.

"That you're an idiot," Sam said.

"Hey, I thought I was just giving her what she wanted."

"What she wanted?" Becca said. Actually, it was more like she yelled it. "Are you kidding me? You were a Navy SEAL, for God's sake. I know you're smart as hell." She was hands on hips now, glaring at him.

Tanner looked at Sam.

"Maybe we should spell it out for him," Sam said to Becca.

"Fine," she said. "Let me do that." She pointed at Tanner and though she was a good eight inches shorter than he, she got right up in his face. "She grew up with quiet, introverted parents. They loved her in their own way, but it was a distant, pat-her-on-the-head kind of way. And everyone who's come into her life ever since has been the same. Loving her in their way."

Tanner opened his mouth to tell her he got that, but she jabbed her pointer finger at him again. "No, you just shush a minute and listen. I mean *really* listen," she said. "Not that I should have to be saying this to you because you knew her before I did and you should've already been clued in." She shook her head in disgust. "She's smart.

So damn smart. In the past, that's alienated her, Tanner, and those smarts of hers don't keep her company. Yeah, maybe she was paid by the athletes to do their homework, but none of them wanted to date her. Especially not the hottest one of them all."

He grimaced.

"Yeah," she said. "You."

"Jesus, Becca. I was older than her," he said in his own defense. "She wasn't on my radar."

"Well, you were on her radar," Becca said. "She was lonely, which made her ripe pickings for a guy to come along and trample all over her heart."

"Eric," Tanner said in disgust.

Becca nodded. "She's grown up a lot since then, but deep inside she's still that lonely little girl looking for someone to love her just for her."

"I want her just for her," he said, thinking of how he wanted her for the rest of their lives. "She knows that I do—" He broke off as a terrible realization sent his stomach dropping into his boots, feeling like it was down for the count.

Did she know?

Because how could she? He'd been careful, very careful, to abide by the rules. Not because she'd laid them down, but because he was a fucking coward. From the beginning Callie had made him promise that sleeping together would change nothing. And he'd given her that promise.

Freely.

Looking back on it, he'd done so with a cockiness that disgusted him now. In the beginning, he'd honestly believed he could stay detached and had just as honestly believed the same of her. There'd been safety in that, the two of them both vowing to remain emotion-free. But that ship had sailed because for the first time in his life, it wasn't enough.

With her, it wouldn't ever be enough. She'd wrapped her fingers around his heart, when he hadn't even been sure the organ still worked. But it did. And she owned it. She owned him.

Without even realizing it, he'd come to trust her with his heart and now he wanted her to trust him with hers. But he'd kept her in the dark. "Shit. I am an idiot."

Becca patted him very kindly on the arm. "They say knowing is half the battle."

Chapter 28

♥

Callie sat at her grandma's kitchen table. The tablecloth was a soft, battered cotton and had been there as long as she could remember. In fact, the entire kitchen brought back memories. The scent of cookies in the oven and last night's roast. The lace hanging in the window. The linoleum floor, with the dent from the time Callie had dropped the deep fryer.

Lots of decisions had been made here, right here, with her grandma sitting across the table offering advice and food. Things like whether she could ride her bike to the store by herself, or if she really needed yet another memory board for her computer, or where to go to college.

But this decision was a biggie. "I think selling TyingTheKnot.com is the right thing to do," she said. "It's not making me happy."

"No, you're not making you happy," Lucille said. "Selling your business won't change that."

"Grandma, you're not helping."

"Well, someone has to tell you how things are."

"I know how things are," Callie said.

"So you know you're being reactive and also a big, fat chicken by turning tail? Selling your business and running back to San Francisco isn't going to fix anything, Callie Anne. You'll still retreat inside of yourself and block people off, good people, great people, including a man who actually loves you. My God, Callie, the man forgot a date, not you as a person."

Well, when she said it that way, Callie felt silly and juvenile. But she couldn't discount her feelings. She couldn't, because she had a habit of letting others discount them for her. "He left me standing there waiting for him on the dock like—" She cut herself off because there was a sudden lump in her throat.

"This is not the same thing as being left at the altar," Lucille said gently. "Tanner wouldn't do that. I'm sure he has a very good reason for whatever happened today."

"I know it," Callie said. "My point is that my overblown reaction is telling. It means I'm not ready for a relationship. And by the way, he never said he loves me."

"Because—and stop me if I'm boring you here—you told him you weren't interested in such things as love."

"Grandma—"

"You're afraid," Lucille said flatly and with frank disappointment. "Call a spade a spade, honey, and at least own up to it. You're afraid to open your heart and let anyone in. And let me tell you what, that man isn't just anyone, he's a man I hand-picked for you, and I'm never wrong. Now I'm serious about retiring from this matchmaking gig and you're going to single-handedly mess up my one-hundred-percent accuracy."

Callie thunked her head to the table a few times. When she lifted her head, she was facing Mr. Wykowski. He smiled kindly. "I'm sure you don't want to hear me say your grandma is right, so I'll spare you that."

"Thank you," she said dryly.

"And I'm sure you also think that as a man, an old one at that, I don't know shit about love."

"Can we take that word off the table?" Callie asked. "Please?"

"But it seems to me," Mr. Wykowski went on, unperturbed, "as if you're judging Tanner by the people in your past."

"I'm not—"

He held up a finger. "Your parents retired early and then later moved away from here, rarely coming back. You took that as a rejection, and rightfully so."

"I'll say," Lucille grumbled in front of the stovetop. "I taught my son better than that."

Mr. Wykowski never took his gaze off Callie. "And then Asshole Eric didn't help things."

Callie choked out a laugh.

"I call 'em like I see 'em," Mr. Wykowski said. "He might have rejected you, but you dodged a bullet there to my way of thinking."

"No shit," Lucille muttered beneath her breath. When she realized that both Callie and Mr. Wykowski were looking at her, she mimed zipping her lips and tossing away the key.

"He didn't deserve you," Mr. Wykowski said to Callie. "But this thing you've got going, being braced for rejection, all you're doing is putting out that negative energy into the universe, and now it's all coming back at you."

"So what do I do?" Callie asked.

"Own your past," he suggested. "Learn from it. Know you deserve better, that the right man will come along and, when he does, you'll give one hundred percent of you."

Callie stared at him. "You sound like a therapist."

He smiled. "I watch *Dr. Phil* while I'm on the treadmill."

"Isn't he the sweetest thing?" Lucille asked.

Mr. Wykowski smiled. "Love you, sweetheart."

"Love you too," Lucille gushed.

Mr. Wykowski looked at Callie. "You see? It's really not that hard to put yourself out there."

"That's hardly fair," Callie said. "You knew she would say it back."

"Not true," Lucille said. "The first time he told me he loved me, I didn't say it back. I didn't, because he'd told me when he was—" She paused and bit her lower lip and blushed.

Mr. Wykowski laughed softly.

Callie covered her eyes. "Subject change, please."

"You love Tanner," Lucille said firmly. "I see it every time you look at him. I hear it in your voice when you speak to him. I can feel it between you when you're both in the same room. The air sizzles."

"There's a difference between attraction and love," Callie said. "A big one."

Lucille barked out a laugh. "Well, of course there is. But attraction"—she used air quotes around the word—"doesn't get devastated by being stood up. Attraction doesn't make you yearn for a person so badly you hurt when you think it's over."

Callie thunked her head on the table again. "I know," she said miserably. "God, I know. And I do love him. I love the way he's working hard to be the best dad he can be in spite of the fact that he doesn't even know what a good dad looks like. I love how he takes care of his mom and not just monetarily. I love how he'd do anything for Sam and Cole. And I love how he looks at me, how he touches me, how he makes me laugh, makes me think, makes me feel…" She shook her head. "Everything." Head still down on the table, eyes closed, she sighed. "I love him like I've never loved anyone before. And I don't think I can handle it. You were right, Grandma. I'm afraid. I'm so afraid that I'm thinking of going back to San Francisco in order to escape facing it. And I'm not proud of that."

There was a single knock at the back door.

Callie jerked and lifted her head, her worst fears realized when she saw the tall, broad shadow standing there.

Chapter 29

♥

Callie jumped up and whirled to face her grandma. "Tell him I'm not here," she whispered. "Tell him I'm already gone. Tell him—"

"That you're a big, fancy liar?" Tanner asked.

She whirled back. The window in the back door was open. He'd bent low and was looking right at her.

He was in a backward baseball cap and sweatshirt, hood up against the wind.

She could see nothing of his expression, but that might also have been because she was holding her breath and her own vision was wavering from a severe lack of air.

He gave a small head shake and she didn't know if that quirk of his mouth was amusement—in which case she'd have to kill him—or annoyance—in which case he could just get in line.

Then he opened the door, calm as you please, and… walked right in.

"Hey, honey," Lucille said to him. "We were just talking about you."

"Grandma!"

Tanner gave Lucille a kiss on the cheek. He turned and shook Mr. Wykowski's hand.

"Do you want some cookies?" Lucille asked him.

"Maybe later," he said, and looked at Callie. "Right now, I'd like a moment alone with your granddaughter if you don't mind."

"Oh," Lucille said in clear disappointment. "But—"

Mr. Wykowski took her by the hand and pulled her toward the door, winking at Callie over her grandma's head.

Callie didn't wink back. Couldn't. "How long were you standing there?" she asked Tanner quietly. "What did you hear?"

"Nothing. I've got some things to say to you, Callie." His voice was quiet steel. "And I need you to look me in the eye and tell me you're going to hear me."

She crossed her arms over her chest but her heart still ached so badly she didn't know how she was supposed to function. Then Tanner was there, right there in front of her, cupping her face up to his. His eyes were dark and serious, oh-so-very serious. Which wasn't to say that she didn't soak in the rest of him, the scruffy jaw, the feel of his hands on her, his scent—which was so unbearably familiar they triggered all sorts of memories and made her ache all the more.

"Say it," he said. "Say you're going to listen."

She reminded herself that she was the injured party here, that she was the one who'd stood on that damn dock like an idiot for an hour.

Yes, an hour.

She was the one who'd put her heart on the line and been burned for it. She was the one who was about to completely lose it.

"Please," he said softly. Intently.

Tanner was strong, of both mind and body. Confident. Smart. Loyal. Tough. God, so tough. It wasn't often he asked for something, anything, and as much as she wanted to push him out the door and go back to her pity party, she found she couldn't deny him anything. "I promise to listen," she whispered.

He didn't waste a second. "I'm sorry about this afternoon. I had an emergency with Troy. I should have called or texted and I didn't, and I hurt you. I can't take that back, but—"

"Is Troy okay?" she asked. "What happened?"

He blinked and then smiled a little. "That right there," he murmured. "You putting Troy first is why I—"

"*Is he okay?*"

"Yeah," he said. "He got in a fight at school, and—"

"Oh my God."

"He's okay," he said. "But—"

"—but he needed you," she said, and let out a breath. "I get that. You put him first and you should."

"Callie, I'm sorry."

"No," she said. "You did the exact right thing putting him ahead of a silly date. You always do the right thing. I wouldn't ever expect otherwise."

He stepped close and stroked his thumb along her jaw, and then beneath her eye, catching a wayward tear she hadn't even realized she'd shed while talking to Lucille and Mr. Wykowski.

"But by doing that, I hurt you," he said. "I hate that."

"That's on me, not you. I was waiting for you and when you didn't show, I…reacted badly."

"You thought I'd left you waiting on purpose," he said, looking extremely unhappy. "In fact, in some ways you've been waiting on me to leave you from the beginning."

"No. I—"

"Truth," he said, holding her gaze, not letting her look away.

"Okay, yes. Fine," she said. "You're right. I've been half braced for that. I figured you'd walk away eventually, I just didn't know when."

His eyes flashed and she knew he was frustrated and probably ticked off, but he listened when she went on.

"So this afternoon when you didn't show," she said, "it sent me spiraling. I went straight to a bad head space and assumed the worst."

"There's something you don't get," he said. "Some men walk away. Not me. I don't operate that way. Yes, I fucked up. I fucked up big and I hurt you, and that was the last thing I ever wanted to do. But I want to fix this. I'm not sure how, but I'm not running. I'm choosing you, Callie. I'm not going anywhere and I want this to work. But if you don't want it too, tell me right now."

She didn't say anything and he stepped in closer so that she was forced to tilt her head up to see him. "You set the parameters for this relationship from the get-go," he said. "And I let you. Do you know why?"

"Because they suited you too," she said.

"Maybe at first, but things change. And now they don't suit me in the slightest," he said. "But I wanted to be with you, and I told myself to take whatever you could give me and be happy with that. But I wasn't, Callie. I wanted more. I was going to get to that tonight, in fact, even though I wasn't sure you would ever admit to wanting the same. Until I heard you talking to your grandma and Mr. W."

"Hey," she said. "You said you didn't hear anything."

"I lied. I heard everything. And I want to hear it again, right now, while you're looking into my eyes."

She sucked in a breath.

"Fine. I'll go first," he said. "I fell early and fast for you, so fast I was dizzy almost every single second we spent together. And I loved it. I love your sweet laugh, I love how frigging smart you are, I love how you took your own strengths and made a successful business for yourself. I love how you take care of your grandma, coming back here to a place that wasn't necessarily filled with happy memories just to make sure she wasn't heading for the crazy house."

"Excuse me," Lucille said through the kitchen door. "I don't mean to interrupt but I'm years away from the crazy house."

Tanner didn't take his eyes off Callie but he did smile. And at the sight, the knot in her chest loosened very slightly.

"I'm going to tell you what else I love," he said. "Even with our audience. You okay with that?"

All she could do was nod.

"Good," he said. He put his hands on her hips and lifted her up to sit on the counter. He pushed her thighs open and stepped between them so that he was flush up against her. "You," he said simply. "I love you."

The knot loosened a little bit more even as her heart swelled against her rib cage so that she could scarcely draw a breath. "You heard me tell my grandma how I feel about you," she said. "That doesn't mean you have to say it back. I don't expect—"

He put a finger over her lips, shutting her up. "You should expect," he said. "And this is me. I say only what I mean, always. You can take that to the bank, Callie. That, and the fact that I love you, I'm always going to love you, and if you need to hear it every day for the rest of your life to believe it, I think I can manage that."

Her eyes filled, and she wrapped her fingers around his wrist, pulling his hand from her mouth. "You said your life was full," she said, "that you had everything you needed."

"I was wrong," he said, gaze darkening and pinning her in place. "I didn't realize I needed you in my life. Now I can't imagine my life without you. I fit with you, Callie. You're my other half, my better half."

"I…" She shook her head. "I'm not even sure what that means."

"It means—" He hauled her in close and pressed hot kisses along her jaw, his voice low, for her ears only as he spoke in between each kiss. "That the next time you and I make love, it won't be because we have an itch to scratch, or because we're convenient, or because of any benefit plan."

"Oh, for God's sake" came Lucille's voice through the door. "They're talking too quietly. I can't hear a thing."

Tanner grinned and his voice lowered even further, his lips brushing the shell of Callie's ear now, sending heat spiraling through her body. "It'll be because we can't live another day without being together."

She opened her mouth to respond to that and his lips

caught hers, his tongue making itself right at home with hers.

"The next time," he said when they broke free for air, "it will be forever. Now." He waited until she looked up at him. "Say it again. Tell me what I want to hear while you're looking at me, talking directly to me."

She waited for the chest pain of anxiety to hit but it didn't. In fact, the words were right there on her tongue, ready to be said. "I love you, Tanner."

He let out a whoosh of air and pressed closer, dropping his forehead to hers, making her realize she hadn't been the only one feeling the strain of a possible rejection.

Then he lifted his head a fraction of an inch. His mouth brushing against hers, he said, "Again."

She cupped his scruffy jaw and met his gaze. "I love you," she told him.

His mouth curved. "Did it hurt?"

She laughed softly. "No."

"Good. Again."

She kissed one side of his jaw, and then kissed the other, and then his chin. And finally his mouth. "I love you," she said against his lips.

He caressed her cheek with his thumb, the palm of his hand warm against her jaw line. "I'm not going to be able to get enough of that." He entwined their fingers and put her hand to his chest so that she could feel his heart beating strong. "It hurt when I thought I'd blown it enough that I might not ever hear that from you," he said.

"You didn't blow it," she told him. "I did, by not letting myself free fall for you even after I knew you'd catch me."

"Always," he vowed, and brought tears to her eyes.

"It's you and me together now," she said, giving him a vow in return. "I won't hold back again."

"I know. But you and I are still in a vulnerable place," he said. "I want a commitment."

She stared at him, her heart surging with emotion. Good emotion. "A commitment?"

"Yeah," he said, and then kissed her.

Just as the kiss got as serious as his statement, including a good amount of tongue and heat, there was a knock at the back door.

"Ignore it," Tanner said. "We're busy. They'll go away."

"Wish we could" came Cole's amused voice.

Callie pulled free of Tanner and looked at the door. Cole, Sam, and Troy stood there, all three of them bent and staring in through the window—although Cole had his hands over Troy's eyes.

"Are they done macking on each other?" Troy asked.

"Yep," Cole said, and dropped his hands. "It's safe."

Callie felt her face heat as she hopped off the counter. "We were just…"

"We know what you were just," Sam said, laughter in his voice, the guys filling Lucille's tiny kitchen with testosterone.

"What the hell are you all doing here?" Tanner asked.

"The kid insisted," Cole said. "Called me for a ride."

"I wanted to make sure Callie knew it was my fault that you forgot her," Troy said. Horror crossed his face. "Wait! Forgot is the wrong word. He didn't forget you," he said to Callie. "Forget I said forget, okay? He got busy kicking ass and taking names at the school and—"

"It's okay," Callie said, and hugged him. "Not your fault."

Troy wrapped his lanky arms around her in return. "So you forgive him, right?" he asked, his voice muffled against her. "You're not going to dump him because of me?"

"Never." Choked up again, she squeezed him tight. "I'm not dumping him. I'm keeping him. I'm keeping you too, if you'll have me."

Troy pulled back to stare at her and then turned to his dad. "You haven't asked her yet?"

Callie looked at Tanner. "Ask me what?"

Cole turned to Sam, palm out. "Pay up."

"Hell, no," Sam said. "He hasn't asked yet. The deal was fifty when and if he asked."

"One hundred, not fifty," Cole said. "And he's going to ask. So pay up."

"Jesus." Tanner pinched the bridge of his nose and then pointed at the door. "Everyone out."

"You sure?" Cole asked. "You might not do it right and need backup."

"Do what?" Callie asked, heart thudding in her chest.

Tanner closed his eyes, muttered something that sounded like "fucking nosy bodies," and then reached for Callie's hands to pull her into him. "I told you I had things to say to you."

"I thought you said them. You told me what you feel for me." She hesitated. "Right?"

"Right." Tanner wrapped his arms around her and pressed his jaw to hers because she looked so damn anxious. "And—"

"Dad."

Tanner gritted his teeth and turned to his son to give him a this-better-be-good look.

"You can't just say 'right,'" Troy whispered. "You have to use the words. The three words. With the biggie. You know, the L-word."

Tanner opened his mouth, saw that Troy was utterly earnest and serious, and bit back his pithy response. He gave a short nod and turned back to Callie. "I love you," he said, and knew he'd never get tired of the immediate response she gave him. She lit up from within, as if he'd just given her the moon. "I also told you my world doesn't work without you in it. I—"

"Wait!"

This time it was Sam interrupting. "You're supposed to be on a knee," he pointed out.

Callie put a hand to her chest as if she were trying to keep her heart inside it.

A gasp came from the other side of the kitchen door, and then it was opened and her grandma and Mr. Wykowski squeezed into the kitchen. "If they're here, I get to be here," Lucille said. "I can't miss this!" She pushed her way through the big bodies until she had a front-row view. "Okay, go ahead, Tanner. Ask her."

Tanner sighed. When he caught Callie's gaze, she was staring at him wide-eyed, her hand over her mouth. She let out a low laugh and shook her head.

He had no idea if that was "I can't believe you're doing this," or "please God, don't do this." Taking his chances, he sank to a knee.

Callie's hand dropped from her mouth and she gaped at him.

"Callie," he said. "You're the love of my life and my closest friend."

"Wait a minute," Cole said. "What am I, chopped liver? Whatever happened to bros before—"

Sam wrapped an arm around Cole's neck and covered his mouth. "Got him," he said to Tanner. "Carry on."

Jesus. Tanner looked at Callie again. "You're it for me," he told her. "To the bone. And I want to be it for you. The end of the line."

Callie's eyes filled but she was smiling. He was going to take that as a good sign. "You've said you never felt particularly special," he said, "but you're the most special woman I've ever met. You're smarter than me, far prettier, and frankly, I'm not going to lie—you should really give this some serious thought because you could do better."

She choked out a laugh.

"Dad! Don't tell her that. You might make her think."

Sam snorted.

Cole grinned.

Tanner did his best to ignore the peanut gallery. "No one will ever love you as much as I do," he told her.

"Nice," Sam said.

Lucille sniffed.

Callie yanked Tanner up and threw herself at him. "Yes. God, yes!"

"Um, honey," Lucille said. "He hasn't actually asked yet."

"Oh, my God." Callie tried to pull back, but Tanner wouldn't let her. No fucking way. He was grinning when he kissed her.

"Callie Sharpe," he said against her mouth, "marry me."

She was laughing and crying when she kissed him back, and from behind her she heard her grandma say, "Well, that was more like telling her than asking, but it looks like she's good with it."

"I don't know," Troy said. "She didn't really answer, did she?"

"The answer is yes," Callie said, staring up into Tanner's warm gaze. "Always yes."

"Good to know," Tanner said.

"Don't forget I'm a minister," Lucille said. "Got ordained on the Internet. I could marry you! Just think of the wedding you could plan for yourself."

Horrified, Callie looked at Tanner. "Do you want a big wedding?"

"I want you, babe," he said. "However that comes. Whatever makes you happy."

"That's a good answer," Sam said to Troy. "You should take notes."

Callie hadn't taken her eyes off Tanner. "After all the weddings I've planned and all the crazy brides I've met," she said, "I don't think I want to plan ours. How do you feel about just picking a day and doing it on the beach?"

Tanner grinned and she smacked him on the chest. "You know what I mean!"

He caught her hand and brought her fingers up to his mouth. "Whatever makes you happy."

"A kiss would make me happy," she said, and he was quick to oblige.

"But you'll let me perform the ceremony, right?" Lucille asked over Callie's shoulder.

Tanner was shaking with laughter when he tore his

mouth free of Callie's and pressed his face into her hair. "This, Callie," he breathed against her.

"This what?"

"I'll never get tired of this. With you."

And with those last few words, she melted into him. "I feel the same," she said softly. "After a lifetime of not belonging, I found my place, my home, and my heart."

Epilogue

♥

On the first day of spring, Callie heard the front door open and remained still. Tanner might be a morning person but she still was not. Eyes closed, she listened to him move about his house. He murmured something and then came Troy's muffled response.

The front door closed again.

It was a Saturday morning, which meant Troy was off to work, prepping the boat for the day's activities.

She didn't hear Tanner move toward their bedroom down the hall, but that was the Navy SEAL in him. Silent but deadly.

Deadly perfect for her.

She felt the bed depress slightly and knew he'd put a knee on it.

"I know you're awake, faker," he said, and she could hear the smile in his voice. Her eyes flashed open to see it dancing across his face.

"And I know you're sneaky," she countered, and rolled to her back. "Why are you tiptoeing in here?"

He fisted the blanket covering her and slowly but inexorably tugged it down, revealing first her shoulders and then her nipples, which puckered in the cool air.

He smirked.

"It's cold," she said.

"Liar." He tore the blankets off her entirely, and when she squeaked and tried to grab them back, he grabbed her ankles, slowly spread her legs, and then made himself at home between them.

She squeaked again because he'd been swimming and was icy cold.

Laughing, he buried his face—and his still-wet hair—into the crook of her neck for a moment before lifting his head and grinning down at her. "So."

Her breath caught at the look of love in his eyes. She'd never tire of seeing it. "So."

"Today's the day you become mine," he told her.

Her heart sighed. "I've been yours all along," she said, and kissed him gently, teasingly, delicately licking his lips with just the tip of her tongue until he growled, tightened his grip, and took over, crushing her mouth to his.

He slid down her body, leading with his mouth. When he found her hot and wet, he groaned his approval. He took her achingly slow and achingly sweet, building her up until she was begging before letting her fly.

Twice.

It took her a moment to come back to herself, and when she did, she found him poised between her legs waiting for her to return to planet Earth. Smiling, she rocked her hips against his. A groan shuddered through him as she teased the both of them. She curled her fingers around the back of his neck as she deepened the kiss until they had to break apart to breathe.

"Look at me," he commanded, and she managed to fix her eyes on his, watching his face as he slid into her in one smooth, hard thrust. All the air left her body as she rose to meet him. "This is forever," he said, and began to move.

"Forever," she gasped, and tried to pull him in even further.

He couldn't get any closer.

But she needed more, needed it desperately but didn't know what or why, and she whimpered in frustration.

Still holding her gaze in his, he bent low over her. "I love you, Callie."

That was it, that had been what she needed. Something deep inside her burst right along with her body. She was pulsing, throbbing, tightening around him, and somehow he filled more of her than he had a moment ago, and not just her body. Her eyes flooded with tears but she didn't try to hold back. "I love you, Tanner."

Gaze burning into hers, he paused. "I'll never get enough of that."

"I love you," she said again, a mindless chant now as she was unable to focus on anything but the sheer necessity of his body inside hers.

He sped up but she still met every movement with one of her own, born of a frightening level of passion. She could hear his ragged breathing in her ear, could feel his heart pounding against her chest. And then he cupped her head so that she met his mouth. The kiss was hot and demanding, as if he needed as much of her as she was begging of him. She gave him everything she had, her hands on his body, her heart his for the taking. Planting her feet, she lifted her knees, pulling him into her.

His control seemed to snap, and he pounded into her a final time, taking them both over the edge.

When she could breathe again, her heart felt so full it was heavy.

No, wait.

That was Tanner's full weight on her, which she welcomed. His hand squeezed her hip and then he rolled to his side, taking her with him.

Tucking her head low, Callie swiped the moisture off her cheeks. She hadn't meant to shed tears, but somehow her emotions couldn't be held in, not today. She cuddled closer and his arms tightened.

"Always," he said into her ear. "Me and you for always."

He got her, and he always would. "Good," she managed to say lightly. "Because you're stuck with me now."

He laughed low in his throat and lifted her face to kiss her, as always able to erase her doubts with just a single touch of his lips.

He held her until his phone buzzed. He looked at it and let out a breath. "They're waiting."

Even a simple wedding wasn't all that simple in the end. The guys were going to get ready at the warehouse. Callie would go to Becca's, where Becca and Olivia would be waiting to help her. "I guess this is it," she said softly. "I'll see you in a couple of hours. On the beach."

It took him another twenty minutes to say good-bye, and she was a limp, sated, boneless mass by the time she showered.

Just like every other morning since they'd gotten together last fall. But unlike any other day, she slipped into the simple white sundress she'd so carefully picked out with Becca's and Olivia's help.

And when it was time to walk down to the beach to meet Tanner, she got the surprise of her life.

Someone had set up a beautiful arch. And flowers. And tables and food…While she stood there gaping, Becca and Olivia filled in the blanks.

"It was Troy and your grandma," Becca said. "In cahoots together, they're unstoppable."

"They put the word out that after all you've done for all your brides, Lucky Harbor needed to step up and do for you," Olivia said.

The flowers were gorgeous, the food looked amazing. "Where is everyone?" Callie asked.

"Hiding in the warehouse," Olivia told her. "They didn't want to intrude if you didn't want company."

Callie pulled out her cell and called Tanner.

"I've seen it," he said.

"Where are you?"

"On crowd control here in the warehouse."

"Let them out," she said. "Let's get this party started."

"You sure you want them all there?"

"The wedding planners should be on-site," she said, and laughed. "In case something goes wrong."

"Nothing's going to go wrong but if it does, we'll handle it," Tanner said with such calm that she took a deep breath and realized it was true.

And the same was true for the rest of their lives. She wasn't naïve enough to think it would be always smooth sailing. Life didn't work that way. But they were solid,

and whatever came, whatever happened, they would handle it, together.

"Turn around," Tanner said, and she did.

He was standing there in front of her, phone to his ear.
Behind him was a crowd of people. He grinned at her and
said into the phone, "Gotta go, babe, I'm going to marry
the most gorgeous, wonderful, amazing woman I've ever
met."

"You sound like a lucky man," she said softly.

"The luckiest."

Becca Thorpe has left the big city for little Lucky Harbor, hoping for a fresh start. She never thought she'd find love too…

♥

Please see the next page for an excerpt from *It's in His Kiss*.

Chapter 1

♥

"Oh, yeah," Becca Thorpe murmured with a sigh of pleasure as she wriggled her toes in the wet sand. The sensation was better than splurging on a rare pedicure. Better than finding the perfect dress on sale. Better than…well, she'd say orgasms, but it'd been a while and she couldn't remember for sure.

"You're perfect," she said to the Pacific Ocean, munching on the ranch-flavored popcorn she'd bought from the pier. "So perfect that I'd marry you and have your babies, if I hadn't just promised myself to this popcorn."

"Not even going to ask."

At the sound of the deep male voice behind her, Becca squeaked and whipped around.

She'd thought she was alone on the rocky beach. Alone with her thoughts, her hopes, her fears, and all her worldly possessions stuffed into her car parked in the lot behind her.

But she wasn't alone at all, because not ten feet away,

between her and the pier, stood a man. He wore a rash-guard T-shirt and loose board shorts, both dripping wet and clinging to his very hot bod. He had a surfboard tucked under a biceps, and just looking at him had her pulse doing a little tap dance.

Maybe it was his unruly sun-kissed brown hair, the strands more than a little wild and blowing in his face. Maybe it was the face itself, which was striking for the features carved in granite and a set of mossy-green eyes that held her prisoner. Or maybe it was that he carried himself like he knew he was at the top of the food chain.

She took a few steps back because the wary city girl in her didn't trust anyone, not even a sexy-looking surfer dude.

The man didn't seem bothered by her retreat at all. He just gave her a short nod and left her alone.

Becca watched him stride up the pier steps. Or more correctly, she watched his very fine backside and long legs stride up the pier steps, carrying that board like it weighed nothing.

Then he vanished from sight before she turned her attention back to the ocean.

Whitecaps flashed from the last of the day's sun, and a salty breeze blew over her as the waves crashed onto the shore. Big waves. And Sexy Surfer had just been out in that. Crazy.

Actually, *she* was the crazy one, and she let out a long, purposeful breath, and with it a lot of her tension.

But not all…

She wriggled her toes some more, waiting for the next wave. There were a million things running through her mind, most of them floating like dust motes through an open, sun-filled window, never quite landing. Still, a few managed to hit with surprising emphasis—such as the realization that she'd done it. She'd packed up and left home.

Her destination had been the Pacific Ocean. She'd always wanted to see it, and she could now say with one hundred percent certainty it met her expectations. The knowledge that she'd fulfilled one of her dreams felt good, even if there were worries clouding her mind. The mess she'd left behind, for one. Staying out of the rut she'd just climbed out of, for another. And a life. She wanted—*needed*—a life. Employment would be good, too, since she was fond of eating.

But standing in this little Washington State town she'd yet to explore, she felt those worries recede slightly. She'd get through this; she always did. After all, the name of this place nearly guaranteed it.

Lucky Harbor.

She was determined to find some *good* luck for a change.

A few minutes later, the sun finally gently touched down on the water, sending a chill through the early-July evening. Becca took one last look and turned to head back to her car. Sliding behind the wheel, she pulled out her phone and accessed the ad she'd found on Craigslist.

Cheap waterfront warehouse converted into three separate living spaces. Cheap. Furnished (sort of). Cheap. Month to month. *Cheap.*

It worked for Becca on all levels, especially the cheap part. She had the first month's rent check in her pocket, and she was meeting the landlord at the building. All she had to do was locate it. Her GPS led her from the pier to the other end of the harbor, down a narrow street lined with maybe ten warehouse buildings.

Problem number one.

None of them had numbers indicating its address. After cruising up and down the street three times, she admitted defeat and parked. She called the landlord, but she only had his office phone, and it went right to voice mail.

Problem number two. She was going to have to ask someone for help, which wasn't exactly her strong suit.

It wasn't even a suit of hers at all. She hummed a little to herself as she looked around, a nervous tic for sure, but it soothed her. Unfortunately, the only person in sight was a kid on a bike, in homeboy shorts about ten sizes too big and a knit cap, coming straight at her on the narrow sidewalk.

"Watch it, lady!" he yelled.

A city girl through and through, Becca held her ground. "*You* watch it."

The kid narrowly missed her and kept going.

"Hey, which building is Two-Oh-Three?"

"Dunno, ask Sam!" he called back over his shoulder. "He'll know, he knows everything."

Okay, perfect. She cupped her hands around her mouth so he'd hear her. "Where's Sam?"

The kid didn't answer, but he did point toward the building off to her right.

It was a warehouse like the others, industrial, old, the siding battered by the elements and the salty air. It was built like an A-frame barn, with both of the huge front and back sliding doors open. The sign posted did give her a moment's pause.

WARNING: PRIVATE DOCK
TRESPASSERS WILL BE USED AS BAIT

She bit her lower lip and decided that, after driving all day for days on end, her need to find her place outweighed the threat. Hopefully...

The last of the sunlight slanted through the warehouse, highlighting everything in gold, including the guy using some sort of planer along the wood. The air itself was throbbing with the beat of the loud indie rock blaring from some unseen speakers.

From the outside, the warehouse hadn't looked like much, but as she stepped into the vast doorway, she realized the inside was a wide-open space with floor-to-rafters windows nearly three stories high. It was lined with ladders and racks of stacked wood planks and tools. Centered in the space was a wood hull, looking like a piece of art.

As did the guy working on it. His shirt was damp and clinging to his every muscle as it bunched and flexed with his movements. It was all so beautiful and intriguing—the boat, the music, the man himself, right down to the corded veins on his forearms—that it was like being at the movies during the montage of scenes that always played to a sound track.

Then she realized she recognized the board shorts, or more accurately the really excellent butt, as she'd only moments before watched it walk away from her.

Sexy Surfer.

Though he couldn't possibly have heard her over the hum of his power tool and the loud music, he turned to face her. And as she already knew, the view of him from the front was just as heart-stopping as it was from the back.

He didn't move a single muscle other than one flick of his thumb, which turned off the planer. His other hand went into his pocket and extracted a remote. With another flick, the music stopped.

"You shouldn't be in here," he said. "It's dangerous."

And just like that, the pretty montage sound track playing in her head came to a screeching halt. "Okay, sorry. I'm just—"

Just nothing, apparently, because he turned back to his work, and with another flick of his thumb the planer came back to life. And then the music.

"—Looking for someone," she finished. Not that he was listening.

On the wall right next to her, a telephone began ringing, and the bright red light attached to it began blinking in sync, clearly designed just in case the phone couldn't be heard over the tools. She could hear it, but she doubted he could. One ring, then two. Three. The guy didn't make a move toward it.

On the fourth ring, the call went to a machine, where a recorded male voice said, "Lucky Harbor Charters. We're in high gear for the summer season. Coastal tours, deep-sea fishing, scuba, name your pleasure. Leave a message at the tone, or find us at the harbor, north side."

A click indicated the caller disconnected, but the phone immediately rang again.

Sexy Surfer ignored all of this.

Becca had a hard time doing the same, and she glanced around for someone, *anyone*, but there was no one in sight. Used to having to be resourceful, she let her gaze follow the cord of the planer to an electric outlet in the floor. She walked over to it and pulled it out of the wall.

The planer stopped.

So did her heart when Sexy Surfer turned his head her way. Yep, Sexy Surfer was an apt description for him. Maybe Drop-Dead Sexy. Either way, he took in the fact that she was still there and that she was holding the cord to his planer and a single brow arched. Whether it was displeasure or disbelief was hard to tell. Probably, with that bad 'tude, not many messed with him. But she was exhausted, hungry, out of her element, and a little bit pissed off. Which made her just enough of a loose cannon to forget to be afraid.

"I'm trying to find Sam," she said, moving closer to him so he could hear her over his music. "Do you know him?"

"Who's asking?"

Having come from a family of entertainers, most of them innate charmers to boot, Becca knew how to make the most of what she'd been given, so she smiled. "I'm Becca Thorpe, and I'm trying to find Two-Oh-Three Harbor Street. My GPS says I'm on Harbor Street, but the buildings don't have numbers on them."

"You're looking for the building directly to the north."

She nodded, and then shook her head with a laugh. She could get lost trying to find her way out of a paper bag. "And north would be which way exactly?"

He let the planer slowly slide to the floor by its cord before letting go and heading toward her.

He was six-foot-plus of lean, hard muscle, with a lot of sawdust clinging to him, as rugged and tough as the boat he was working on—though only the man was exuding testosterone, a bunch of it.

Becca didn't have a lot of great experience with an overabundance of testosterone, so she found herself automatically taking a few steps back from him, until she stood in the doorway.

He slowed but didn't stop, not until he was crowded in that doorway right along with her, taking up an awful lot of space.

Actually, *all* of the space.

And though she was braced to feel threatened, the opposite happened. She felt…suddenly warm, and her heart began to pound. And not in a terrified way, either.

He took in her reaction, held her gaze for a moment, then pointed to the right. "The front of the building you're looking for is around the corner," he said, his voice a little softer now, like maybe he knew she was torn between an unwelcome fear and an equally unwelcome heat.

She really hoped the heat was mutual, because it would be embarrassing to be caught in Lustville by herself. "Around the corner," she repeated. Did he know he smelled good, like fresh wood and something citrusy, and also heated male? She wondered if she smelled good, too, or if all she was giving off was the scent of confused female and ranch-flavored popcorn.

"What do you need with that place?" he asked.

"I'm the new tenant there. Or one of them anyway."

His expression was unfathomable. "I take it you haven't seen it yet."

"Not in person," she said. "Why? Is it that bad?"

"Depends on how long you're staying," he said. "More than five minutes?"

Oh, boy. "I don't actually know," she said. "It's a month-to-month rental. Lucky Harbor is sort of a pit stop for me at the moment."

His gaze searched hers. Then he nodded and moved back to his work. He plugged the planer in and flicked it on again.

Guess their conversation was over. She was on her own. And if that thought caused a little pang of loneliness inside her still-hurting heart, she shoved it deep and ignored it, because now wasn't the time to give in to the magnitude of what she'd done. Leaving the warehouse, she turned right.

To her new place.

To a new beginning.

The handy neighbor who's come to help Olivia with her store is charismatic, sexy—and determined to uncover her secret.

♥

Please see the next page for an excerpt from *He's So Fine*.

Chapter 1

♥

For a guy balancing his weight between the stern of his boat and the dock, thinking about sex instead of what he was doing was a real bonehead move. Cole Donovan was precariously perched on the balls of his feet above some seriously choppy, icy water. So concentrating would've been the smart move.

But he had no smarts left, which was what happened when you hadn't had a good night's sleep in far too long—your brain wandered into areas it shouldn't.

Sex being one of those areas.

He shook his head to clear it. It was way too early for those kinds of thoughts. Not quite dawn, and the sky was a brilliant kaleidoscope of purples and blues and reds. Cole worked with a flashlight between his teeth, his fingers threading new electrical wire through the running lights on the stern. He only had a couple hours before a group of eight was coming through for a tour of the area.

That's what Cole and his two partners and best friends

did—they hired out themselves and their fifty-foot Wright Sport boat, chartering deep-sea fishing, whale watching, scuba diving…if it could be done, they did it. Sam was their financial guy and boatbuilder. Tanner was their scuba diving instructor and communications expert. Cole was the captain, chief navigator, mechanic, and—lucky him—the face of Lucky Harbor Charters, mostly because neither Sam nor Tanner was exactly a service-oriented person.

They'd had a warm Indian summer here in the Pacific Northwest, but October had roared in as if Mother Nature was pissed off at the world, and maybe in need of a Xanax to boot. But business was still good. Or it had been, until last night. He and Tanner had taken a group of frat boys out, and one of the idiots had managed to kick in the lights running along the stern, destroying not only the casing but also the electrical.

Cole could fix it—there was little he couldn't fix. But as he got down to it, a harsh wind slapped him in the face, threatening his balance. He kicked off the dock so that he was balanced entirely on the edge of the stern. Still not a position for the faint of heart, but after five years on oil rigs and two more running Lucky Harbor Charters, Cole felt more at ease on the water than just about anywhere else.

He could smell the salt on the air and hear the swells smacking up against the dock moorings. The wind hit him again, and he shivered to the bone. Last week, he'd been out here working in board shorts and nothing else, the sun warming his back. Today he was in a knit cap, thick sweatshirt, cargo pants, and boots, and he was wishing for gloves like a little girl. He shoved his flashlight into his pocket, brought his hands to his mouth, and blew on his fingers for a moment before reaching for the wires again.

Just as they connected, there was a sizzle and a flash, and he jerked, losing his footing. The next thing he knew, he was airborne, weightless for a single heartbeat...

And then he hit the icy water, plunging deep, the contact stealing the air from his lungs. Stunned, he fought the swells, his heavy clothes, himself, eyes open as he searched for the flames that surely went along with the explosion.

Jesus, not another fire. That was his only thought as panic gripped him hard. He opened his mouth and—

Swallowed a lungful of seawater.

This cleared his head. He *wasn't* on the oil rig in the Gulf. He *wasn't* in the explosion that had killed Gil, and nearly Tanner as well. He was in Lucky Harbor.

He kicked hard, breaking the surface, gasping as he searched for the boat, a part of him still not wholly convinced. But there. She was there, only a few feet away.

No flames, not a single lick. Just the cold-ass swells of the Pacific Northwest.

Treading water, Cole shook his head. A damn flashback, which he hadn't had in over a year—

"Omigod, I see you!" a female voice called out. "Just hang on, I'm coming!" This was accompanied by hurried footsteps clapping on the dock. "Help!" she yelled as she ran. "Help, there's a man in the water! Sir, sir, can you hear me? I'm coming. *Sir?*"

If she called him "sir" one more time, he was going to drown himself. His dad had been a *sir*. The old guy who ran the gas pumps on the corner of Main and First was a *sir*. Cole wasn't a damn *sir*. He was opening his mouth to tell her so, and also that he was fine, not in any danger at all, when she took a flying leap off the dock.

And landed right on top of him.

The icy water closed over both of their heads, and as another swell hit, they became a tangle of limbs and water-laden clothing. He fought free and once again broke the surface, whipping his head around to look for the woman.

No sign of her.

Shit. Gasping in a deep breath, he dove back down and found her doing what he'd been doing only a moment before—fighting the water and her clothes, and herself. Her own worst enemy, she was losing the battle and sinking fast. Grasping the back of her sweater, Cole hauled her up, kicking hard to get them both to the surface.

She sucked in some air and immediately started coughing, reaching out blindly for him and managing to get a handful of his junk.

"Maybe we could get to shore first," he said wryly.

Holding on to him with both arms and legs like a monkey clinging to a tree, she squeezed him tight. "I've g-g-got y-y-you," she stuttered through already chattering teeth, then climbed on top of his head, sending him under again.

Jesus. He managed to yank her off him and get her head above water. "Hey—"

"D-don't panic," she told him earnestly. "It's g-g-gonna be o-o-okay."

She actually thought she was saving him. If the situation weren't so deadly, Cole might have thought some of this was funny. But she was turning into a Popsicle before his very eyes, and so was he. "Listen, just relax—"

"H-hang on to m-me," she said, and…dunked him again.

For the love of God. "*Stop* trying to save me," he told her. "I'm begging you."

Her hair was in her face, and behind the strands plastered to her skin, her eyes widened. "Oh, my God. You're trying to commit suicide."

"What? *No*." The situation was ridiculous, and he was frustrated and effing cold, but damn, it was hard not to be charmed by the fact that she was trying to save him, even as she was going down for the count herself. "I'm trying to keep you from killing me."

The flashback to the rig fire long gone, Cole treaded water to keep them afloat as he assessed their options. There were two.

Shore or boat.

They were at the stern of the boat, much closer to the swimming platform than to the shore. And in any case, there was no way his "rescuer" could swim the distance. Though Cole was a world-class swimmer himself, he was already frozen to the bone, and so was she. They needed out of the water…fast.

With a few strokes, he got them to the stern of the boat, where he hoisted her up to the platform, pulling himself up after her.

She lay right where he'd dumped her, gulping in air, that long, dark hair everywhere. Leaning over her, he shoved the wet strands from her face to better see her and realized with a jolt that he recognized her. She lived in one of the warehouse apartments across from Lucky Harbor Charters.

Her name was Olivia Something-or-Other.

All he knew about her was that she hung out with Sam's fiancée, Becca; she ran some sort of shop downtown; she dressed in a way that said both "hands off" and "hot mama"; and he'd caught her watching him and the guys surfing on more than one occasion.

"Y-y-you're bleeding," she said from flat on her back, staring up at him.

Cole brought his fingers to the sting on his temple, and his fingers indeed came away red with his own blood. Perfect. Just a cut though, no less than he deserved after that stupid stunt of shocking the shit out of himself with the wiring and then tumbling into the water. "I'm fine." It was her he was worried about. Her jeans and sweater were plastered to her. She was missing a boot. And she was shivering violently enough to rattle the teeth right out of her head. "You're *not* fine," he said.

"Just c-c-cold."

No shit. "What the hell were you thinking?" he asked, "Jumping in after me like that?"

Her eyes flashed, and he discovered they were the exact same color as her hair—deep, dark chocolate.

"I th-th-thought you were d-d-drowning!" she said through chattering teeth.

Cole shook his head. "I didn't almost drown until you jumped on top of me."

"What h-h-happened?"

"I was working on the electrical wiring and got shocked and fell in."

"S-s-see? You needed help!"

He absolutely did not. But arguing with her would get them nowhere, except maybe dead. "Come on, the plan is to get you home and warmed up." Rising to his feet, he reached down and pulled her up with him, holding on to her when she wobbled. "Are you—"

"I'm f-f-fine," she said, and stepped back to look down at herself. "I l-l-lost my favorite b-b-boot rescuing y-y-you."

She called that a rescue? "Can you even swim?"

"Y-y-yes!" She crossed her arms over her chest. "A l-l-little bit."

He stared at her in disbelief. "A *little bit*? Seriously? You risked your life on that?"

"You were in t-t-trouble!"

Right. They could argue about that later. "Time to get you home, Supergirl."

"B-b-but my b-b-boot."

"We'll rescue the boot later."

"We w-w-will?"

No. Her boot was on the ocean floor and DOA. "Later," he said again, and grabbing her hand, he pulled her across the platform, through the stern. He needed to get her off the boat.

She dug her heels in, one in just a sock, one booted.

"What?" he asked.

Still shivering wildly, she looked at him with misery. "I d-d-dropped my ph-ph-phone on the dock."

"Okay, we'll grab it."

"Y-y-yes, but I d-d-didn't drop my keys."

"That's good," he said, wondering if she'd hit her head.

"Y-y-you don't get it. I th-th-think I lost my k-k-keys in the w-w-water."

Well, shit. No keys, no getting her inside her place. This wasn't good. Nor was her color. She was waxen, pale. They couldn't delay getting her out of the elements and warm. "Okay, plan B," he said. "We warm you here on the boat." Again he started to tug her along, needing to get her inside and belowdecks, but she stumbled against him like her limbs weren't working.

Plan C, he thought grimly, and swung her up into his arms.

She clutched at him. "N-n-not necessary—"

Ignoring her, he got them both into the small galley, where he set her down on the bench at the table. Keeping his hands on her arms, he crouched in front of her to look into her eyes. "You still with me? You okay?"

"Y-y-y—" Giving up, she dropped her head to his chest.

"Not okay," he muttered, and stroked a hand down the back of her head and along her trembling frame.

Truth was, he wasn't much better off. His head was still bleeding, and his shoulder was throbbing. He had nothing on her, though. She was violently trembling against him. Easing her back, he got busy. First he cranked the heater, then he opened their linens storage box, pulling out towels and blankets, which he tossed in a stack at her side. "Okay," he said. "Strip."

VISIT US ONLINE AT

WWW.HACHETTEBOOKGROUP.COM

FEATURES:

**OPENBOOK BROWSE AND
SEARCH EXCERPTS**

•

AUDIOBOOK EXCERPTS AND PODCASTS

•

AUTHOR ARTICLES AND INTERVIEWS

•

**BESTSELLER AND PUBLISHING
GROUP NEWS**

•

SIGN UP FOR E-NEWSLETTERS

•

**AUTHOR APPEARANCES AND TOUR
INFORMATION**

•

SOCIAL MEDIA FEEDS AND WIDGETS

•

DOWNLOAD FREE APPS

Find out more about Forever Romance!

Visit us at
www.hachettebookgroup.com/publishing_forever.aspx

Find us on Facebook
http://www.facebook.com/ForeverRomance

Follow us on Twitter
http://twitter.com/ForeverRomance

NEW AND UPCOMING TITLES

Each month we feature our new titles
and reader favorites.

CONTESTS AND GIVEAWAYS

We give away galleys, autographed copies,
and all kinds of exclusive items.

AUTHOR INFO

You'll find bios, articles, and links to personal websites
for all your favorite authors—and so much more.

GET SOCIAL

Connect with your favorite authors, editors, and
other Forever fans, and share what's important to you.

THE BUZZ

Sign up for our monthly romance newsletter,
and be the first to read all about it.